Deadly News

A Britton Bay Mystery

Jody Holford

LYRICAL UNDERGROUND
Kensington Publishing Corp.
www.kensingtonbooks.com

LYRICAL UNDERGROUND BOOKS are published by

Kensington Publishing Corp.
119 West 40th Street
New York, NY 10018

All Kensington titles, imprints, and distributed lines are available at special quantity discounts for bulk purchases for sales promotion, premiums, fund-raising, educational, or institutional use.

Special book excerpts or customized printings can also be created to fit specific needs. For details, write or phone the office of the Kensington Sales Manager: Kensington Publishing Corp., 119 West 40th Street, New York, NY 10018. Attn. Sales Department. Phone: 1-800-221-2647.

Lyrical Underground and Lyrical Underground logo Reg. US Pat. & TM Off.

First Electronic Edition: October 2018
eISBN-13: 978-1-5161-0866-4
eISBN-10: 1-5161-0866-3

First Print Edition: October 2018
ISBN-13: 978-1-5161-0869-5
ISBN-10: 1-5161-0869-8

Printed in the United States of America

THE PRIME SUSPECTS

Molly picked up the paper and unfolded it, looking down at the printed copy of an email exchange. It was between Elizabeth and Vernon. The recently departed writer had been threatening to reveal what he knew of Elizabeth's relationship at the next public town meeting and to Alan's wife. Molly scanned the emails. He didn't even seem to want anything. He just continued to tell her he knew and that knowing was to his advantage. Elizabeth's responses were short and concise: *You're a vile man with nothing better to do than harass people. I'm warning you, don't do this.*

Molly's fingers tightened on the paper. Tears filled her eyes. She was sorry that Vernon died and she didn't condone affairs, for whatever reason, but how could the man be so malicious? To live his life just looking for ways to hurt people. *What goes around, comes around.* Though it didn't make her feel like a good person to think it, the sentiment was all too true in his case. Had Elizabeth or Alan felt the same way? Both of them had come in late this morning. So had Clay. Her stomach clutched at the thought of all of these people—that she was coming to know and like, well, most of them—having motive to kill Vernon…

Not till we are lost do we begin to find ourselves. —Thoreau

Chapter 1

Fated or not, Molly Owens was rethinking her decision to plant roots in the seaside town of Britton Bay. Or at least accepting the job as editor of the town's small, failing newspaper. The name of the little city by the ocean had called to her, but at the moment, tension pumped through the room like a stereo with too much bass as Alan Benedict introduced her to his staff of four.

All eyes were on her, making her stomach clench in tight spasms. At least Alan's voice was steady and kind.

"Molly has a double degree in journalism and literature. She's a remote editor for several large-scale magazines and has even worked with a couple of publishing houses as a freelance editor. We're very lucky she's agreed to join the *Britton Bay Bulletin*. As you all know, I've been spread a little thin lately and Molly is going to be my right hand."

"Welcome. Again," Elizabeth Grover said, a tight smile on her unpainted lips. They'd met when Molly had arrived this morning.

Elizabeth was probably in her fifties, and Molly knew she wrote most of the small pieces for the online and print versions of the paper. After accepting the position via email and phone interviews, Molly had done a bit of research on both the staff and the paper. Elizabeth was somewhat reserved, even though she'd been nothing but polite.

The young man seated to Elizabeth's right gave a different kind of smile—one Molly didn't want to dwell on for too long. The kind that most people—women especially—would look away from. Molly held his gaze, unwilling to show discomfort. From the corner of his upturned lips, a dark blue pen cap was sticking out. He pulled it out to speak.

"Nice to meet you," he said, running a hand through his blond, slightly shaggy hair. "I'm Clay. I'm only here part-time. I do some of the photography and the social media. What there is of it, anyway."

Laughing like he'd shared a joke, Clay put the cap back in his mouth—a plastic toothpick. Molly nodded and locked eyes with the man to Clay's left. It was his scowling face that suppressed any joy she might have felt over a position she'd been excited to take. She almost preferred the lecherous grin of the younger man to the simmering anger burning in this man's eyes.

"You want to introduce yourself, Vernon?" Alan asked, sending Molly an apologetic look.

She tried to smile reassuringly, but nerves zipped around her stomach like horses on a racetrack. *Breathe. You're meant to be here.*

When he said nothing, she filled in the silence. "I've read several of your articles, Vernon. You've got a great knack for headlines," Molly said, hoping her olive branch wouldn't be whacked down with a chain saw.

The older man, who looked a little like an unfriendly Albert Einstein with white tufts of hair growing from either side of his head like rainbows over his ears, snorted derisively.

He looked up from the furious spirals he was drawing with a black pen on a bright yellow Post-it note. "Well, gee, thanks. Means a lot coming from someone your age. What are you? Twenty?"

Molly curled her fingers together on top of the long mahogany table. Like the paper, she bet that in its glory days, it had been a thing of beauty. Now, it was weathered and scarred, marks creating a map of lines over the once glossy surface. She wasn't sure what had happened to the newspaper, or the table, but clearly, someone hadn't cared for it in the way they needed to. Though Vernon might not realize it and definitely didn't want to acknowledge it, she was the perfect person to bring it back to its former glory.

Molly straightened her shoulders and didn't shy away from his eye contact. "I'm twenty-eight, actually. I understand you're all a bit of a family already and I'm just hoping I can find my place here. I look forward to working with each of you."

She turned to the last person at the table; a teenage girl. "I'm sorry. What's your name?"

"This is Hannah," Alan said, a smile spreading across his handsome, weathered face. "She's my niece. She's doing a work-experience practicum. Hannah is in her final year at Britton Bay High and runs the school newspaper. Has for the last two years."

Hannah smiled brightly and gave a small wave. "I'm free labor," she said with a laugh.

Some of the tension slipped from Molly's shoulders. Three out of four not visibly hating her were numbers she could live with. Living in L.A. had given her an extra layer of skin so Vernon wasn't going to get under it, if that's what he was hoping.

Alan leaned back in the black leather chair, his fingers pressed together under his chin. Molly noted the way Elizabeth stared at him, watching the man's every move with unnerving awareness. When her gaze drifted to Molly, the woman gave a slight start, like she knew she'd been caught. Elizabeth stood and reached for the water at the center of the table and poured Alan a glass, the ice ringing against the rim.

"Thank you," he said, his eyes holding Elizabeth's. His fingers wrapped around the drink, the prominent wedding ring on his finger clinking against it.

Molly loved watching people the way she loved reading books. Their actions and reactions were stories in themselves. She noted, as Elizabeth continued to pour for everyone else, the woman did not have any rings on. Accepting the water, Molly thanked her and gratefully downed half her glass. The dryness in her throat was as distracting as the tension in the room.

Glancing around once again, she marveled at how she'd ended up sitting in a nondescript conference room in a town that shared a name with her childhood best friend. All because she'd stumbled across an online ad posting the job at a time when her life was going the exact opposite of the way she'd planned. There was only one window in the stuffy room and though it was cracked open, the air coming through was dry and heavy. Again, L.A. was good preparation for hot days and cold shoulders.

Alan set his glass down, smiling at his staff. With a full head of salt-and-pepper hair, he reminded Molly of a more reserved version of her dad. It was, to her, another sign that she'd made the right decision to pick up and move. Of course, that choice had been kicked into high gear after walking in on her live-in boyfriend taking his ex-girlfriend on a naked tour of their sheets. *Molly's* sheets. That experience had been more like a boot in the face than a simple sign. Sometimes believing that everything happened for a reason sucked.

Elizabeth settled back in her chair, sipping delicately at her water. Despite the death-glare Vernon was giving her, Molly still believed she was right. With its cobblestone streets and easy access to the water, Britton Bay was a place she could see herself staying.

"Are we done with the meet and greet? I'd like to get back to work," Vernon said, pushing back his chair.

Molly glanced at Alan and saw his slight nod of encouragement. Opening the files in front of her, she passed handouts to each of them, pleased to see her hand was steady.

"This is a great article on responsibility, fairness, and accuracy in reporting. Elizabeth and Vernon, you have great personality and voice in your writing, but if we want to broaden the *Bulletin*'s readership, which is what Mr. Benedict has hired me to help with, we need to make sure that the stories you're sharing have all of these things. Every time."

Despite practicing this speech, her voice wobbled as she closed the file and looked around the table. Molly cleared her throat and hoped her expression exuded a balance of professionalism and confidence. Thankfully, no one could *see* the way her heart hammered painfully against her rib cage.

Vernon didn't touch his handout. He glared at Mr. Benedict. "My understanding was that you're here as a copy editor? Maybe a fact-checker. If you're leaving the paper entirely, Alan, we have a right to know. Is she assigning stories now?" He hooked his thumb at Molly as if she were a mannequin and not a real person listening to his derisive tone.

Molly turned to face Alan. Sitting forward, he folded his hands in front of him. "Molly will essentially take over what I've been doing. To be honest, she's better suited to it than I am. She has the ability, background, youth, and the understanding required to make the *Bulletin* stand out among its competitors. We used to be one of the most read papers on the Oregon coast and we all know those numbers have dwindled. I won't say it's not my fault, because in part, it is. Maybe if I'd had the same passion for reporting as my father or grandfather, I'd have done a better job keeping us afloat. But I made a commitment to my family and the way I see it is, Molly's our best chance at me keeping my promise. While she's doing that, my goal is to up our revenue and get more businesses—especially some of the new ones, working with us. So to answer your question, her job title is…vast. She'll do a little bit of everything and yes, that includes assigning stories."

When she'd contacted Alan about the job, they'd had a long conversation about the newspaper's history, as well as his family's, in the town. He'd followed his path, as his father had expected him to, but in today's market, he wasn't giving the public anything they couldn't easily live without. From what she'd seen, the *Bulletin* posted articles that barely passed as puff pieces: What was on sale at the market, what the local kids had been up to in their free time, and an up-to-date account of city hall's agenda. Hardly captivating stuff.

Molly hoped to deepen and strengthen the news they were sharing, regardless of Vernon's reluctance, which was seeming a lot like jealousy at this point. Alan hadn't mentioned anyone in-house wanting the position, but why would he? If he had, would she have thought twice? No. If Alan thought she was the best person for the job and Vernon had an issue with that, it wasn't her problem. At least, she hoped it wouldn't be.

"I, for one, would like to see this newspaper last for another hundred years, so I'm happy to take your advice, Molly," Elizabeth said.

"We talk a lot about the impact of the digital world on hard-copy news in class," Hannah said.

Molly nodded, appreciating the interruption to Vernon's pouting. "It doesn't make things easy, but we can work with it. Clay, I've seen your reach on social media and we'll talk about widening the *Bulletin*'s audience there. Your web edition of the paper only shares one quarter of what's in print. That needs to change immediately. Not only is it more convenient for most readers, it gives the businesses advertising with you a wider audience. I know I'm new here, but from what I've seen in the last couple of days, there's a younger demographic moving in. We can appeal to that. Which means mobile-friendly editions of the paper, coupons that can be scanned by the cashier. And most importantly, news that people want to read. The town itself will be drawn to their hometown paper. *If* we make it more appealing."

Molly had taken a look at the town's history and population. It had grown and changed over time, with a few families having remained for several generations. However, young couples and new families were settling in the town, realizing it offered a lot of perks for less cost than many of the other cities along the coast. She loved the idea of bringing a small-town circulation back to life. Mostly, she loved the idea of moving forward and putting all of her attention into something with a real chance at success.

The conversation turned to current articles that had already been assigned by Alan. It was a good opportunity for Molly to ease her way in, see how they worked and the approach they took to getting their stories finished. So far, she hadn't seen much that required a lot of fact-checking because the paper was more of an observation journal than a media source. If she could help them fine-tune their current pieces, they could start making a shift in the right direction.

"Are we done?" Vernon stood abruptly. He picked up a black notebook covered with multiple Post-it notes in a variety of colors. Other than the one he'd drawn circles on while she'd spoken, they were filled with scrawled notes.

Mr. Benedict huffed out an impatient breath and looked up at him. He'd mentioned during the interview that he had some personal issues going on and would be leaving her with a fair amount of responsibility. Which was fine with her and best she accept it sooner rather than later.

"You're working on a few stories, but Alan said there's a special celebration this summer and you're working on a heritage piece, correct?" Molly asked, checking her notes.

Vernon all but sneered as he looked at her. "Yes. I'm doing a timeline of the Phillips family's history in Britton Bay. It'll be a lead-up to the annual Phillips Festival."

Which was boring on its own, seeing as it occurred every year. "I think that's a great place to start. What about an interview with the family members? Maybe even a cross-generational one, if that's possible?"

"Oh, there isn't a soul in the Phillips family who doesn't love to talk," Elizabeth said. Her bright smile went a long way toward making the drab office a happier place.

"Why would we interview people we could talk to any day of the week? They're not royalty," Vernon argued, gripping the back of his chair with both hands. His fleshy knuckles turned white.

"They'd tell you differently," her boss said.

"I read up about them. They have a long, unique history here in comparison to some of the other families. Would you be interested in setting up an interview, Vernon? If not, I could maybe pursue that angle. I certainly don't have as much writing background as you, but if I did the interview for you, you could use my notes. Plus, it'd be a great way to meet some people," Molly said, her voice syrupy sweet. She'd had just about enough of his toddler behavior.

"I think I can do my own damn job. You want an interview, I'll get one. I'm sure people will be jumping all over our paper to read about what Clara Phillips bought at the Stop and Shop," Vernon growled.

When he walked out of the meeting room, a silence ensued. Molly bit her lip and tried to breathe softly. Evenly, rather than expelling the deep sigh she'd like to.

"He gets a little grumpy without his coffee," Elizabeth said.

Clay snickered in between chewing on the cap. "Or if he's awake."

Hannah laughed. Molly kept her expression neutral and tried to focus on the people who actually wanted her here.

"Clara Phillips? Married to the mayor?" Molly asked, thinking back to her research.

"She is," Hannah answered. "Their daughter, Savannah, is my best friend."

Molly smiled. Hannah and Savannah. It was cute, just like the teen. Gears turned in Molly's head. A fresh start. A fresh point of view and a good way to test out her staff's capabilities. "How would you like to ask your friend a few questions for the paper?"

Hannah's eyes widened. She looked at her uncle and then back at Molly. "For real?"

Molly laughed. "Completely. Might be nice to get a young person's perspective on what it's like to grow up in a family so well known in a small place. On top of that, she's got the responsibilities that go along with being the mayor's daughter. And she'll definitely open up to you more than someone else. Why don't you put together some questions, and we'll go over them together and determine what you should ask. Once you do, I'll work with you on writing up an article. It'll give me a chance to see your writing."

Alan beamed at Molly, but his smile paled in comparison to Hannah's. "I'd love that. Thank you. I've got to get to my second-period class, but I'll start on the questions after school."

"Great. It was nice to meet you," Molly said truthfully.

"You too."

She kissed Mr. Benedict on the cheek and left the room. When she did, he checked his watch, his brows furrowing, forming little creases on his forehead.

"I… uh, need to get to a meeting. I'll leave the day in your capable hands," Alan said, standing.

When he stood, Elizabeth's eyes followed him. Molly watched, fascinated as the woman tried to be subtle about her staring.

"Elizabeth, in addition to running the regular classifieds next week, I'd like you to do a small piece on requesting some local opinions on a few different topics. Make sure they aren't controversial issues for now, but let's invite the town to take part in their paper. Maybe we could even run some fun polls."

Elizabeth nodded, but her eyes continued to dart to the open door Alan had left through. It didn't surprise Molly when a moment later, Elizabeth excused herself from the table and said she had to get to work.

Molly gathered her papers, hoping Clay would leave as well. She wasn't quite ready to deal with his role yet, as she hadn't figured out exactly what he did. The paper had a subpar website, a Facebook page with no information, and twenty-five followers on Twitter. Besides that, the way he looked at her made her skin itch.

"So. You're from California?" Clay pronounced the 'i' like an 'e' and Molly had to refrain from rolling her eyes.

"I am."

She stood and picked up the work she planned on attending to first. There would be no issue with her doing her share. She'd always taken work very seriously, which was how she'd ended up here, at twenty-eight.

"I could show you around. Lived here all my life," Clay said, also standing.

He wore dark jeans that hung too low and an oversized plaid shirt. Molly seriously hoped the sloppy style wasn't the "it" thing among the men in Britton Bay. *Not that I care. All work, no play.* That was her new mantra. She'd bet from the meeting, work would be enough to keep her plenty busy.

"I kind of like the idea of exploring the town on my own, actually. Thank you, though."

"No worries. You change your mind, I'm your guy," Clay said.

Not in this lifetime or any other. "I'll keep that in mind."

She was grateful Alan had given her an office of her own, regardless of its small size. When she sank down into the inflexible chair, she let out the deep breath she'd been holding. Pulling a dark blue notebook out of her messenger bag, she made a note: *Day one of new job: Not so bad. Every adventure has bumps. I have to start somewhere.*

Trying to stay in the moment and be positive was Molly's newest goal. She figured it was better than plotting out ways to torture her ex. Though that had its appeal, she realized, after the shock wore off, she'd been more upset about her sheets and her pride than she was over losing him. It was eye-opening, not to mention disconcerting, to realize, at almost thirty, that she had no idea what she wanted out of life.

She worked through the day, pouring over old editions of the paper, making notes of articles that drew her attention. She made a list of several article options for the next edition of the paper, highlighting ways to make the pieces interesting and relevant. From what she'd seen, they didn't have a reporter, per se. Which meant she'd be taking over that role as well, until she could get Vernon or Elizabeth to take that on. The interesting thing about the *Bulletin* was despite the decline in popularity, it still survived financially. She'd been offered a decent wage and figured the others must earn enough to get by as well. Molly suspected Mr. Benedict's personal accounts kept the paper afloat.

Mr. Benedict would continue to handle the books, the final say, and the staffing, but most other things would fall under Molly's domain. She wondered again about the personal issue carving chunks out of her boss's attention and time.

When Vernon slapped some papers down on her desk, Molly surfaced, glanced at the clock, and realized most of the day had gone by.

"Story on the addition being added to the high school and my outline of the timeline. I'll see if I can chat with Vanessa Phillips—Clara's mother. Maybe she can tell me about her bridge club or garden society meetings."

Molly measured her words in her head before standing up and coming around the desk. Vernon shuffled backward, keeping space between them. She'd have invited him to sit down in one of the two chairs in front of her small desk if he wasn't acting like he couldn't wait to be away from her.

"Thank you. I'm looking forward to looking these over," she said, gesturing to the printouts. "I'll have some notes to you in a couple days. Listen, I feel like we got off on the wrong foot. I'm really excited to be here and to be part of returning the paper to its former glory. It'll take some hard work on all of our parts and an adjustment to doing things differently." Such as actually reporting *news*.

Vernon shook his head. "Nobody cares about what we write. We're all here earning a wage. Who cares what we print? You're young and looking to make your mark on the world. As soon as you get bored, you'll move on and we'll go back to printing flyers and obituaries. While you're here, it's just more work for us and we'll end up back where we've been stuck for years."

He didn't wait for her to respond. He walked out of her office and Molly frowned. She wasn't sure what made a person so jaded, but she truly hoped it wasn't contagious.

Mr. Benedict returned by the time Molly was ready to call it a day. She said good night and walked out the back door to where she'd parked her bright blue Jeep TJ. Climbing in, she'd driven out of the lot and down a couple of blocks before a strange sound made her cringe. The car started bumping along like she had square tires. Nerves had her checking her rearview, grateful to see no one was behind her. She was on Main Street, which had shops and eateries littered along both sides. Remembering the service station she'd seen a couple of blocks down, she gritted her teeth and forced her Jeep to hobble through the stoplight and in that direction.

Metal on concrete pierced her ears as she pulled into Sam's Service Station. Molly didn't even drive it all the way to the building, near the open bays. Once she was off of the road, she parked and turned the vehicle off.

She was out of the Jeep and walking around it, irritation and worry duking it out in her chest as she looked at one flat tire after another. What the heck?

"Now that's one way to make an entrance," a thick, amused voice said from behind her.

When Molly spun around, her breath caught in her throat. The man walking toward her, wearing a pair of dark blue coveralls and wiping his hands on a grease rag, was tall, with wide shoulders, and thick, dark hair. His smile had more wattage than the sun setting behind him. Her stomach flip-flopped like it had no memory of just being wronged by this very gender! *Traitor.* The closer he came, though, the more she couldn't blame her fickle stomach for its leap. *No harm in looking.* Ha. She knew where that belief could lead.

"Hi there," he said, stopping close enough in front of her that she could see his happy eyes were green.

"Hi." Apparently words had disappeared along with her common sense.

"You've got some tire trouble," he said, nodding toward the Jeep.

"Looks like it."

"You're new in town," he said, still smiling. Something about the way he locked eyes with her made it impossible to look away.

"I am. Molly Owens," she said, offering her hand.

He glanced down at his before accepting. His grip was solid and warm. Welcoming with a zip of heat that traveled up her arm.

"Sam Alderich. Welcome to Britton Bay, Molly. Mind if I take a look?"

Her pulse kicked into high gear as she held his gaze and his hand. It took her one flustered second to realize he meant *at the vehicle.* She pulled her hand back and he chuckled as she moved aside. Heat warmed her neck and her face. Sam crouched down and made an "hmm" sound before going to the next tire. He walked all the way around the vehicle before coming back to stand in front of her.

"Looks like you didn't get the welcome you deserved," Sam said.

Her eyes widened. "What do you mean?"

He gestured to the Jeep. "I'd say someone let the air outta all your tires on purpose."

Chapter 2

Molly only needed one guess to figure out who might have deflated her tires. She shook her head, wondering how a full-grown man could act like such a petulant child. She hadn't seen him leave the office during the day, but she had been buried in newspapers. *Who else could it be?* She hadn't had time to make anyone else mad. Not that she had plans to.

"I can take care of this for you right now," Sam said, his smile never wavering.

"Are you sure?" She looked around him to where all three bays were busy.

He arched an eyebrow. "It's just air. I'm going to grab my portable compressor, though. Don't want you on those rims any more than necessary."

She hoped she hadn't ruined them. Watching Sam walk away, she tried to focus her thoughts on something other than the view or why *someone* would take the time to vandalize her jeep.

Molly thought about what she needed to do that evening when she got back to the hotel. She'd checked in three days ago. It was quiet and comfortable, despite the lumpy bed. It would do until she had a couple of days off. The price was reasonable and there was free Wi-Fi. Her stomach growled, reminding her that food needed to be on her agenda. Soon. She'd checked out Morning Muffins on Main Street—which she'd definitely be visiting again, but so far, she'd stuck to the small greasy diner beside the hotel for her dinners. Maybe tonight she'd try the Come 'n Get It Eatery.

"So, where you from?" Sam asked as he rolled a red air compressor behind him. He walked and talked like he had all the time in the world. Molly never moved slowly. Even when she wasn't moving, she tended to fidget—bouncing her knee up and down or tapping her fingers. She liked to move, which helped her fit in while in California. But the pace here was...different.

"Lancaster, California. I'm working at the *Britton Bay Bulletin*," she said, watching as he went to work on the driver's-side tire.

He glanced up at her after he'd attached the hose. "I heard Alan was looking for an editor."

Before she could respond, he flipped a switch and a loud, bumpy sound emanated from the machine. Her tire puffed back to life. Sam switched the machine off and pulled it to the next tire. He worked his way around and in under ten minutes, she was ready to go.

"How much do I owe you?" she asked, wishing she could think of something better to say.

He laughed and her stomach dipped again. "For air?"

Her cheeks warmed and she nibbled on her lip for a second. "And your time."

Sam's gaze held her still. "No charge for either. You find a place to stay yet?"

Molly's brain switched gears. She did like the hotel, but it would probably be a good idea to have a kitchen. "No. I haven't had time to look."

Sam pulled a pen and a scrap of paper out of the top right pocket of his coveralls. He wrote something on it and passed it to her, the tips of his fingers brushing against hers. *Geesh. Get a grip.*

"Katherine owns the bed-and-breakfast on LaMonte Street. She's looking for a tenant for her carriage house. Nice area and the place is more than big enough for one person."

He paused, frowned at her and she thought it didn't suit him. "Unless, you moved here with your boyfriend or... uh, husband or something."

His cheeks flushed a little, which Molly found endearing.

"No. Just me. Thanks for this. And the air."

"No problem. Welcome to Britton Bay."

She climbed into her Jeep as he hauled the compressor away. Molly took a second to remind herself that she was all work, no play now. A new town, a new start. And dinner.

* * * *

Come 'n Get It Eatery was snuggled between a gift shop and the post office. Just on the edge of Main Street, it was a great spot to people watch. The wall of windows looked onto the street with the ocean and the pier in the distance. Molly hadn't driven by once without seeing a crowd in there.

She parked the Jeep and walked up the patterned concrete, very aware that the newcomer would draw attention. Being an army brat, she was used to being the newbie, but flutters still niggled in her stomach as she pulled open the diner door. A bell jingled loudly, announcing her arrival.

Inside, there were booths and tables and bar-style seating along the front window. Spinning stools with blue vinyl covering matched the booths. Old-style diner chairs were pushed in—or being sat in—at the round tables. Laughter rang out over the music that hummed in the background. Country. Small towns loved their country music. Behind the long countertop at the back of the restaurant, a woman with bright red hair, pulled up into a loose bun on top of her head, waved at Molly.

"Go ahead and seat yourself, hon," she called.

Molly made her way to the far side of the restaurant, smiling at people as she walked by. She settled on one of the stools at the window so she could watch the sun sinking over the water as she ate her dinner.

"You're new in town," the redhead said as she approached. She carried a plastic menu with her and plopped it in front of Molly.

Up close, the woman's skin was flawless. Pale, with bright blue eyes, Molly wondered if anyone could ever be sad in her presence. She pulled a pad out of the apron that hung on her ample hips. Dressed in jeans and a light blue top with ruffles on the sleeves. Molly stuck more to short-sleeve dress shirts and wondered for a half second if she could pull off ruffles. Probably not.

"I am. I'm Molly Owens. I just started at the newspaper," she said, knowing she'd only have to do this a few more times before people would just know who she was. Her father had been in the army most of Molly's life and though they'd mostly lived in larger cities, she was no stranger to small towns or how they worked. Word of mouth was the fastest form of communication in any place with less than a dozen stoplights.

"I'm Calliope Jacobs, owner, waitress, chef, janitor, you name it. Welcome to town, Molly."

"Thanks. Your restaurant has a great reputation. What do you recommend?"

Calliope leaned closer and pointed to the menu. "My personal favorite is the crispy fish burger. Comes with double-dipped sea-salt fries."

Now that she'd sat down without work in front of her, Molly realized she was exhausted and starving. Grateful not to put any thought into it, she nodded.

"I'll try it. And a cola, please."

"You got it. How's the newspaper? Don't you let Vernon scare you," Calliope said.

At least it wasn't just her—that ought to be comforting, but she was still irritated over her tires. "I'm trying not to. Mostly, it's good, but today was my first day."

"I mean it—don't you let him bug you. That man could take the fun out of an amusement park."

Molly arched her brow, her lips twitching, which must have been all the prompting the woman needed to continue.

"He was in here the other day arguing with Callan Blair. I had to tell the two of them to take it elsewhere, you know? Have you met Callan? Easygoing guy from what I've seen. But Vernon got him all riled up. That man could rile up a saint."

Molly shook her head, trying to follow along with Calliope's quick pace. Apparently not everyone in the small town moved at a slower pace. Molly hadn't had time yet to meet many people.

"He owns the Sit and Sip a few doors down. Great place for a milkshake. My husband plays cards with him and Vernon and a few other guys. Good group, mostly." She leaned close like Molly had earned the right to a secret. "Behind his back, the guys call him Vicious Vernon because he's so grumpy, win or lose. So don't you take anything he says or does personally. We're a friendly place, but every town has its share of crab apples."

Trying to take it all in, letting the information roll around in her head, Molly decided she quite liked Calliope and her straight-talking ways.

The redhead straightened. "Alan's a good man. Sometimes goes about like his head is in the clouds, but you'll like working for him. You find a place to stay?"

Molly smiled again, trying to keep up. "Actually, Sam Alderich told me the woman who owns the bed-and-breakfast is looking for a tenant." Thinking about Sam made her skin feel warm.

The waitress-slash-owner made her eyebrows dance. "He'd be right and he'd know, seeing as that's his mama. Beautiful place she's got there and I've seen that carriage home. There's been many a day I wished I could rent it myself when my husband comes home in a stormy mood."

Molly wasn't sure what to think of Sam recommending his mom's place, but she supposed it made sense. She liked that Calliope was giving it a stamp of approval.

"Let me go put your order in and check on the other customers. We're short a waitress tonight, but I fully plan on asking you way more questions than is polite," Calliope said.

Molly just laughed as the waitress walked toward the kitchen. Turning back to the window, she sighed. She rolled her shoulders a couple of times and stretched her neck. Everything was going to be fine. One bad apple didn't really spoil the bunch—at least not from what she'd seen. There were plenty of people in Britton Bay she'd like to get to know more.

It took effort not to pull her files out of her satchel, but she knew she'd never take a break if she didn't force it on herself. Her mom was always telling her there was nothing wrong with sitting still. Except, it tended to make Molly edgy.

A man and woman came out of a shop across the street. The woman looked up at him and laughed at something he said. A couple of doors down, an elderly man was sweeping the sidewalk. There was a wide range of shops lining both sides of the street. In the distance, Molly saw a few people bicycling along the boardwalk that surrounded the beach. The coastline seemed to go on forever. *First day off, I'm going to park myself on that beach and read a book.* Or research and edit, or people watch, but still, she'd do it from the cozy comfort of the sand with an iced tea beside her.

Covering a yawn with one hand, she tapped her fingers on the countertop with the other. A man behind her was telling a joke and the woman with him was already belly laughing. In the far corner booth, a young couple sat across from each other, sharing a plate of fries. Calliope stopped by their table with a bill and said something that made them both smile.

She brought Molly's cola and placed it in front of her. "Okay. I'll give you the rundown first. Of course, I'm going to tell you there's no finer establishment to eat than mine, but should you want something different, Morning Muffins is the best breakfast spot on the coast. I've got the waistline to prove I verified that. Stay away from Dot's Bakery. It's just a hobby for her and really, she should have taken up needlepoint. There's a town council meeting every second Thursday. It's the best place to get gossip. If you're grocery shopping, head to the edge of town to the Greedy Grocer. Best prices around. If you're into chain stores, you'll find most of them just outside Britton Bay, but you can find most of what you need right here. It's always better to stay local. Corky Templeton is our town crazy and we all take good care of him. Swears he's been hit by lighting six times and to be honest, I don't doubt it. You'll see him around and every time he talks to you, he'll leave in a hurry, thinking someone's after him. He means no harm, but he's a lot to take in on the first meeting."

"Cali, you gonna talk all day or bring that girl her dinner?"

Molly's eyes went to the back of the diner. She could only see the portion of the yeller's face that wasn't covered by the chrome pass. He gave a wide toothy smile and a wave.

"That's my man, Dean. Cooks like a dream and does plenty of other things well too. But I'll tell you, come football season, I may crash at that carriage house of yours."

Calliope started to turn when the door swung open again. Molly's eyes widened and she couldn't help thinking there must be something special in the water surrounding Britton Bay. The woman walking in was nothing short of striking, in a Jackie O sort of way.

"Hey there, Clara," Calliope called.

Clara Phillips Black. *Guess Vernon was right about being able to talk to them anytime.* Molly had a pretty good memory, especially since they'd spoken about Clara's family today, but with all the information Calliope liked to dish, she'd need to jot down names if she had any hope of remembering everyone she was meeting or hearing about.

Calliope leaned close again and Molly felt like she was in high school, whispering while the teacher was turned away.

"That's the mayor's wife. Her great-great-great-granddaddy and his brothers were the founders of Britton Bay. She's the last one in her line still in the area. Takes great pride in the cachet her family's name brings. Goes on a little too much about it now and then, but she loves the town and she and her husband take good care of it. They have a daughter. Savannah. Little socially awkward, but nice enough girl."

Clara came their way as Molly marveled at how much Calliope knew. She was better than any Google search.

"Hi Calli. I'm just picking up an order. It's study night," Clara said. She turned her smile on Molly. "Hi there. You're new here."

Molly held out a hand. "Molly Owens. I just started at the *Bulletin*. It's a pleasure to meet you."

"Oh, that's right. I knew Alan had brought someone in for the position. Well, let me officially welcome you to our little piece of paradise. You'll love it here, I'm sure of that."

Other than a grumpy old man and some flat tires, the mayor's wife was right.

"Hey there, Clara. Got your order here," Dean called from the pass.

Clara looked over, then back at Molly. "Again, welcome."

"Thanks," Molly said.

Calliope walked alongside the woman to get Molly's meal. Her stomach rumbled impatiently. She really needed to do a better job at keeping a routine. Or starting one.

Calliope was back inside a minute, a wide smile on her face. She waved as Clara left, takeout bag in hand. Knowing there was dine-out service could be dangerous to Molly's waistline and budget.

"There you go. It's on the house. Dean says I need to let you eat in peace—so I will—but you drop by again soon and I'll take a break and grill you proper."

Shaking her head, beyond amused, Molly beamed. "I will absolutely do that. Thank you. This smells delicious. Do you guys advertise in the *Bulletin*?"

Calliope's lips straightened. "Hmm. Haven't in a long time. Me and Dean were thinking of sponsoring some adult slow-pitch teams though, so maybe we ought to consider it. I'll talk to him. Go on, dig in."

Molly did just that. Her mouth watered as she took her first bite. It was fresh with perfectly crispy batter. The fries were golden brown and served with a sauce that added a hint of sweet. She was rethinking her need for a kitchen. If she could afford to eat out every night, she wouldn't bother with a rental.

Once she finished, Molly left a tip and waved to Calliope and her husband. She'd escaped the questioning for today, but she didn't doubt the cheery redhead would hold true to her word. As she approached her Jeep, she took a deep breath, then expelled it as she walked around it once. All four tires were fine. *What? You think he was going to follow you around giving you flats?* It wasn't the worst welcome she'd ever had, she remembered as she followed Sam's directions to the bed-and-breakfast.

When she was in fifth grade, her father had been stationed in Texas. Her classmates there had welcomed her by putting a tack on her seat. It had pierced her left butt cheek, making her yelp and hop up. Humiliated, she'd run from the room. To this day, she never sat down without giving the seat a quick glance. Four flat tires were nothing she couldn't handle.

Thinking about her dad made her miss him and her mom. He'd retired and they were living in Arizona now. Molly had lived there while she'd gone to college, but had moved to California for a job. And a man. Only one of which made her happy.

Slowing the Jeep for the light, she took a right onto LaMonte Avenue. A quaint residential street, lined with trees and black lampposts. Each house looked like a gingerbread home. In spring. Pastel colors and window shutters made Molly feel like she was driving down a lane in the game

Candy Land. At the end of the street was a pale blue Victorian-style home. Parking on the road, she walked up to the white steps of the wraparound porch, to the front door.

She knocked, then wondered if she should have called first. Like she'd been expected, the door opened and a dark-haired woman greeted her with eyes and a smile she'd already seen once today. Sam hadn't mentioned this was his mother, but there was no denying he was her son. He got his rich, dark hair from her, along with the eyes and slightly playful smile. Strands of gray weaved through the thick side braid she wore.

"Hi. You must be Molly. Sam called and told me you might come by. Then Calli called and said you were on your way," the woman said.

The town seemed to be making her mind up for her. But Molly trusted her gut, and like Calliope Jacobs, this was going to be someone she liked. She extended her hand. "I didn't expect them to do that. I am Molly. You must be Katherine."

Sam's mother nodded her head and stepped aside, dropping Molly's hand so she could step in. "I am indeed. Come on in. I'll make you a cup of tea and then I'll show you the carriage house. It's fully furnished, but I can store whatever you don't want in there."

She shut the door behind Molly, who looked around the stunning entryway. Dark hardwood floors matched the wide mouldings on the walls. A short, wide staircase was directly ahead of her and to both sides, arched doorways led into other areas of the house. The air smelled of cinnamon, making Molly feel like she'd wrapped herself in a cozy blanket at Christmastime. Even without seeing the carriage house, she knew it would be a replica of the fine craftsmanship of the main house. Clearly, ambiance mattered to Katherine.

As Sam's mom chatted about the history of the bed-and-breakfast and her current guests, Molly bit back a yawn. After her tea, she'd head back to the hotel for a final night, but Molly knew, before she even took a seat at the beautifully finished farmhouse table, that she'd found her home. The way Katherine put her at ease was one more sign. She would be happy here.

Chapter 3

The next few days went by in a blur of learning and adjusting. After she settled into the carriage house, making the space her own, Molly forced herself to take a walk each evening. Sitting all day wasn't bad for her just physically, but it tended to make her feel a little too slothlike. It'd be too easy to get into the habit of coming home, eating, and surfing channels or the internet until she fell into bed with a book. The fresh air was welcome and her walks let her familiarize herself with the area.

If she cut through a park near the bed-and-breakfast, there was a trail leading to some steps down to the ocean. Surprisingly, Molly rarely saw anyone on it. Maybe it was the time of day she was walking, but it made her feel like she'd discovered her own, secret little path. Other than the occasional birdsong and the distant sound of the water, she was alone with her thoughts.

This was the routine she'd needed to establish and as she came up on the ocean, stopping to toss a few rocks into the waves, she was glad she'd forced herself out again this evening. She waved at an older couple holding hands as she passed them along the sand. Taking a deep breath of sea air, Molly breathed the stress of the last few days out of her shoulders.

The last few days had been…productive, but tense. Together, Clay, Elizabeth, and Molly worked to get the current week's paper to press. Though Alan was in and out of the office quite a bit, he insisted she worry more about the following edition rather than the one they were on. Elizabeth was great while Alan was there, but any time he stepped out, she lost focus. Vernon kept to himself at his little desk, working on his laptop, writing in a notebook or jotting down notes on his endless supply of Post-its—which apparently no one else had permission to touch. At one point, he even put in earbuds to drown the rest of them out. Along with developing her own routine, she was learning theirs.

She was trying hard not to push everything on them at once. Several times, she'd had to bite her tongue when Vernon rebuked an idea she gave for further developing a story. It was like he was scared to add a little depth, or—God forbid—an actual source. Molly wasn't sure if he was just that set in his ways or merely determined to butt heads with her. And everyone else around him.

Resuming her walk, appreciating the freshness of the air and the sound of gulls swooping in the distance, she made herself think of more pleasant things, like her new home. The carriage house was tucked in behind a couple of oak trees at the back of the bed-and-breakfast property. Katherine told her it hadn't yet been rented, as she'd just had it fully finished and furnished a couple of months prior. The constant yawning on Molly's part had cut the first evening short, but she had a feeling, like Calliope, Katherine would soon find a way to chat her ear off. Molly was looking forward to it.

As Molly padded out of the sand and onto the concrete walkway that lined the beach, she noticed a man leaning under the hood of his car. He was broad-shouldered with dirty-blond hair, and she wouldn't have paid much attention if he hadn't suddenly slammed the hood down and kicked the front tire several times. Though she couldn't hear the words he was saying, she guessed they weren't too pleasant.

Car trouble sucked. She knew that firsthand, but his reaction seemed a little over-the-top. There were a few other cars in the lot, but no other people. If there had been, she may have offered assistance in the form of her cell phone. Which would have been unnecessary, she noted, as he pulled one out from his back pocket. Molly turned in the other direction as the man stalked away from the car.

Things might take some getting used to at work, but her car was running, she had some money in the bank, and a great place to live. *Not too bad. Plenty to be happy about.* Still, there was a restlessness nagging her, quickening her step. Nothing a good book—or an engaging article from one of the *Bulletin* writers—wouldn't cure.

With her first week in the area disappearing like a snap of her fingers, Molly was feeling truly settled. The heat of the sun was already pressing down when she parked in one of the spots behind the *Bulletin*. Dropping her satchel and her laptop on her desk, Molly went to the small kitchen in the back of the office to make some coffee.

Her phone rang and she swiped the screen, smiling at her friend Tori's image. Excitement flooded her veins. It had been too long since they'd spoken.

"Hey. I was going to phone you tonight."

Tori chuckled. "Sure you were. I was worried your new job had swallowed you whole. How is it?"

Molly looked around the room she was in. The building was old, like the newspaper itself. It didn't stand out with character the way many of the other buildings in the neighborhood did, but the inside was spacious and comfortable. It made her happy to be there.

"It's good. I like the office. Most of the people are nice. The food here is crazy good. How's Hollywood?"

She'd met her best friend when she'd done some freelance editing for her. They'd met up in person to discuss her script and hit it off instantly. She'd been the one thing Molly had been sad to leave behind when she'd cruised out of L.A.

"The same. Busy, but good. You sound good. I worried you wouldn't," Tori said.

Molly stared at the coffee, willing it to drip faster. "I'm fine. Honest. How do you have time to worry?" She knew what kind of hours her friend spent in writers' rooms, chugging coffee like it was water.

"I get a chance to squeeze in a thought of you now and again. What do you mean, *most people*?"

Molly laughed, grabbing a mug. *Of course she'd zero in on that.* "There's one guy who seems to wish I'd gotten lost on my way here. But apparently he hates everyone, so it's not just me."

"Couldn't be you anyway. Clearly, he has a problem. I miss you."

"Me too. But this was a good move. I'm going to be happy here," Molly said. She removed the not-yet full carafe and poured a half a cup. *Mmm. Happier now.* Moving to the fridge, she grabbed the cream.

"That's all that matters then. I gotta go. Love you."

"You too."

Molly hung up and doctored her half cup of caffeine and enjoyed it while waiting for the rest to brew. She wandered, cup in hand through the empty office. It was peacefully quiet with no one else there.

There was a conference room, a few offices, a small kitchen, one bathroom, and a central area at the front of the building. It looked out onto the street and housed partitions to separate the employee desks around the edges of that room. In the center, a large island-type counter, bigger than any kitchen-style one, allowed them all to gather around and organize layouts and designs. Molly couldn't wait to do that. *First priority after pouring an actual full mug of coffee.*

Second, would be figuring out a way to tell Vernon his timeline could have been done by any person who had the ability to use Google. Elizabeth's pieces were fairly straightforward to edit. They could use some spice and a few more powerful sentences, but until Molly got her finger on the heartbeat of the Bay, current-event types of stories would have to do. The rich, bitter taste of the coffee made her feel more alive. Heading to her office, she opened up her laptop.

Messages from her mom and Tori popped up on her personal email. She was used to missing her parents since they hadn't lived in frequent-visits distance for a while. She typed a quick email to say she was fine. Her parents would want more details, but they'd have to settle for a quick hello. If she didn't give them something, they'd be on her doorstep just to see for themselves she was okay. Molly wouldn't mind curling up on the couch with a hot chocolate and telling her mom about this cute little town. *Later. You can update them later. Right now, get to work.* She opened up a new email account specifically for the office staff. One of the biggest problems, in her opinion, was the lack of communication between Alan and his writers. He let them print what they wanted without offering guidance or input. By the time they got their stories to him, it was too late to edit or change much. Not if they wanted to make the deadlines. He'd told her, when they'd spoken on the phone, that he knew this wasn't how to make it a success, but his heart wasn't in it.

Molly wondered if that was because his heart was too tied up in Elizabeth. *A week in and now you're going to be a gossip?* She wanted her staff to rely on facts, so she should do the same. She had no proof that Alan and Elizabeth had a thing going, but boy, did she suspect it. *Coveted glances, unspoken words.* He'd mentioned his wife in passing a few times, but Elizabeth hadn't mentioned a spouse or partner. *None of your business and just because you're jaded doesn't mean Alan is messing around.* She hoped he wasn't, though, because he seemed like a very nice man and that would change her view of him.

Molly made it through her first coffee in record time and made herself take time to enjoy the second mug. By the time Elizabeth, Vernon, and Clay showed up, she was ready to show them how great the *Bulletin* could be.

"What's all this?" Elizabeth asked, stowing her purse in the drawer of her desk. Her normally neat hair was coming out of its tight ponytail. As if she knew she looked a bit frazzled, she smoothed out the front of her cream-colored blouse. Vernon looked her over and Molly's stomach twisted at the smirk he gave his co-worker. Perhaps she wasn't the only one suspecting things.

Refocusing all of them, she walked to the white board that hung on the wall to the right of the picture window. On top of an agenda for the day, she'd also listed several story ideas for the upcoming edition. Ones she fully expected them to pursue. Vernon didn't even look at the board. He opened up his laptop and ignored her while Clay opened the main computer housed on the layout desk. They'd do the page planning today, run with the stories they had. The next issue was due to go out in three days, but Molly continued to suggest tweaks and small changes. If she could get Vernon to follow through on an interview and get a look at Hannah's as well, there'd be some more interesting pieces hitting the news soon.

The actual press was in the basement of the building. It was small in comparison to some of the monsters Molly had seen, but the *Bulletin* only produced a twelve-page paper. It was more than adequate for their needs.

Keeping her eye on Clay, she noted that he moved around the graphic software with ease. She might get a creepy vibe from him, but he knew what he was doing.

"I'd like each of you to sign up for a GotMail account. We'll use it to communicate within the office. You'll send your articles and assignments this way and then I can edit and get them back to you quicker."

Vernon snorted. "Figure we're going to stop talking to you so fast we need to email?"

Molly waited until he was looking at her and smiled at him. "Actually, I plan on keeping you all so busy that between running down stories and writing, you might not have time to speak."

From the corner of her eye, Molly saw Elizabeth cover her mouth with one hand. She heard Clay snicker behind her, but held Vernon's gaze. Having the newspaper generate more readers would only benefit all of them. Without it, she still had her freelance gigs. But what did they have?

Looking over to Elizabeth, she gestured to the whiteboard. "I'd like you to contact Calliope Jacobs at Come 'n Get It. Tell her we'd like to run a full-page ad for free next week. I want you to go interview her and her husband. We'll run a ten-question interview alongside food and drink features. Clay, I'd like you to go with her and get some photographs of the diner. Set up your emails first and give them to me. I'll email you the questions I made up last night, Elizabeth."

There was a second of silence before she nodded. "Of course."

"I'll finish up the layout while I wait for you," Clay said. He looked at Molly, shifting the ever-present pen cap to one side of his mouth. "I already have a GotMail account."

Turning to face him, she took a quick breath and hoped she didn't make all of them hate her. "The sole purpose of it needs to be work-related. If it's a personal account, I'd like you to start a second one."

He smirked. "Yes, ma'am."

Satisfied, she turned to walk to her office. Stopping at Vernon's desk, she lowered her voice. "I'd like to see you in my office."

She was seated behind her desk and looking through his timeline when he finally strolled in. Dressed in a horizontally striped golf shirt and dress pants, Molly figured at least he looked professional, even if, so far, he hadn't acted that way. It was time to set things straight.

He sat in front of her and she didn't waste any time. She didn't want to give herself the chance to chicken out. Ideally, she'd liked to have confronted him with Alan standing at her back, but she wasn't exactly sure where her boss was this morning.

Folding her hands in front of her on the desk, she met his bored gaze. "I don't want to have tension between us. We're a team and need to act as such. You might not like it, but I'm in charge of articles and assignments now. If you have a problem with that, you'll need to take it up with Alan. My hope is, once you lose the chip on your shoulder, we'll work well together. I've read several of your old articles from a few years ago and there's some great writing there. But in the past couple of years, you've gone from reporting to summarizing. Your timeline is oversimplified. There's nothing in it that a Google search wouldn't show. You said you'd contact Vanessa Phillips. I'd like to see your interview questions. When are you meeting with her?"

He shifted, settling one foot on his knee. "Any reason I can't just do a phone interview? I don't care who is in charge, but I don't need a babysitter."

That was a lie. He cared. Molly could see by the banked fire shimmering in his eyes that anger fueled his attitude.

"Maybe not, but you need some guidance on what you're delivering to *Bulletin* readers. I want you to go to her home and make the readers feel like they went with you. At one time, delivering news mattered to you. I want it to matter again."

Vernon dropped his foot and leaned forward. "I bet you wish I cared what you want."

"I care what she wants," Alan said from the doorway.

Molly glanced up, nerves prickling her skin. She hated confrontation. Alan was an imposing figure, standing tall in a navy blue suit. His graying hair was lightly gelled back from his face. He looked tired. And mad.

"Alan. Nice of you to show up," Vernon said.

Eyes widening, Molly looked back and forth between them. *Maybe he should do some research on manners.* She'd never speak to a superior in that tone. Not if she wanted to keep her job. Vernon wasn't even doing his job. Why did Alan put up with his insolence?

"Cut the crap, Vernon. We're all working toward the same thing. It's either we turn the paper around or we close it down."

Vernon's shoulders relaxed slightly and he stared at Alan, as if trying to see if he was lying. Looking at Molly, he shrugged. "Fine. I'll see if I can go meet with the old bat. Maybe even this afternoon if it doesn't interrupt her teatime. I'll take Clay with me so he can photograph the house. I'm sure our readers would like to see how the other half lives."

He stood and pushed past Alan. Molly called after him. "I'd like the rough version of the interview in by tonight, please."

He lifted a hand as he continued walking. "Yes, boss."

Alan frowned at her and took the seat Vernon had vacated. "I'm sorry."

"For what?" Like she didn't know. A heads-up about Vernon certainly would have prepared her better.

"He's good at his job. They all are. I just haven't been demanding they prove it lately."

Molly sighed. At least he was honest. "I can pull back a bit. I know I've assigned more than they're comfortable with, but it pays to look ahead. Still, I can move slower so they don't feel like I'm changing everything."

Her boss leaned back in his seat, adjusting his tie. "No. You're ripping off the Band-Aid. I've learned the hard way that trying to protect everyone's feelings doesn't necessarily save them in the end."

The sadness in his voice made Molly's heart ache. She was pressuring everyone else to dig deeper. She needed to take her own advice and get to know her colleagues better. *Cut yourself some slack. It hasn't been that long.*

Before she could say something comforting—even if it would have sounded trite—he stood and brushed invisible lint off of his trousers.

"I'm contacting a few businesses today. Having you here means I can focus more on the marketing aspect. Don't worry; I plan to pull my own weight," he joked.

She appreciated the lighter tone. "I fully expect you to," she teased.

* * * *

By late that Thursday afternoon, Molly was the best kind of tired—the kind that came from working hard and having something to show for it. With no argument, Clay and Elizabeth had gone to interview Calliope and Dean. As expected, the answers to their questions were as full of life as the woman herself. Without a doubt, Molly could picture Calliope flaunting the full-page ad and interview around the restaurant.

Vernon had said nothing else to her that morning. He'd stepped out for lunch, leaving through the back and returning the same way. They all noted the snarl on his face, as it kept everyone from speaking to him. Molly was relieved when Vernon had left for the interview, taking Clay with him.

The office was quiet and as Molly poured over the layouts on the computer, she was pleased with the progress. This week's paper, which went out on Sunday mornings, was nearly ready to go. Next week, they'd have Calliope's interview and Mrs. Phillips's interview as features. Small changes would lead to big improvements. She hoped.

The front door opened and Hannah walked in, her smile leading the way. With her light blond hair pulled back, she was youth personified. She wore slim-fit jeans and a T-shirt, making Molly think of the all-American girl.

"Hey, Molly. Oh. Wait, should I call you Ms. Owens? I'm sorry," she said as the glass door drifted closed behind her.

Molly waved her suggestion away. "Of course not. It's nice to see you. You look like springtime and summer rolled into one. How was school?"

Hannah lifted her purse off of her shoulder and hung it on the coatrack tucked in a corner. "It was good. Same as always. One class after another, high school boys being dumb, track-and-field practice, and way too much homework."

Molly smiled, not wanting to tell the perky girl that despite graduating, boys could still be plenty dumb. Instead, she took a safer route. "You're on the track team?"

Hannah walked to where Molly was seated at a high stool beside the layout center. She peered over her shoulder and Molly caught the scent of lavender in her hair. If she were to check, her own hair would probably smell like hotel shampoo. She'd even brought it with her when she'd packed her stuff for the carriage house. She really needed to do a thorough shop. Get some nice smelly conditioner and some new bodywash. Her travel-size one was down to its last drop. Her mother would fret if she knew how wrapped up Molly had been. Balance had never been her strong suit. *You should make a list. Toiletries and groceries. Might want to worry more about feeding yourself than smelling nice.*

"Oh! Is that Calliope? She looks adorable. I'm surprised you got Dean in the photo. He's the shy one of the two," Hannah said.

Molly laughed. "He'd have to be. I can't imagine anyone being more outgoing than Calliope Jacobs."

"Yeah. She's good friends with my mom. I've been going to that diner since I was a toddler. Have you tried their sea-salt caramel pudding yet?"

Molly's stomach grumbled. *You will not eat out again tonight.* "No. But it sounds delicious. You guys sure like your country music and sea salt."

Hannah giggled and pulled a paper out of her pocket. "Well…yeah."

She handed the paper to Molly. They'd gone over a few questions yesterday and she took a moment to look through Savannah Black's responses. Hannah had written the answers verbatim, which tickled Molly's insides. Adorable. Whether Alan knew it or not, he had a budding writer in his niece. She'd made little notes in the margins for possible photos that could accompany the piece.

"This is excellent, Hannah."

The young girl clasped her hands together. "Seriously?"

Molly nodded. This was exactly the kind of energy they needed. "Completely."

Clapping her palms together in quick succession, Hannah bounced up and down once. "I'm so happy you like it. Thank you for giving me the chance."

Her attitude was far more appealing than another writer's on staff. "You're going to get more than one. I'd like you to write a list of sporting events happening at your school. Cross-reference the two closest high schools to this county to see if there's any overlap in games, playoffs, or highlights. Do you attend many sporting events at your school?"

Hannah nodded, going to the mostly empty desk that sat alongside Elizabeth's. "Obviously I attend the ones I participate in. That's basketball, track, and swimming. But I've gone to several football games with friends. It's kind of a Friday-night thing during the season."

"That makes sense. I think we should be sharing more about local athletes and events. You want to do another interview? Maybe with one of your track teammates or one of the football players?"

Hannah's eyes sparkled all the way across the room. "Uh, there's one player I wouldn't mind interviewing. He's the quarterback and there's rumors he's already being scouted by Ivy League schools."

Why the heck weren't these things hitting the paper? Surely that was more interesting than the two-for-one sale at the grocer. "That sounds ideal. Of course, you'll need to make sure you can keep the interview one hundred percent professional."

Molly tried to keep a straight face as Hannah bit her lip. "What do you mean?"

Lips twitching, Molly looked back at her screen. "Something tells me this football player might be as easy on the eyes as he is good at the game."

The young girl's laugh had Molly smiling for the rest of the day.

* * * *

Molly intended to check out the Greedy Grocer, but as it was more convenient, she picked up all of the items she'd put on her list from the Shop & Stop. The bed-and-breakfast—*home, start calling it home*—made her feel calmer just by looking at it. The large lot had trails and trees and flowers everywhere. Birds sang overhead and the sun peeked around white, fluffy clouds. Her hideaway was tucked in between two tall oaks and had a cute little cement path leading to the door. She let herself into the small unit with the key Katherine had given her the first night.

Molly shut the door with her foot and off-loaded her bags onto the gleaming white countertop. It had been a great day and excitement continued to swirl in her chest and stomach. Unloading her groceries and tucking them away in the cabinets, she left out a bag of chips. Opening it, she shoved several in her mouth. When she'd left L.A., she'd taken her clothes, some linens, her laptop and other devices, and not much more. All she'd really wanted was to leave her tarnished memories behind.

Finding a furnished place was another sign she'd made a good decision. The space was adorably decorated, with vintage pieces, such as the light blue table under the window and the funky side table between the couch and armchair. The bedroom fit a double bed and a dresser. Barely. She unloaded her groceries and lined the wall of the tub with her new soaps.

When she finished, she set her laptop up on the counter, wondering if she should purchase a small desk. *Counter and couch will work.* No need to make the space feel overly crowded. At the moment, it had a home-sweet-home vibe. She snapped a few pictures on her phone and sent them to her parents and Tori.

Munching on chips, she pulled up her email, pleased to see each of the staff had sent her an "I signed up for GotMail" message. What didn't please her was the lack of an interview from Vernon. He'd left in the early afternoon and it was nearing seven now. He should definitely have finished since she'd only asked for the transcript of the interview for now. She opened the Word file where she'd saved everyone's contact information.

Finishing a mouthful of chips, she dialed Vernon's phone number and pressed her cell to her ear as she got herself a soda from the fridge.

"Hello?" Vernon's voice was gravelly and she wondered, not for the first time, if he was a smoker.

"Hi. It's Molly. How'd the interview go? Can you send me an email with the answers?"

Shuffling noises made her brows pinch together. Was he looking for his notes? "Uh, yeah. I'm working on it. It's pretty dull, as I told you it would be."

She pressed her lips together tightly and breathed through her nose. "I'm sure we can find a way to spice it up. Did she give you anything of interest? From what I've heard, the family loves to talk about themselves."

"A couple of grainy old photos. Some journals. Not much anyone would be interested in. There's some pictures of her as a teen and she went on about meeting Charleston Phillips and how special the family is until I wanted to poke sticks in my ears. Old Lady Phillips seemed like she'd taken the edge off with a glass or four of wine."

Molly's fingers clenched around the phone. *Great.* She wasn't sure if Vernon's assessment could be trusted since he hadn't wanted to go in the first place. Personally, Molly found the idea of journals and photos very interesting and, if presented properly, she thought the readers might as well. It was part of their own history. Vernon coughed into the phone.

"I'm not going to be in tomorrow. Think I caught something from the old lady. I'll see you Saturday."

Irritation made the hair on the back of her neck stand up. He was so abrupt.

"Is that something you need to clear with Alan?"

Vernon's throaty chuckle grated over her skin. "I don't think he'll complain. In fact, I don't think he'll say anything about it at all."

Molly's brows nearly touched. She did not understand this man, but staffing and sick days were not her concern. Still, she didn't like the nagging suspicion he was avoiding her.

She set her soda on the counter and pressed her palm flat against the cool surface. Through clenched teeth, she asked, "Are we going to stay at odds? Because it's tiring."

"Get used to it, sweetheart. Life is tiring." She heard him shuffling and he didn't bother to cover the phone when he called out, "Keep your pants on. I'm coming. I have to go. Got a visitor."

He hung up on her and the shock of it had her staring at her screen. All she could think was who would visit him willingly? Maybe it was food delivery. What an annoying, self-absorbed jerk. Molly worked not to judge people based on one or two incidents, but it was becoming impossible to see Vernon as anything other than a miserable old man.

Grabbing another handful of chips, she chewed angrily, trying to work her way back to a good mood. She thought of calling Alan to get Ms. Phillips's home number. Maybe she should have gone with her gut and interviewed the woman herself.

Giving up on work, Molly decided to change into her comfiest pajamas and binge watch *Veronica Mars*. It would take a lot more than one dour, has-been reporter to chase her out of this sweet little town. She'd find her way and her place and she'd do her job well. She'd make friends and keep them. Heck, maybe she'd even swing by to get her oil checked whether it needed it or not. The memory of the mechanic's warm smile was enough to incite her own. There were plenty of nice people in town.

Molly wouldn't turn tail and run because one man in a town of many had decided he hated her. For no reason at all.

Chapter 4

On Saturday, Molly wasn't late, but she definitely wasn't early. Intent on sticking to a routine that didn't include rushing into the office just to show she was there first, she swung into one of the diagonal parking spots outside of Morning Muffins. Sam Alderich stood at the counter, one jean-clad hip against it, chatting with Bella Reid, the baker and owner of the delectable-smelling shop.

"Good morning. Molly, right?" Bella asked, her dark, pixie-cut hair making her look more like a wood nymph than a baker.

Sam's eyes met Molly's and that tumble in her stomach she'd felt the first time, returned. She gave a small wave, hoping her cheeks weren't flushing pink just from seeing his happy smile.

"Morning, Bella. And yes, it's Molly. Hi Sam."

"Hi Molly." His eyes were lit with amusement and she wondered if he woke up with that mischievous grin.

"What can I get for you?" Bella asked as Molly approached the counter. Sam didn't move over one inch, so the scent of his cologne and…him washed over her, smelling almost as good as the coffee and muffins. She was extremely pleased that she'd showered with the subtle, berry-scented shampoo she'd purchased.

"I'll take a double-blueberry scone and a jumbo latte," Molly answered.

While Bella grabbed her order, Sam sipped his coffee, glancing at her and making nerves zip up and down her spine. *Nothing to be nervous about. He's just a guy. And you don't care because you're all about work.* All work or not, it would be hard not to notice the way his jeans hugged him perfectly or how at ease he was in his own space. In her space.

"How's the Jeep?" Sam asked.

"Great. Thanks. And for the carriage-house recommendation."

"No problem. I didn't say anything about her being my mom because I didn't want it to be weird, like—Hey, my mom has a place. She likes having you there. Says you're good people."

Molly laughed as she angled toward him. That sounded like something Katherine would say. Sam's dark hair fell onto his forehead just a little, making her fingers itch to push it back. *Fingers to yourself!* She did not, however, make any attempt to put space between them.

"You look just like her," Molly said.

Both of his dark eyebrows rose as Bella came back with her coffee and scone.

"I look like my mom? Um…thank you?" Amusement colored his tone.

Bella laughed and Molly peeked at the floor, wishing it would slip out from under her. Heat rose over every inch of her skin, but she made herself look up at him as she tried to explain.

"I just—she has—eyes. You have her eyes." *And you're just making it worse.*

She pulled a five-dollar bill out of her pocket and set it on the counter. The nice thing about small towns was five bucks would cover it. The not-so-great thing was despite feeling like she'd just stuffed her hands into her mouth up to her elbows, there was nowhere to hide.

"I'm just teasing. I knew what you meant," Sam said.

When her eyes met his again, the warmth in his gaze settled her nerves. Bella pushed the five dollars back to her.

"First time is on the house," Bella said.

Because she wasn't done being ridiculous, Molly said, "But I've been here before."

Bella's light laugh filled the awkward space. "First time *I* serve you."

Molly grabbed her bill, her stuff, and started backing away. She hooked a thumb over her shoulder, pointing to the door.

"I should go. You know, news to report and all that jazz."

Sam smirked and Bella smiled like Molly hadn't just made a fool of herself.

"Have a good day," Bella called.

"See you around, Molly," Sam said.

Molly waved and got into her Jeep with measured movements. The last thing she needed was to drop her coffee or her breakfast right there in front of them. She resisted the urge to lay her head on the steering wheel. *Get over yourself. It's no big deal.* Right. What was a little foot-in-mouth-disease while talking to the one guy in town who made her heart hammer like a woodpecker gone mad? *You don't even know him. Stop it.* Taking her own advice, she started her vehicle and headed to the paper. The other nice thing about small towns was it took less than three minutes to get there. Maybe she should start walking to work.

Inside, she looked through her email while she inhaled her scone. Bella Reid was a culinary magician. Molly savored the last bite, thinking Guy Fieri should bring his red convertible to Britton Bay and check out the local food hot spots. He wouldn't be disappointed.

Washing down the scone with a long swallow of coffee, Molly checked the time on the computer. Where was everyone? They seemed to have an erratic start time, but Molly figured that was because she'd practically been showing up at dawn. As if she'd summoned company, she heard the front door bell jingle. Through her open office door, she saw Clay come strolling in, no pen cap in his mouth this morning. Maybe he ate something different for breakfast today.

"Morning," he said, not meeting her gaze.

"Morning," she replied, finishing up an email.

When she joined Clay, he was working with the layout of next week's edition on the computer. It was looking good. Glancing at the time again, she wondered where Alan, Elizabeth, and Vernon were. No one had been bothered by Vernon's absence yesterday, but today should have been business as usual. It was nearly nine. With the current edition printing today, Molly hoped they'd be able to follow up on some of the stories they were looking at.

When Elizabeth and Alan came in together at nine-thirty, Molly glanced up from her desk where she was proofing the articles Elizabeth had written on the local happenings around town.

"Good morning," Elizabeth called out, going straight to her desk.

"Morning."

Alan went directly into his office, offering only a small wave. Molly tried very hard not to speculate and distracted herself with wondering, again, where Vernon was.

"Is Vernon often late?" Molly asked as she walked to Elizabeth's desk.

Her hair was wound into a tight bun and she wore very little makeup. She was a pretty woman regardless, but the way she held and carried herself made her elegant as well.

She pursed her lips. "No. Not that I can recall. Want me to phone him?"

Molly shook her head. "No. I'll do it."

She left them to their work while she phoned Vernon and left a message on his voicemail. When he hadn't responded an hour later, she swung by Alan's office.

He was running his hands through his hair, staring down at a piece of paper that had clearly been folded several times. When she knocked on the door, he startled, closed up the paper, and forced a smile.

"How's it going?"

"Mostly okay. Vernon is late and Elizabeth says that's not the norm. I'm wondering if maybe someone should swing by his house."

Alan frowned, checking the time. "He's never late. I was surprised he even took a day off yesterday. Two in a row isn't his style. Did you phone him?"

Molly nodded, curious about the paper under her boss's hand.

"I can go over," Alan said. His tone was heavy.

"Why don't I go? I need to learn my way around and I'm worried that he's not here because I've hit him over the head with a bunch of new expectations."

She wouldn't feel guilty for doing the job she was hired to do, but maybe she could have tread a little lighter. Her eagerness, to others, might seem like forcefulness.

"You're only doing what I've asked you to. But sure, why don't you run by his place. You can take Clay with you," Alan offered.

It was Molly's turn to give a false smile. "I won't be long and he's working on the paper."

Alan nodded and when Molly walked away, she looked over her shoulder, toward the open office door. He'd unfolded the paper and was frowning at it. Obviously, not happy news. *None of your business.* Curiosity was in her nature, though, so it was hard not to wonder. Plus, she genuinely liked him. Whatever it was he'd read, hopefully it wasn't anything too bad.

Once she was in her Jeep, Molly followed the GPS instructions and drove away from Main Street into a more residential neighborhood. She passed Britton Bay High and the library, as well as city hall, the police station, and a few parks. The bus stops she saw had large, barrel-style planters on either side of them and were bursting with colorful flowers. A couple people were out walking or doing yard work. Idyllic, she thought. It was a sweet little town; big enough so that she would never know everyone, but small enough to feel like she knew many.

Vernon lived in a duplex about ten minutes from the paper. His aging, gray Toyota sat parked in the gravel driveway. She pulled in behind it, wondering if he was just having a tantrum. *Cut him some slack. Maybe he wanted and deserved the editing job and some girl swoops in from California and takes it?* She didn't do a lot of swooping, but she could empathize with the idea of things not working out as he might have hoped. Still, it didn't excuse not showing up for work.

Taking a deep breath and hoping the ocean air was filled with courage, she knocked with three hard raps on the door. She waited. Looking around from her spot on the concrete steps, she noted the yard was well cared for. The house itself was in good repair, painted a soft gray. She couldn't picture him home on the weekends doing yard work or puttering around. *You don't know him.*

Since finding her ex with *his* ex, Molly worried maybe she wasn't the best judge of character. The thought was unsettling. As was the silence. She knocked again. Had he looked out the window and seen her Jeep? The window to the right of the door had dark curtains over it. She pressed the doorbell and listened to the cheerful chime.

Her hand went to the doorknob before she even thought through how silly it was to turn it. But when she did, she found it unlocked. She snorted out a breath of surprise. Small-town living. No way would she have left her door unlocked in her old place. Or this one. Some city-girl habits were too well ingrained.

Uncertainty clawed at her chest. If Vernon wasn't a fan of her, coming into his house after he'd ignored her would not win him over. Straightening her shoulders, she opened the door a little wider.

"Vernon?" She put one foot in and tried to peek through the small opening she'd made. "Vernon? It's me, Molly."

The smell of alcohol hit hard. Molly scrunched up her nose. Maybe he wasn't pouting at all. From the smell of things, he was sleeping one off. The idea made her angry. If he didn't like her, *fine.* But don't use it as an excuse to be utterly irresponsible.

Molly opened the door wider and stepped into the house. She didn't shut the door behind her, figuring the place could do with some air.

"Vernon? Are you awake? You're late for work," she called.

An unwelcome thought jumped into her brain—what if he was with someone? *Oh please don't let me see that.* Slowing her steps, listening just in case, she shuffled down the narrow hallway. When she got to the end of it, there was a kitchen in front of her, a sunken living room to the right, and another hall to the left. From where she stood, she could see a television, a chair, and a wood-burning fireplace. Molly rounded the corner, wondering if he'd passed out on the couch.

When she saw Vernon lying on the floor near an antique pine desk, she stopped in her tracks. Idiot. He'd never even made it to the sofa. He'd just passed out right on the carpet. Taking the two steps down and then moving toward him, Molly's frustration rose like bubbles in a boiling pot. What a child.

"Wake up. This is ridiculous. Vernon! You need—"

Her words stuck in her throat as if she'd swallowed them wrong. Her vision blurred: The sight of Vernon lying facedown danced in front of her like an old film reel. He was lying in a pool of deep, rusty red liquid. Molly's stomach revolted, but she forced herself to lean closer.

"Vernon. Can you hear me? It's me, Molly. Vernon!"

She pressed her fingers to his neck, knowing by the cool feel of his skin that she'd find nothing. Had he hit his head? How could that kill him? She looked around frantically, wrestling with the zipper on her purse. She pulled out her phone just as her eyes landed on a stainless steel mug—one of those big, sturdy ones that she'd seen at construction sites. It was lying close to the body, on its side. Panic launched in her chest like a rocket. There was blood on the bottom of it.

She dialed 911. Small towns had that, right?

Without realizing it, Molly had edged backwards, away from Vernon's body. She hit the step with her ankles and lost her footing, falling and landing on her backside, as an operator picked up.

"Nine-one-one. Fire, police, or ambulance?"

Molly backed herself against the wall, unable to take her eyes off of the man she'd come to maybe form a truce with.

"Ambulance. Police. Both. I think there's been a murder," Molly said into the phone. She didn't recognize her own voice.

Chapter 5

Molly wasn't sure what to do in the moments between the phone call and the arrival of the police. Her eyes scanned the room endlessly as she tried to avoid focusing on the dead body. The dead body. She'd lived in major metropolises around the world and never had she stumbled into a crime scene. *A crime scene. Oh my God. Breathe.* Her eyes fell on Vernon again.

The stillness of his body stole her breath. Aside from the stainless steel cup lying a foot from Vernon's head, there was an upturned glass with a stain surrounding the carpet around it near the back of the desk. If she had to guess, she'd say there had been scotch in it—the stench still hung heavy in the room. It was making her stomach pitch. Molly pressed one hand to her stomach, while clutching her phone with the other. The tiny chip on the corner of the case—from dropping it on the cement—dug into her hand, but she didn't loosen her grip. The sting of it against her palm was tangible evidence she was alive and seeing this now. Alive. Unlike Vernon. Molly drew in a ragged breath, pushing back against the wall and somehow managing to find enough strength in her wobbly legs to force her up.

She couldn't look at him any longer. Keeping her back to the wall, needing the support it offered, she eased her way along until she was back to the intersection of the hallway. *Just leave. You can wait outside. One foot in front of the other. Go.* Molly hesitated, her legs feeling loose and uncooperative. Leaning over, she placed her hands on her knees and hung her head, breathing slow and deep. Nausea roiled in her stomach like she'd downed a liter of scotch herself.

A car door slammed outside. Molly lifted just her head, which felt heavy. Her eyes landed on a piece of plastic. Scrunching her brows together, forgetting the weakness in her lower limbs, she took a step closer to where the hallway led out of the house. Nestled in the carpet, resting along the white molding like it had recently been dropped, was a pen cap. Her heart seized. She got close enough to see the indentations in it—the *bite marks*—then froze as uniformed officers entered the house.

The officer who spoke first seemed very young. Or maybe Molly just felt very old in this moment.

"Ma'am? You're the one who called in a possible murder?"

The officer behind him had his hand on his gun, but the one who spoke just had a hand up, palm out, his body in the ready position. Ready for what? *For apprehending you! You just found a dead body. Oh God. Do not pass out. Calm down, you're going to hyperventilate. Pull yourself together. You're being ridiculous.*

"Ma'am? I'm Officer Beatty. Are you the one who called nine-one-one?"

She stood tall, breathed in and out through her nose. "Yes. My name is Molly Owens. I'm new in town and work at the *Britton Bay Bulletin*. I was coming to check on Vernon East because he didn't show up for work this morning."

Another officer appeared behind the two. Officer Beatty stepped toward her and reached out, took her arm. "Why don't you come with me while these officers secure the scene?"

It was a demand phrased as a gentle question, which Molly appreciated. She nodded and went outside, gulping in the fresh air like she'd been starved of it. How did everything outside look just the same as when she'd come in? Like a man wasn't dead on his living room floor; the world was exactly as she'd left it.

"You all right?" The officer let her arm go and pulled a notepad from his breast pocket.

"Compared to what?" Molly asked.

His dark hair matched his dark eyes, which crinkled around the corners with empathy. "Seeing a dead body never gets easier."

"I hope I don't find that out for myself."

"I need to ask you some questions," he said. The radio on his shoulder crackled and he spoke into it, asking for a Sheriff Saron to come to the address.

Molly sank down to the concrete steps and wrapped her arms around her knees, surprised by the chill in the air.

"Okay, Molly. What time did you arrive here?"

Molly answered the questions about her timing, her reason for showing up, her relationship to the deceased, and when she'd last seen him. No, she hadn't touched anything or seen anyone, hadn't been there long, hadn't heard anything strange. By the time Officer Beatty finished asking questions, two more squad cars and a truck with *Sheriff* written on the side pulled up to the house.

"Ma'am," the sheriff greeted. "Heard you found Vernon East. Not an easy thing to see. You doing all right?"

Molly nodded. "Yes, sir. Uh, I need…to go back to work. Can I go? Can I tell…who will tell Mr. Benedict and Vernon's coworkers?"

The sheriff and Officer Beatty exchanged a look and the officer stepped forward. "Why don't I take you back to the newspaper office and I'll inform them. I need to question them anyway."

"All right," Molly agreed.

She looked back at the house and then at the driveway. Her thoughts felt jumbled, like they were trying to wade through Jell-O. "I'll need my Jeep."

Officer Beatty gave a quiet smile. "Mind if I drive? I'll get one of the other guys to bring my cruiser back to the station later."

Molly dug through her purse and handed over her keys. Feeling as though she was moving in slow motion, Molly walked to the passenger side and climbed in. She didn't chat as Officer Beatty drove the short distance to the office. Nor did she say anything when he parked out front. Once out of the vehicle, she saw a blond-haired woman watching from across the street. She was arranging plastic-wrapped flower bouquets in large, silver buckets. The colors popped in a rainbow of petals. Molly stopped and stared at the woman, surprised by the way life carried on, regardless. An older gentleman walked toward the woman, a cute cocker spaniel bouncing along beside him. When he waved to the woman, she spoke to him and pointed at Molly.

"Ma'am?" Officer Beatty's voice broke through the haze.

"Molly. It's Molly."

He opened the door to the newspaper, gestured for her to go first. The others must have seen her through the window with the officer. Elizabeth and Alan were already walking toward her.

"What on earth? Molly, what's wrong?" Elizabeth's face was a study in confusion.

"Chris, what's going on? Why are you bringing Molly in?" Alan asked, speaking directly to the officer. Molly briefly wondered how they knew each other. *Small town.*

Clay turned his chair to face them, but stayed in his seat. His expression was blank—no surprise, no emotion. Between his lips, he held a dark blue pen cap, just like the one on Vernon's carpet. Molly's stomach tightened painfully.

Like a spectator, she listened as the police officer told them what had happened. Elizabeth covered her mouth with one hand and leaned on Alan. Her boss just shook his head, as if he refused to believe what he'd just learned.

"This can't be," Alan said, his voice hoarse. He turned to Clay. "Weren't you with your father yesterday?"

Molly snapped out of her fog like she'd been prodded with a branding iron. His father? Clay's father. Clay glanced at Molly, then at Alan.

"No. Dropped him off at his house the day before. After the interview with old lady Phillips," Clay said.

Officer Beatty pressed his lips together and breathed through his nose. He walked over to Clay. "I apologize. I didn't realize you were his next of kin. I'm sorry for your loss."

Clay shrugged and Molly stared, uncertainty whipping up a frenzy in her stomach.

"He's your father?" That explained the pen cap, didn't it? If Clay had been visiting his father, it would make sense. Maybe he'd dropped it when he said good-bye. Had he been the visitor?

Why hadn't it been mentioned, though? It seemed odd no one had mentioned the connection. Her question was ignored when Officer Beatty spoke to Clay. "When was the last time you were in your father's house? Did you go in the other night when you dropped him off? Notice anything unusual?"

Another shrug. "No. It's been months. We're not exactly close."

Months? Clay was lying. She could feel it. She could *see* it.

"Molly, honey, you look like you should sit down," Elizabeth said.

She shook her head, waved a hand in front of her. "I'm fine."

Why hadn't Clay said he was Vernon's son? *Would you admit to that parentage?* Guilt slapped at Molly immediately. Regardless of how unkind he was, no one deserved Vernon's fate.

"Is Mr. East married? To your mother?" Officer Beatty asked Clay, whose lip curled up.

"He's been married twice since Clay's mom. Gretta Reynolds hasn't lived in Britton Bay for years. Vernon has been single for the last five," Alan said.

Molly sat in Elizabeth's chair, listening as more questions were asked and answered. She couldn't stop seeing the image of Vernon lying on the floor, blood surrounding his head. What had happened? Had Clay hit his father with the coffee mug? Had they argued? If not Clay, then who? And why? And why now?

"Was Vernon working on anything controversial?" Officer Beatty asked. Did he not read the paper? The most scandalous thing about the recent stories was how dull they were. Molly looked up to see Alan was looking at her. "Uh, he wasn't working on anything abnormal. He interviewed Vanessa Phillips but said there wasn't much interesting about her answers. Did the meeting seem strange in any way, Clay?"

All eyes went to the sullen man. A stab of pity pierced Molly's heart. His father had just died. Which hadn't seemed to catch him off guard. He looked more...irritated than sad. Had he known before she did?

"Other than being boring, it was fine. She seemed a bit tipsy, I guess. But if I had her cash, I'd be drinking the good stuff too. We went to the mansion, they talked, I took some photos, and she gave us a photo box of old newspaper clippings and pictures. She raved about her amazing family."

Molly hadn't seen a box anywhere. When they'd spoken, Vernon had mentioned photos and journals. He'd seemed unimpressed, but had he found something in the box he hadn't shared? Something important? Molly's insides froze. The last time she'd spoken with him, he'd said he was working on the story. If his death did have something to do with the box...something to do with interviewing Vanessa Phillips...Molly was the catalyst. She'd pushed him to do the interview. To do some actual reporting. *Oh God. It's my fault.* A small sound left her lips, drawing all eyes to her.

She was responsible for Vernon East's death.

Chapter 6

It's not your fault. It's not your fault. Molly inhaled, sucking in a sharp breath when she realized how tight her chest felt.

"Molly?" Elizabeth put a hand on her arm.

Molly shook her head. "I'm fine."

"Under the circumstances, I think we should close the office for the day. Clay, let me drive you home," Alan said.

Elizabeth continued to stare at Molly and she told herself, once again, to get it together. She didn't need mothering. She needed to figure out if Vernon's death was her fault. The professional part of her brain jolted. *This* was news. *You're a terrible person.* But it was true. They needed to report on this and tell the town what had happened. This wasn't the sort of thing to be passed around as midday gossip. Though, no doubt it would be.

"I don't need a ride. I have my car. I'm going to head to my mother's house in Portland," Clay said. He had his hands shoved in his pockets and was looking down at his scuffed sneaker.

"I'm sorry for your loss," Molly muttered.

When their eyes met, she saw a flash of pain, which was quickly squelched by anger. "Not much of a loss, is it?"

"Clay!" Elizabeth glared at him.

He walked out the front door and the officer didn't stop him. Why would he? Only Molly knew he'd lied. *You think he lied. You don't actually know. Don't jump to conclusions.*

"I'd like his contact information and his mother's if any of you have that. Yours as well," Officer Beatty said, pulling out his notepad.

Molly had already given hers. She didn't want to go home to the carriage house to be alone, but she couldn't stay in the office right now. She gathered her things and asked for permission to leave. She didn't mention the story to Alan. She'd do it on her own, once she could pull in a breath without it getting stuck between her ribs.

She left her Jeep, deciding the walk would do her good. She'd come back later for her laptop. Slinging her messenger bag over her chest, she set out along Main Street, looking for any sign that the world had shifted—changed—with the absence of one person. She'd edited news stories on death, but there'd always been several degrees of separation. Now she'd be writing about the body she found. The little hairs on her neck stood straight.

"You lose your Jeep?"

Molly turned at the sound of Sam's voice. The tone and tenor was inviting—soothing like a cup of tea that warmed her from the inside. He stood outside one of the work bays. Behind him was a bright red car with its hood popped. Another mechanic was working beneath a dark truck that was hoisted in the air.

Sam wandered over when Molly just stood on the sidewalk, staring at him. She hadn't even realized she was walking past the service shop. She needed to jump out of this haze, but she couldn't shake it. She couldn't stop seeing Vernon's lifeless body. If she closed her eyes, it would be all she saw. A shiver raced over her body.

"Hey, you okay?" Sam's green eyes narrowed as he looked her over, like he could see on the outside what she felt inside.

"Vernon's dead," she answered.

Sam's eyes widened and he stepped closer. "What?"

Obviously, it was too much to keep contained because her words flowed like lava, filling him in on her morning, right there on the side of the street. Cars drove by, a few honked, people called out to one another, and in the distance birds squawked as they circled the pier.

Sam listened without interrupting, his lips parted in small *o*. When she finished, Molly felt like the weight of a grand piano had drifted up from her shoulders.

Sam bent his knees and put a hand on her shoulder so they were eye to eye. "Stay here a second, okay?" he said.

Molly nodded. Her phone buzzed in her back pocket, but she stood still, watching Sam speak to the other mechanic. He was back at her side in seconds. He took her arm and turned her in the other direction.

"Come on," he said.

"Where are we going?"

"Let's go grab a drink. You look like you could use the company."

She couldn't deny the *company* part. "It's too early for a drink," she said.

Sam laughed, dropping his arm, but staying close, as they walked side by side. "It is absolutely never too early for a milkshake."

He held the door of Sit & Sip open for her and despite the jumbled state of her thoughts, she inhaled the fresh, crisp scent of his cologne. If only she could trap that smell, maybe she could forget the acrid odor of scotch and stale air. The cool air danced over her skin, making goose bumps come alive.

"Hey Sam. Who's that you have there?" The guy behind the counter offered a salute-type wave. His dark blond hair was cropped close. He was tall and imposing and didn't look much like he was the type to serve up milkshakes. He also looked familiar—he was the man she'd seen getting irrationally mad at his vehicle, by the water the other day.

"Hey Callan. This is Molly Owens. She just moved to town."

Molly was grateful Sam kept it at that. News would spread soon enough. Callan...her mind backtracked, flipping through information. He'd fought with Vernon and he had a temper she'd witnessed. Grateful the work side of her brain even functioned at the moment, she wondered if there was a connection.

"Welcome to Britton Bay, Molly. What can I get you two?"

Sam looked down at Molly, a compassionate twinkle in his gaze. "Trust me?"

She blinked once, then nodded. He ordered one vanilla bean milkshake and one Oreo cookie shake, telling her they'd switch halfway. While Callan made their drinks, Molly forced herself to look around at what she knew was another hot spot in the area. It had retro diner–style tables with splashes of red, white, and blue on the walls and floors. Vintage posters for ice cream, soda, and summer fun adorned the walls. Her eyes kept sneaking back to look at the owner. His relaxed posture as he worked and the hint of a smile on his lips didn't scream *murderer*.

"You can't find a seat once the kids get out of school," Sam said.

Molly looked up at him, trying to dig herself out of the fog that wouldn't lift. He'd stayed close to her and she appreciated the warmth. He'd asked if she trusted him and on a gut level, she did. Even without the lure of how his gaze made her stomach tap-dance, he had a vibe that radiated steadfastness. When he tilted his head, bringing it slightly closer to hers, she realized she was staring.

"Here you go," Callan said, pulling both of their attention. He set the drinks on the counter and smiled at her.

Molly thanked him, taking one of the shakes. Sam paid and took the other. Just as they settled in a booth at the back of the restaurant, near a window, but away from the door, Callan called out over the low music pumping through the speakers.

"You on for poker next Friday or too scared to lose more money to me? Scared Vernon off. My guess is he won't be scamming any of us again."

Sam cringed when he looked at Molly. Did Callan know with absolutely certainty how right he was? Molly stared at him, trying to assimilate the two impressions she'd gathered of this man. Was he the easygoing, good-looking shake server or the car-kicking temperamental motorist? Both? Did it even matter?

"I'll be there. Your luck has to run out soon enough."

Like Vernon's, Molly thought. Her thoughts drifted to the conversation she'd had with Calliope. She hadn't mentioned what Vernon and Callan had argued over. Scamming them, perhaps? If he hadn't shown last night, maybe he'd been killed before the game. When her eyes drifted to Callan again, he was wiping the counter, whistling softly.

"Vernon wasn't at poker last night. Did he always play?" Molly asked.

Sam nodded, taking a drink of the vanilla shake.

Molly took a sip of hers and started to speak, but stopped and stared at it. "Oh my God, this is delicious."

"I know," he said, a small smile tilting up his lips.

His smile was a distraction for sure, but murder was a bigger one.

"Did Vernon get along with everyone?"

Sam scoffed. "Do you mean *anyone*?" He shook his head and frowned. "Sorry. That was insensitive. No. Vernon didn't go out of his way to make friends, so I wouldn't say he got along with the others. But he liked to play and until last night, never missed a game."

Unspoken words settled between them. Vernon obviously had a good reason for missing the game. Molly wondered how close Callan and Sam were. She sipped at her milkshake as the words formed. "What about him and Callan? Calliope said they argued at her diner last week."

Sam frowned, then gave a one-shoulder shrug. "Both of them are a little hotheaded. If they argued, it was probably just temper over something small. Callan thought Vernon was cheating. I'm not so sure. Are you okay?"

She stared at him and the need to tell someone how she felt clawed at her chest. "I can't help feeling like I'm responsible for Vernon's death. I pushed him to go interview the Phillips woman. He takes a day off yesterday, which he apparently never does. Then he ends up dead."

Sam reached across the table and covered Molly's hand with his. There was a spark of warmth that travelled up her arm, but there was also a welcome comfort in his touch. Later, when she was alone, she could think about how much she enjoyed the dual sensation.

"Molly, I can't even imagine how hard it must have been seeing Vernon. But it's not your fault. The police will figure this out. Sheriff Saron is a good guy. He's good at his job. And I went to school with Officer Beatty. The truth matters to them and they'll find it. You didn't kill Vernon and nothing you did prompted his death. And as for Callan, he was at the game last night."

The words soothed Molly to a small degree, easing the ache in her chest. Tears stung her eyes. She didn't have to like the man for death to be sad. But without knowing Vernon's time of death, could Callan really be ruled out? The man humming behind the counter did not seem like he'd kill and then carry on to a poker game. Sam pulled his hand back, slowly sliding his fingers along her skin and they both returned to their milkshakes. When he made it halfway through his, he switched, making her laugh.

"What if I don't want the vanilla?" He was distracting her when she shouldn't be letting herself get distracted. She had the distinct feeling he was doing it on purpose.

Sam gestured to the half shake now in front of her. "Taste it and then tell me you don't want it."

The creamy explosion of flavor made her sigh. Taking a long sip, she closed her eyes, wondering where these had been all her life. When she opened her eyes, Sam's expression was smug.

"Told you." He checked his watch.

"I've pulled you away from work," she said, wondering what she'd do with the rest of her day.

"No. Not at all. I do need to get back, though."

They finished their shakes and Molly appreciated the quiet without the solitude. When she stood, she saw Callan eyeing her in a way that made her nerves jump. Was he a man who would hurt someone to get what he wanted? Maybe she needed to ask Calliope more about the argument the amazing shake maker had had with Vernon. But not now.

Sam and Molly walked back to his service station. When they got there, he stared at her a moment. Her thoughts were still on Vernon, but more specifically, on his easy dismissal of the story he'd been working on. What if he'd lied? If he'd found something truly interesting, she was the last person he'd share it with.

Sam touched her shoulder. "Listen, I was going to swing by my mom's tonight after work. Do you maybe want to take a walk later or something?"

Molly blinked, realizing that if what she wanted was where she thought it might be, she could use his help. She bit the inside of her lip. He was good-looking and sweet. He'd shown her more kindness and compassion in twenty minutes than her ex had in their entire relationship—which she knew didn't speak well of her previous choices. Maybe she hadn't been the best judge of character in that instance, but it didn't mean her entire radar was skewed. It was easy to see and feel that Sam was different. Enticingly different. There was a chance they could go on an actual date some time. Unless she completely scared him away with her idea.

"Uh... you thinking about it?" He pushed a hand through his dark hair and lowered his gaze. She wondered if any woman had turned him down for a date, then wondered if any woman had asked something as crazy as she was about to.

"No. I'd like that, but...I—listen, there's something I need to get," she started.

His eyes came back to hers. "Okay."

Molly took a deep breath. "Vernon got a box of photos and things from Vanessa Phillips. But they weren't anywhere in the living room. Which is where his desk was and where he was."

Sam arched a brow. "Okay."

"I think they're in his car. Which I'm guessing is locked."

Both brows arched. *Your talent to end something before it has a chance to begin is truly remarkable.* No. She couldn't think like that. A man had been murdered and it was quite possible it had something to do with what he'd found. In order to get the police to look in that direction, she needed to see what he'd stumbled across.

"Molly?"

She inhaled and exhaled hard and fast. Clutching her hands together, she blurted out her question. "Do you know how to break into a car?"

Chapter 7

Sam's mouth hung open and in the instant Molly thought he'd tell her to go fly a kite, preferably far away from him, he smirked.

"You're an interesting woman, Molly Owens. I'll pick you up at nine. I'm thinking the cover of night works best for your nefarious plan," he said.

He shook his head, as if he couldn't believe her suggestion. Or his own agreement. A man who'd come along willingly, without looking at her like she was a loony tune, could be trouble for her heart. But this wasn't about her feelings. It was about figuring out what Vernon was up to. Being able to spend time with Sam was just a welcome bonus.

Molly walked back to the newspaper office and went around the back. She was almost at the door when someone shuffled behind her, making her jump and turn, smacking her back against the concrete building. She looked around and saw nothing in the back alley, other than a dumpster offering the faint scent of days-old garbage. Further down, cars were parked behind the various shops, but it looked as if the *Bulletin* staff had gone home. Molly wasn't ready to. She heard another noise and though her stomach danced like a bouncy ball, she continued to scan the area.

When she heard a growl, she thought *racoon*, but when a little white tail wagged into view her heart leaped. The rest of the body, starting with the back end, shuffled into view and Molly watched from a distance. The dog, a white and black breed she couldn't identify, was pulling on something behind the dumpster. It continued to tug and Molly's heart kept its steady pace. Giving one final tug, the dog fell on its haunches as a small stuffed bear, or what was left of it, flew through the air.

Laughter rumbled from Molly's chest. She let out a fast breath, opening her palm over her erratic heartbeat. The pup whimpered like he couldn't understand how the toy had bested him. Its head was barely attached and the stuffing coming out of the bright purple belly made Molly think of an exploding eggplant.

"It's okay, bud. That thing is probably dirty anyway," Molly said, taking a tentative step forward.

The pup, as if just realizing it had an audience, bounded over, tail wagging and tongue leading the way.

Molly crouched down, unable to hold back a smile. *What a cutie.* "Hey. You lonely? Where's your owner?"

She checked for a tag and found nothing but fur. Her—oops, *his,* little black nose was surrounded by a patch of white, while the rest of his head, including adorable floppy ears, were black. Molly glanced around once again while she gave the little guy some rubs.

"Aren't you friendly? Where'd you come from?"

Wondering if she should go to the various shops and ask around, Molly sighed. Despite it being barely noon, her energy was at an all-time low. Likely, word of Vernon's murder would have gotten around by now and with it, news that she'd found the body. She wasn't ready to repeat the story a dozen times and knew the best way to avoid that was to get the story out officially. Pulling her work key from her pocket, she let herself into the building. Holding the door open and whistling to the pup, she smiled when he followed her. *Ahhh, blind trust.*

Had Vernon trusted whoever killed him? Molly left the main overhead lights off inside. The back door led to a small room where staff hung their coats and old copies of newspapers piled up. She wandered through, having no trouble seeing with the way the sunshine poured in through the picture window. The pup followed behind her as if she'd taken him on an adventure. She smiled down at him. When she looked up, her eyes landed on Vernon's desk. Thoughts of how he'd died, when, and at whose hands assaulted her mind. Would she have had so many questions if she hadn't been the one to find him? Probably. It wouldn't have sat well regardless, but being the one to see him like that…to find him like that…added layers to her interest.

Walking slowly, she rounded Vernon's desk and sat in his chair. He had a desktop computer, but she'd only seen him work on his laptop. Hmm. His laptop…had it been on his desk? She didn't want to close her eyes and try to picture the desk, because everything else would come rushing forward. She didn't remember seeing it.

No one was in the office, but still, Molly opened the first drawer of Vernon's desk with a quiet slowness. Inside, she found pens, paper clips, several packs of gum, Post-it notes in every color, and an unused pocket calendar. She shut that one and opened the next. A bottle of scotch, nearly empty, rolled forward. The memory of the scent in the air had her swallowing down a nauseous feeling. At least he was consistent. She went through the whole desk and found nothing of consequence. Leaning back in his chair, her throat tight, she glanced around and realized the pup was not at her side.

Oh no. Please don't use the floor as a bathroom. "Pup. Come here, pup." She found him in Alan's office, curled up on the leather love seat that sat against the far wall. Molly smiled.

"Aw. You're a sweetie. Did you wear yourself out with your bear battle?" The pup's ears perked, but he kept his head down. Molly sat on the couch and pet him. In seconds, he was snoring softly. Perhaps it was silly, but the dog's presence settled some of the unease she was carrying around. Molly rested her head against the back cushion, her eyes staring up at the popcorn ceiling. How had this happened?

Murder was something people read about in papers; something she'd instruct her staff to write about. *Not* something she got up close and familiar with. She should call her parents. Tori. Someone. Her mind drifted back to Sam. It would be easy to let her thoughts focus on the way his fingertips had felt against her skin or the way he looked at her like no one else was around. *Stay on task. But which task?* Molly sighed loudly, gaining the pup's attention. She pet his head and he closed his eyes again. So easily content. Maybe she should go home. Instead, she sat, restlessness coursing through her veins.

She bounced her knee up and down distractedly and looked around Alan's office. It was welcoming, in a masculine way. His desk was a large, dark, plain rectangle. On the shelves behind his desk there were dozens of books and framed photographs. There were awards for the paper. Molly stood to have a closer look.

Picking up one of the pictures, she studied it. She knew very little about her boss, but she'd guess by the way the group stood together in front of a large, white boat, the first picture was his family. Alan stood, suntanned and smiling—which made him look far less reserved than he did in the office—with his arm around a petite blond woman. Beside her was a younger blonde resembling the first and on Alan's other side was a dark-haired, tall boy who looked ready to be a man. Had to be his wife and kids. There were more photos of him with the same people. He looked so…happy in those photos. So why the affair? *You don't know he's having an affair! Stop jumping to conclusions.* God. Molly felt like she'd landed in a prime-time soap opera. Possible affairs, death, and broody, suspicious young men.

Definitely not anything she'd counted on when she'd said yes to the job in this quiet little cove of a town. Molly turned, resigned to going back to the carriage house. At least there, she'd be able to do something productive. Working for a newspaper meant delivering the news and Molly was the perfect person to do it. The one who should have been the most removed. She didn't want to bother Alan with the printing press, so she'd do an article and post it on their website, Facebook page, and Twitter. *Like anyone even has Twitter in this town.* Other than the mayor, his wife, some of the teachers at the high school and their students, Molly didn't think it was a strong source of communication in Britton Bay. But it was a way to share the story.

When she finished that, maybe she could get some laundry done, answer some emails, or make something for dinner that didn't come out of a box. Feeling steadier with a plan, she turned to leave and saw the crumpled paper Alan had been reading earlier, sitting on his desk. Still folded, like he'd tossed it there earlier. *Mind your own business. Don't do it.* She inched closer. *Don't.* Why'd he leave it right there? *On his private desk in his private office? Don't!* But she did.

She picked up the paper and unfolded it, looking down at the printed copy of an email exchange. It was between Elizabeth and Vernon. The recently departed writer had been threatening to reveal what he knew of Elizabeth's relationship at the next public town meeting and to Alan's wife. Molly scanned the emails. He didn't even seem to want anything. He just continued to tell her he knew and that knowing was to his advantage. Elizabeth's responses were short and concise: *You're a vile man with nothing better to do than harass people. I'm warning you, don't do this.*

Molly's fingers tightened on the paper. Tears filled her eyes. She was sorry that Vernon died and she didn't condone affairs, for whatever reason, but how could the man be so malicious? To live his life just looking for ways to hurt people. *What goes around, comes around.* Though it didn't make her feel like a good person to think it, the sentiment was all too true in his case. Had Elizabeth or Alan felt the same way? Both of them had come in late this morning. So had Clay. Her stomach clutched at the thought of all of these people—who she was coming to know and like… well, most of them—having motive to kill Vernon.

Molly put the paper back and called the pup. She put a sign in the window that described the dog and said to contact her at the paper if he'd been lost. For now, she was desperate enough for company to bring him home.

The pup didn't seem to mind the car ride. He sat in the front seat, paws on the windowsill and watched Main Street go by. When she pulled up to the bed-and-breakfast, she drove around back to the parking spot near her place. Her smile bloomed without warning when she saw Katherine pouring drinks for a couple sitting on the back deck. The yard was well manicured, with strategically placed flower beds that created little walkways. The dog barked and Molly bit her lip. Perhaps she hadn't thought this through. She didn't even have a leash. When she got out of the car, she rounded the hood to grab the pup.

Katherine said something to her guests and met Molly at her car.

"You poor thing. How are you?" Katherine pulled her into a hug before she could open the door. Molly welcomed the embrace and the comfort. The dog went nuts against the window, clawing at it and yipping excitedly.

Before Molly could answer, Katherine laughed. "Who is your friend?"

When Katherine pulled back, Molly missed the feeling of warmth. She missed her own mom, her dad, and her best friend. Especially in this moment. She sniffled and gave a watery laugh.

"He was fighting a stuffed bear outside the *Bulletin*. No tags. I didn't want to just leave him and I wasn't up for going door-to-door to find the owner. I left a note in the window of the news office. I'll ask around tomorrow, but I should have checked with you first. I'm sorry."

Sam's mom waved Molly's concern away. "I'd have done the same thing. Let's get the little guy out of there."

She opened the door and the frantic dog practically jumped into the woman's arms, making Katherine belly laugh.

"You are an excitable little guy, aren't you?"

"I really didn't think this through. I don't have anything for him. Maybe I should take him to a shelter?" Molly pulled her laptop and bag from the Jeep as she spoke. Not what she wanted to do, but she really had no right to have brought a pet home.

Katherine continued to snuggle the pup. "I was so sad when we had to put our dog down last year. She was fourteen years old and the sweetest thing. I still have her kennel and dish. Why don't I dig them out?"

Molly's heart squeezed tightly, stealing her breath. "Are you sure? Thank you. I don't want to put you out."

Katherine's eyes met hers. "Honey. After the day Sam told me you've already had, please don't worry about it. In fact, I saved you some lunch. It's just terrible what's happened and I can't even imagine seeing what you saw."

Molly bit her lip to staunch the tears, but still had to blink rapidly to hold them at bay. She barely knew these people and had already asked this woman's son to break into a vehicle. Toning down the crazy would not happen if she burst into tears.

A car door shut and both women turned to see the sheriff walking toward them. Molly's gut seized.

"Afternoon, Katherine. Ms. Owens."

"Good afternoon, Sheriff," Katherine greeted. She leaned into Molly. "Let me just take the pup with me for now and you can get him settled after you're finished here."

Molly nodded and held the sheriff's gaze as he came closer. The couple on the deck watched curiously and Molly couldn't blame them.

"How you doing, Ms. Owens?"

She attempted a smile. "I'm okay and please call me Molly."

"All right then, Molly. You've picked a good place to settle. You're new in town. Where you from?"

Appreciating the small talk as it gave her shoulders a chance to unwind, she forced a deep breath in and out. Not knowing what to do with her hands, she shoved them into the pockets of her dress pants. "Lancaster, California." She looked around the yard. "I agree. This place is perfect."

"Katherine wouldn't have it any other way." He looked toward the house where the woman in question was showing off the pup. Molly skin warmed. Was that more than simple admiration she heard in the sheriff's voice?

He looked down again, meeting Molly's curious gaze. "Can we chat inside?"

Tension burrowed back under her rib cage. Leading the way, she let them both into the carriage house. Grateful she'd gone shopping, she opened the fridge and pulled out two cans of cola.

"You want one?"

"Actually, I won't be here long, but thank you."

Nice as he was, she was glad he wouldn't be staying. She put one can back and busied herself with grabbing a glass and ice. He waited patiently, which she supposed was part of his job. He had a friendly face to go with his seemingly laid- back nature.

"Alan says you and Vernon didn't hit it off," the sheriff said.

Molly's fingers wrapped around her glass and the cold pressed against the cut her cell-phone case had caused earlier.

"No. He definitely wasn't happy with my arrival."

The sheriff nodded and pulled out his notepad, writing that down. He flipped a page before looking up again, his light blue eyes pinning her to her spot.

"Did you argue?"

She'd done nothing wrong, but it took effort to keep the defensiveness out of her tone. "We talked on the phone Thursday night. He was pursuing a story I'd asked him to dig deeper on, but he told me it was boring and uneventful. When I asked him to send it to me, he snapped at me and hung up." Realization rocked her back on her feet. "Am I a suspect?"

Sheriff Saron's deep chuckle soothed the nest of bees buzzing around her stomach.

"No. Not at the moment. Can't imagine the first item on your agenda when moving to a new town is murdering a complete stranger."

"No. I can promise it won't be on my agenda even after I'm settled," she said. Then realized she'd just made a joke about murder and she froze. "God. I'm so sorry. That was a horrible thing to say."

"No need to apologize, Molly. There's no right or wrong after you've seen something like you did and I'm impressed at how well you're holding up."

Ha. He doesn't want to be around ten minutes after he leaves. She wanted to curl up into a ball on her bed, maybe with a cute little puppy snuggled into her side.

"We will have to get your fingerprints to exclude them from the crime scene. It'd sure be helpful if you popped by the station sometime today or tomorrow."

"I can do that." She bit the inside of her cheek. "Do you have any suspects?" *If not, I have a few.*

Should she mention the pen cap? The emails? She was really ringing the crazy new-girl bell with her suspicions and suggestions. Maybe it was better to keep them to herself.

"Nothing conclusive yet. We don't get much of this sort of thing around here. We're going through everything by the book, but it takes time. It's not like you see on television. There's no one who owes me any favors that'll make them push through the evidence faster."

Just tell him. He watched her, his eyebrows lifting in slow motion.

"Something on your mind?"

"It's probably nothing."

"Some people's nothing can be a tiny piece of a puzzle."

She pushed her drink around the countertop in small circles. "It's just… on my way out the door at V—Vernon's, as I was leaving to wait outside for the police, I noticed a pen cap. It was chewed."

One side of his lips tipped up. "Lots of people have a habit or two that involves chewing on something."

Her shoulders tightened. "Clay does. He chews on a pen cap constantly and I know I have no right to point fingers because I don't know anyone and I'm not trying to stir up trouble, but I thought it was strange that he said he hadn't been in the house and then I saw that. When he got to work this morning, it was the first and only time I'd seen him without a cap in his mouth."

The sheriff's lips tipped downward now and he made some notes on his pad. "Hmm."

Hmmm, what?

"I'll make sure it's picked up. Clay and his daddy have a long history of not getting along. Officer Beatty said he went to visit his mama out in Portland, but we may need him to head back here for questioning. I'll talk to him. Regardless of their poor relationship, it's still his father, so I imagine this is a hard hit. Especially if he lied about his whereabouts."

There. She'd done it. Did it count as some sort of civic duty? Of course it did. The tension slipped down her back, but she knew she wouldn't fully relax until Sheriff Saron, nice as he was, left.

"Anything else?"

"Not that I can think of." She took a long swallow of her soda, appreciating the way it eased the dryness of her throat.

Avoiding his assessing gaze, she could admit to herself that it was easier to tell the sheriff about Clay because she didn't altogether like him. It was unfair, but if she had to choose, she could see Clay losing his temper far quicker than she could picture it of Alan and Elizabeth. She didn't want to think either of them were capable of an affair—or worse. But what if she was wrong? The town thrived on gossip. Maybe everyone knew about her boss and co-worker. *Probably not about the emails, though. At least not yet. And now that Vernon is gone, no one will. It's not your job to protect them.* But she didn't want to take responsibility for sharing their private information, either. Especially when she didn't really know anything.

"Okay, then. You take care and if you think of anything else, I want you to call me." He took a card from the back of his notepad and set it on her countertop.

She saw him out and then leaned against the closed door, shutting her eyes and focusing on her breaths. When a knock sounded behind her, she actually jumped. Molly gave herself a second before opening the door.

Katherine stood in the doorway, a small beige kennel in one hand and the end of a leash in the other. The pup hurdled forward, jumping up on Molly's legs and making her smile.

"I'd say he missed you. Everything all right?" Katherine asked.

Molly moved aside so she could come in. She knelt down and let the pup off its leash. The pup jumped and tried to lick her face. "Calm down, you." She ruffled his fur, which he seemed to enjoy. He rolled over, belly up, his dark eyes begging for more.

"You've got yourself a steadfast friend there," Katherine commented.

Molly met the woman's gaze. "It would seem so. At least until his owner claims him. Thanks again for letting me bring him here."

"No worries. Have you eaten?"

"No. Sam took me for a milkshake this morning," she said.

Katherine's eyes sparkled. "Another steadfast friend. He's a good boy, my Sam. Just like his daddy was."

Molly stood up, walking to the small kitchen area. "Was?"

There was such a sadness in Katherine's smile, Molly felt the woman's pain. "He died about five years ago. Heart attack. My one true love."

Tears filled Molly's eyes. So much sadness in the world. The pup plopped his butt down on Molly's foot. She looked down and laughed. And so many little reasons to smile. What a balancing act.

"I'm so sorry," Molly said, truly meaning it.

Death certainly made a person grateful for their own blessings. Tonight she would definitely make the time to chat with her parents.

"Thank you. Sam and I, we do okay, even though we miss him. I started this place with the insurance money and Sam started his shop. Our way of making his memory carry forward."

"That's really lovely. You have a beautiful place here and everyone I've met speaks so highly of you."

Katherine blushed. "That's nice to hear. I always say, you get back what you give."

Molly thought about that and her thinking shifted to Vernon. It could be true of him as well, which was a terrible thought, but not entirely wrong.

"Anyway, I should get going. I've brought you some lunch and I expect you to eat it. After you're good and settled, I'll have you up to the house for dinner, but any time you like, come by for breakfast. I serve it for my guests from seven to nine in the morning every day. It's simple; muffins, yogurt, granola and fresh fruit, but it's a good way to start your day."

"Thank you, Katherine. Truly, for everything."

"My pleasure, dear. Get some rest," Katherine said, giving Molly a quick, hard hug.

As she walked to the door, she called back, "And eat," making Molly laugh.

She thought for sure she'd break into tears once she was alone. The pressure of warring emotions was giving her whiplash. But she didn't. Instead, she took the dog through the back door to the small fenced yard that was secluded from the rest of the bed-and-breakfast property. Trees edged the entire property and Molly knew she'd have to get out and explore the grounds. The steady trickle of water meant there was a stream or brook close by and she'd yet to figure out where. The pup bounced around the yard, easing a good portion of the pressure in Molly's chest. He'd probably love a walk through the trees, especially if they found the water.

"I think I'm going to call you Tigger for now. All you do is bounce."

To prove it, the little guy bounced over to her and jumped up, putting his paws on her knees. Molly picked him up and snuggled him close. Moving around for her dad's job made having pets too difficult and as an adult, she'd only lived in apartments. It hadn't occurred to her, how much she'd enjoy having a furry companion.

Inside, she finished off her soda and looked at the lunch bag sitting on her counter. She hadn't even seen Katherine carry it in. Inside was a delicious-looking sandwich, an apple, and a bag of plain chips. Molly was reminded of the lunches her mom used to pack her. Tonight, when she phoned them, she'd remember to thank them for just being great. For loving and supporting her. It made Molly sad to think of Clay's relationship with his father and the flip side of that was gratitude for the one she had with her own parents.

While the pup dozed at her feet, Molly curled up on the couch with her notebook. Her thoughts were circling like a tornado and she needed to get some of them down.

She trusted the sheriff—he seemed like a strong leader and a good man. She wondered if Sam had ever caught the interested glances the man sent his mother's way. A smile tipped her lips as she wrote the date. The thoughts bouncing around in her head were exhausting her and she knew, if she didn't write it down, she wouldn't be able to put any of it aside. She wrote a quick note about the morning.

Indescribable. Vernon, who seemed to hate me on sight, is dead. I found his body this morning. He was murdered and I'm terrified it has something to do with the interview I demanded he get from Vanessa Phillips. But,

*seeing as I'm not a cop, I could be wrong and there's more than one person
on the list of suspects.*

She tapped her pen on the page, leaving random dots. *Stop it. The
police will do their jobs.* But worry gnawed in every recess of her mind
and despite trusting the sheriff and his men, she couldn't help herself.
Molly wrote Vernon's name in a circle and drew a line, connecting Clay's
name. Noting the pen cap and that the sheriff would look into it, she wrote
Callan's name. Putting a little star by his name, she reminded herself to
speak to Calliope. *Ask what the fight between Vernon and Callan was
about.* She made note of Callan's display of temper and his words from
this morning: *Vernon won't be scamming them anymore.*

Sadly, she drew two more lines, putting Alan and Elizabeth's names at
the end, then drew a connecting line between them with the word *affair*
and a question mark. The thought turned her stomach. She made a note of
the email exchange and Elizabeth's warning. Should she have told Sheriff
Saron? What if there was nothing to it and she started a rumor about two
good people? Or, what if the sheriff decided she was just a newcomer
looking to stir up trouble? *Or what if he appreciates you sharing any
information that could be relevant?*

None of these things were connected to the interview she'd asked for
or the documents she hoped to grab tonight. So why was she obsessing? If
one of these people killed Vernon, it had nothing to do with Molly. Except
then she was in close proximity to a murderer. They all were. Closing the
notebook, mostly because her brain hurt from thinking about it, she stared
at her laptop and heaved out a deep sigh.

Pulling up the *Bulletin*'s web page, she started to write. It took her a
while to get the details down without putting in too much. Sheriff Saron
probably wouldn't look at her so kindly if she mentioned the pen cap or
how Vernon had been found lying in a drying puddle of scotch. Keeping
the article short, Molly wrote that Vernon had been found dead in his home
and the authorities were looking into the details. She attached several links
to Vernon's older articles and copied and pasted his biography from the
site. Since most people knew what she hadn't, she included the fact that
Vernon was survived by his son, Clay Reynolds, who was unavailable
for comment.

Because he'd left town. The sheriff hadn't seemed concerned over this,
but it didn't sit right with Molly. After posting the article and sharing it
on social media, she texted Alan and let him know. She didn't receive a
response.

Eyes burning, she closed her laptop and set it on the coffee table. It'd be a while before Sam came over. Glancing over her shoulder, she decided her bed was too far away. The fleecy-soft beige blanket her mom had given her last Christmas was draped over the back of the couch. Handy, since she felt like burrowing under it now.

When she did, the dog—Tigger—took it as an invitation to join her. Together, they fell into sleep. Likely, it was only her that suffered from a nightmare.

Chapter 8

Vernon was there on the floor in front of her and all she could think was, "I need to get out of here," but when she tried the door, it wouldn't budge. Gripping the knob harder, she twisted and turned it, but got nowhere. She could hear the cops banging on the other side and Molly slammed her fists against the heavy wood to no avail. When she tried to scream, to tell them she was in there and needed help, no words came out. Someone was calling her name.

"Molly! Can you hear me?"

A dog barked, yanking Molly out of her nightmare. The knocking was real and so was the barking. Tigger was off the couch and at the door, yapping excitedly. Molly shuffled after him and answered.

Sam filled the doorframe, standing there in the dimming light of the evening. He was wearing jeans and a light gray sweater. Molly blinked. How long had she slept? The dog darted between Sam's legs and out into the yard.

He stared after the dog, then looked back at Molly with a tummy-tumbling grin. "Hey. Did I wake you?"

Feeling abnormally shy and not quite awake, Molly tucked her hair behind her ear and stepped out into the yard.

"Hi. I didn't mean to sleep so long. I was just going to lie down. I found this guy outside the *Bulletin* this morning."

Sam stood by her side, watching the pup zip around in circles. "My mom's half in love with him already."

Glancing up, her eyes met his. He had pretty great eyes. "Your mom is fantastic."

He shrugged, his smile soft and sweet. "I like her."

Molly laughed, then looked over at Tigger as he picked a fight with a flower. He barked, jumping toward it.

"Come on, Tigger."

Sam chuckled. "Tigger?"

Pointing a finger, she laughed at him. "You watch. All he does is bounce."

It was nice, standing with Sam in the soft breeze of the evening, sharing laughter over the silly puppy. Certainly nicer than the start of her day. They went indoors and luckily, Tigger followed. Molly's stomach growled loudly and her cheeks heated.

Sam's sweet smile woke her up all the way. "My mom told me to ask if you'd eaten."

She took the lunch bag out of the fridge, not meeting his gaze. "I fell asleep. She doesn't need to look out for me, even though it's sweet that she wants to. She packed me a lunch."

Molly unloaded the bag. The pup flopped onto Sam's feet.

"She'll do that. She can't help it and there's no use trying to stop her. My mom would feed and house the world if she could. Hey there, little guy. You're tough, aren't you?"

Molly looked to where Sam was crouched, rubbing the dog, and couldn't help but think they made a cute pair. "He picked a fight with an ugly stuffed bear today. That's how I found him."

A deep laugh came from Sam as the pup rolled over, showing no decorum at all. Indulging the pup, Sam continued to rub his belly. Molly bit into her sandwich and sighed before realizing she had absolutely no manners.

"Can I get you a drink? Half a sandwich?" Though she really didn't want to share. Turkey and ham with cheese, lettuce, and just the right amount of mustard made it delicious.

"I'm good. My mom just fed me. You sure you want to do this tonight?" He stood up and took a seat across the counter.

Finishing her bite, she nodded. "I feel like I have to. The sheriff stopped by today to ask a few follow-up questions. He said they don't have suspects yet, though I don't know that he'd tell me if they did. I can't ignore the timing on Vernon's death. Even if it seems unrelated, it's too coincidental. Plus, I can't stop thinking about the box he got from Vanessa. It wasn't in the house—well, at least not in the living room." The memory of his body lying there floated back and a shiver wracked Molly's spine.

Molly's pulse sprinted when Sam leaned closer. "I can understand that, but I hope you aren't still blaming yourself, because it's truly not your fault."

"Thank you. I feel like I need to do this and I'm glad you're coming with me. I'll just finish this off and we can go. Your mom gave me a kennel for the pup. I think I'm going to miss him when the owner claims him. I put up a notice in the *Bulletin* window."

She took another large bite, grateful she hadn't had to make it herself. "I saw you also put an article up on the website. Word is all over town."

Molly nodded. That was the point. Better to report facts than people speculating any more than they already would.

Tipping her head, she fought back a grin. "Do you usually check the website?"

His gaze locked with hers and the air between them crackled. "Not often. Just wanted to see if the new editor was doing her job."

The smile he gave her, slightly lopsided and all-the-way cute, caused a carefree feeling in her chest. One she hadn't felt in far too long. "Pretty soon I'll have you all stalking the website and our Twitter feed."

Sam gestured to Tigger. "Have you thought of what you'll do if no one claims him? There's been quite a few stray dogs around in the last couple of months. I know the police were checking into it a while back."

Molly frowned and looked at Tigger. She tossed him a piece of bread and a chunk of meat. She'd need dog food if he stayed. "He doesn't seem like a stray."

"Maybe not. He's pretty cute. Definitely a keeper."

Locking her eyes on Sam's, all too aware of the dangerous flutter expanding around her heart, she nodded. "I agree."

* * * *

They took Sam's truck—a newer Chevy Silverado—to Vernon's house, or just past it.

"Where are we going?" Molly asked when they passed the street. Tapping her fingers lightly on the armrest of the passenger door, she tried not to think of what driving these roads had led her to just this morning.

Sam glanced her way. "I was thinking it would be better to park about fifteen minutes away. There are some walking trails not too far from here. I figured we'd park there and then if anyone sees us, we'd just say we were going for a walk. Not to seem lame or anything, but this being my first try at breaking and entering, I didn't want to roll up right in front of Vernon's house."

Guilt tugged at Molly's conscience. "I'm sorry. This was a terrible thing to ask of you."

Sam glanced at her. "Would you have done it with or without me?"

"Yes." No sense lying.

He sent a quick grin before turning up a gravel road. "Then I'm glad you asked. Tell me something about yourself that has nothing to do with your job."

Molly pressed her fingers flat on her lap, holding them still as the truck bumped over the ground. "Um. All right…I'm an army brat. Single child. My parents live in Arizona; my dad is retired now. I can cook but prefer not to, especially now that I've tried Come 'n Get It. I like Hallmark movies and thrillers. I'd rather shop online than in a store. My Jeep is my prized possession and I love candy more than any adult should. How's that?"

He chuckled and took another turn. The road led upward and became more wooded. "Pretty good."

Molly waited. He pulled over in a treed area and cut the ignition. Out of the truck and around the hood before she had her seat belt off, he opened the door for her and held a hand out so she could get down. *Ignore the sparks. Ignore the sparks.* She tried, but when he let go of her hand, she felt the loss of warmth.

Sam grabbed a backpack and slung it over his shoulders. Molly eyed it, wondering if she should have brought something with them. "What's that?"

His eyes darted over her head. Putting his hands in his pockets, he mumbled, "Authenticity. If we run into someone and say we're hiking, we'll have some gear to make that seem true."

The worry and sadness Molly had been carting around off and on all day lifted for a few blessed seconds. She smiled so wide her cheeks ached. "That's really cute."

He rolled his eyes. "Great. Just what I was going for."

It might not have been what he was aiming for—guys, for some reason, didn't warm to the adjectives *sweet* or *cute*—but it was exactly what Molly needed.

They walked side by side down a path named Captain's Creek Trail. Molly was still battling happy butterflies when she asked, "What about you? Tell me something about you."

The air was warm, but not as hot as it had been earlier in the day. The graveled path was wide and easy to stroll along. Wildflowers and trees lined both sides, surrounding them with the best of nature's scents. If she didn't think about what they were actually going to do, things would seem quite normal.

"Not much to tell. Born and raised here. Not at the bed-and-breakfast. We lived north about twenty minutes, basically on the border of Britton Bay and Astoria. When my dad died, about five years ago, he left some money and my mom insisted I take part of it. I went to college. Majored in business. But I hadn't found my thing yet. I loved tinkering with cars. Something my dad taught me, but I'd never considered doing it full-time. Worked at a few garages and enjoyed it. Starting my own, at twenty-four, seemed pretty cool so I gave it a shot."

"I'm sorry about your dad," Molly said.

The sky had grayed overhead, the outlines of stars beginning to pop. Sam's eyes were darker in the moonlight. "Thanks. It's still hard. But I think of the garage as a way of honoring him. He thought I could do anything."

Molly smiled. "I doubt he was wrong."

They walked quietly for a few moments, Sam leading them through a trail and past a small stream. Tigger would have loved the walk, but probably would have made their task harder. She'd have to see how he did when he joined her on one of her own walks—if his owner didn't claim him first.

"What else? Tell me something else," she said.

"Okay...I'm twenty-nine. An Aquarius, if you're into that sort of thing. I like fishing, but hate hunting. If you tell anyone that, I'll deny it. We have some pretty avid hunters around here, but it's just not my thing. I hate cooking and mooch off my mom way more than I should. I live about four minutes from my shop in an apartment. I've been outside of Britton Bay to travel, but never wanted to plant roots anywhere but here. Oh, and I love double-stuffed Oreos."

Molly's laugh seemed to echo around them. "A very redeeming quality. I too am a fan."

"You have to worry about anyone who isn't, right?"

She agreed and this time, when the fluttery warmth of being close to him overtook her senses, she let herself enjoy the sensation instead of trying to fight it.

He pointed to a trail that led down a little hill. Molly saw the houses in Vernon's neighborhood from where they stood and spotted his house without any trouble. Her stomach churned, the tension inching its way back through her body while memories slapped at her. The smell of scotch. The sight of his body. Fun time was over.

"You ready?" Sam asked. He moved closer to her, as if he could sense her discomfort.

"No. You sure you're okay with this?" Guilt tugged at her.

He shrugged. "You have a good reason to want the stuff. It'll cut through the red tape asking for it would inevitably bring. Hopefully, you'll find what you're looking for and then you can give it back to Mrs. Phillips."

"Yes. Unless the cops decide they want it."

"You could worry about that if and when it happens."

"Good point," she said. She took a deep breath.

"One thing," Sam said.

Molly looked up at him and held her next breath. They were standing so close she could see the trace of stubble on his wide, strong jaw.

"I get to pick the activity next time we hang out."

She exhaled around a laugh. "Deal."

There was no one else around when they made it to the street. Unlike the houses closer to the water, these houses were fairly nondescript. Plain boxes with triangle tops, like a child's drawing in grade school. The yards were well maintained, however, and the streetlights flickered on. Vernon's car was still in the driveway as it had been that morning and his home was dark. What would happen to it now? Again, she was struck by the realization that everything seemed the same despite the fact that nothing was.

Sam shifted closer to her as they neared the car. They moved to the side and peeked in the passenger side. Sure enough, a box bursting with photos and news clippings sat in the seat.

"That's it," Molly whispered.

Sam edged back, removed the pack he was carrying. "I figured. This should only take a second."

He pulled a long, flat metal tool out of the bag and handed her the open sack. Looking around once, he stepped closer to the car and slipped the tool into the small space between the window and the doorframe. He jimmied it around until there was an audible *pop*. Removing the tool, he handed it to her, opened the door, and grabbed the box. He passed that over as well, then leaned back in. He handed her a yellow Post-it note.

"That was on the seat. Might have fallen out of the box," he said in a low voice as he locked and shut the door.

Molly glanced at the note. It had Vernon's handwriting and only had one word: *Macintosh*. Him and his Post-its. She frowned and pressed it to the top of the box. Before working to stuff the box of photos into the bag, Sam's hand came to her shoulder and nudged her forward.

"Let's walk while you put that away."

He leaned in and held the bag so it was easier to slide everything in. Some of the photos and clippings fell to the bottom of the backpack, but they'd been shoved in the box haphazardly anyway, so she didn't think it was a big deal. *Unless they're evidence and you're tampering with them.* When they got several hundred feet away, closer to the entrance of the trail leading them back to Sam's truck, he stopped and his breath whooshed out.

Molly's heart hammered faster than Tigger's tail. "Thank you."

Sam nodded. "No problem. We should go."

They walked back to the truck quicker than they'd walked to Vernon's. When they were settled inside and turned around to head back to the B and B, Molly leaned back in the seat.

"I thought that would be harder," she said.

Sam's laugher made her turn her head to study his profile. "Says the woman who wasn't jimmying open the door."

She bit her lip. "Right. Sorry."

"I'm just teasing. And actually, it would have been a lot harder if he had a newer car. So, what now?"

She hadn't thought past getting the stuff. "I guess I go through it and try to figure out if anything in here is a story worth killing for."

"Right. And if you find nothing?" Sam slowed down for a stoplight.

"Hopefully the police will."

"Seems crazy to think there's someone in this town that would actually take a life."

It was crazy anyone would take a life anywhere, but she imagined it felt even stranger to Sam, as he'd grown up in this quiet spot. *How well do you ever really know anyone?*

"I don't think it was planned. I don't know if that makes it better or worse, but it didn't seem like someone went there with the intention of killing him. He did have a habit of making people squirm."

Molly bit her lip, wondering if she should tell Sam about Elizabeth and Alan.

"That's the truth. A lot of people steered clear of him for that exact reason."

When Sam turned down the street that led to the carriage house, Molly leaped. She needed to start trusting her own judgment again. "I think he was blackmailing Alan and Elizabeth."

"What?" He whipped his head to look at her.

"I found a printout of an email conversation between Vernon and Elizabeth today when I went back to the paper for a bit."

Sam let out a low whistle as he pulled his truck up beside her Jeep. He shifted into *park* but kept the engine on. Turning a bit in his seat, he watched her for a moment.

"Alan loves his wife. He's a good man. It would surprise me if he was cheating on her."

Molly undid her seat belt and swiveled toward Sam. She didn't want to put tension between them by throwing around accusations about people he cared for. She hadn't considered that, but she also felt like his thoughts

on the subject carried weight. While a piece of her was relieved to share
the opinion with him, she couldn't ignore the facts.

"I agree. But when Elizabeth wrote back, she didn't deny it. She warned
him not to say anything."

Sam's frown deepened. "By *warned*, do you mean threatened?"

Her pulse slowed as she nodded. "It had the feeling of a threat, but so
did his. She could have just been replying in kind."

Sam's hand tightened on the steering wheel. "I don't know Elizabeth other
than to see her. But Vernon had a way of making people uncomfortable,
so it's possible he could have pushed too far. I just really can't see Alan
hurting his family that way."

"Yeah."

They held each other's gaze for a moment or two and the tone shifted,
creating a different kind of tension in Molly's body. The stars littered the
sky outside and the glow of the moon splashed through the windows of
his truck. Sam reached out his hand and took Molly's. He stared down at
their linked fingers for a moment.

Through unfairly-long lashes, he glanced up at her. "Can I ask a favor?"

Her heart tripped. "Sure."

"Be safe."

She laughed. "I can do that. Or at least try."

Sam squeezed her hand and then released it.

Molly grabbed the backpack. "Thanks for tonight."

"I'd say anytime, but I really would rather do something different next
time."

"Me too. I'll see you around?" She tried to sound at least a little
nonchalant.

"Definitely."

She watched him drive away, then went to let Tigger out of the kennel.
His level of excitement at being reunited had Molly giggling. She opened
the back door for him to run out. The motion lights installed on either
side of the door flashed on. Molly leaned on the doorframe, resting her
head against it, her mind on Sam. Tigger brought over a small stick and
dropped it at her feet.

"Little late for fetch, bud," Molly said, crouching to pick up the stick.
He and his rapidly thumping tail disagreed, making her laugh.

That laughter died in her throat when she looked down. Tigger growled
at her, nudging the stick with his nose, but Molly's attention had shattered.
The flowers—the beautiful flowers that decorated the grounds of the bed-

and-breakfast—including Molly's area, were trampled. Not just trampled like they'd accidentally been pushed at with a lawn mower.

Molly narrowed her gaze, pulling her phone out of her pocket to shine a light directly on the spot. Large boot prints left marks and the remains of flattened flowers. She looked to the other side, but those flowers were fine. It was only the ones beneath the window that peered into the living area that had been rumpled. Panic snapped at her, an elastic band whipping against her skin. She took a couple of photos and called Tigger in abruptly.

Whimpering at the tone of her voice, he came in slowly, cowering. She shut the door behind them and locked it, her heart stampeding in her chest.

"It's okay, bud. I'm not mad at you."

Should she call the police? *Because of some trampled flowers?* She could be overreacting. Maybe it was one of Katherine's guests wandering around and they just went too far. *Over the fence?* Maybe they thought it was a common area or wanted to see inside the cute cottage.

"That makes sense," she said to Tigger. She shut the blinds on the window next to the back door and went to the kitchen to get some cereal. With milk for her and dry for the pup.

"That totally makes sense. They were wandering down and saw this adorable little carriage house. It's like a cottage in the woods. They probably wondered if it was for rent, like the rooms."

Her heart started to maintain a normal rhythm. Her breathing evened out and Tigger's tail sprung back to life as he chowed down on Cheerios. Feeling certain she was overreacting, Molly finished her breakfast-for-dinner. When her eyes fell on the backpack, she closed them. *Not now. Tomorrow is soon enough.*

Checking her phone, she saw her mom had phoned. The backpack—everything else—could wait. Molly needed to hear her mom's voice more than she needed answers right that minute. She just hoped she could keep her own voice from cracking as she told her about everything that had happened.

When her tears finally did catch up with her, there was a good chance they'd drown her.

Chapter 9

The next morning, Alan was already in the office when Molly arrived. She brought Tigger with her, thinking maybe someone knew who he belonged to. The dog had snuggled close enough to be a second skin the night before. When Molly spoke with her parents, the pup read her voice and her tears and stayed near. She didn't need the added responsibility of a pet, so it was silly to be wishing she could keep him. *Silly never stopped you before.*

Molly hung her coat in the back and went to Alan's office. He was standing at his desk, looking down at it. One hand rested on what she now knew was the email correspondence. The other hand was in the pants pocket of his suit. He looked…sad.

The pup, no better at sitting still than Molly, whined. Alan looked up and gave her a ghost of a smile.

"Good morning," he greeted. "Who's that you have there?"

"Hi. Actually, I was hoping someone here would know. I found him yesterday by the dumpster. I put a note up in the window so maybe someone will claim him, but he doesn't have any tags."

Alan came around the desk and crouched down. "Hi there. Oh, you're friendly, aren't you?"

Tigger fell over himself trying to prove he was, making Alan laugh. Molly was happy to know he'd found at least one spot of joy today. He stood up and leaned on the desk.

"Is everyone coming in?" What was the protocol for death of a colleague? Molly had never considered the idea. Other than her grandparents, who had died when she was little, she'd never lost anyone. Not that Vernon was her someone, but death was always somewhat removed in her life. Never on her doorstep.

"Clay isn't. I think he's gone to see Gretta. His mother."

He thought? Had he spoken to the young man? The footprints from the night before flashed in her head. *Not connected. Not connected. He's not even in town.*

Alan sighed. "They're planning a funeral for Thursday. Elizabeth will be in shortly and I told Hannah to stay home."

"I'm really sorry," Molly said. The words did nothing, so why did people feel compelled to say them? *Because there is nothing else to say.*

"Me too. Thank you for getting the news online last night. This is exactly why we need you. There was a time I could count on Vernon for such things. But life and…I don't know, maybe circumstances, hardened him. You didn't see the best side of him, but Vernon could be a good man. He was rough around the edges and could hold a grudge like no one I know, but he had his moments."

"I'm sure he did. A man doesn't get married three times and father a child without having moments of…happiness and connection. The police spoke to you?"

"They did. They asked me about you and I mentioned you and Vernon didn't get along, but it was the same for everyone." His eyes went to the paper again. He fidgeted with it.

Molly's stomach swirled. Everyone, including Elizabeth and Alan. Even more so for them than her. Did Alan feel protective of Elizabeth? It would certainly seem so, even to a casual observer. But enough to confront Vernon? In anger? While she never thought much about her curious nature before, all of the questions were beginning to drive her crazy. Every one led to another. She was rethinking her decision not to say anything to the police. She wanted to believe she'd pick up on some sort of killer vibe, but truthfully, she didn't know any of these people.

"I'm sure the police will get things sorted out quickly. I mean, I know Vernon had enemies, but not many of them could have actually wanted to see him dead."

She watched his expression, which remained blank—unreadable. Alan picked up the paper and shoved it in his pocket, making Molly's chest tighten. His brows scrunched together and he pinched the bridge of his nose, sighing loudly, then looked up to meet her gaze. "What a mess. Everything is such a mess. I'm sorry I've brought you into all of this drama and conflict, Molly. Things will turn around. I hope you'll give it time."

Molly's breath hitched. He hadn't addressed her comment at all. Because he didn't agree that not many people had reason to want Vernon dead? This man didn't seem like a killer, but who knew what pushed someone to murder? If his marriage was at stake...*cheating alone would put his marriage in jeopardy.* But would he kill to keep that secret? Would Elizabeth? A few emails didn't seem like enough motivation to take a life. *Who decides what just cause is? Especially when hearts and emotions are involved. No.* Sam told her Alan was a good man. For now, she could trust Sam's assessment. She wasn't feeling so certain about her own judgment.

She was missing something. Vernon knew something, but Molly didn't know how to figure out if it had been enough to get him killed. Realizing Alan was waiting for a response, she tried to smile, but fell short.

"I'm not going anywhere. I like it here, despite the circumstances. The paper has gone out, right? Are you sure you want to be here today? I can work on the leads and layout on my own."

Even having found the body, she was more removed than any of the others and truthfully, she wouldn't mind being by herself. Too many questions swirled in her mind and it was too hard to think clearly while she was worrying about *who* she was working with. Had Vernon threatened Elizabeth more viciously in person, maybe prompting Alan to take action? But he was at the office when Molly found Vernon. Didn't mean he hadn't stopped by the night before. Maybe Vernon had been lying dead for hours when Molly found him. The questions and possibilities were hurting her brain. But what if the police asked *her* about Alan and Elizabeth? She had a feeling neither of them told the authorities about the emails.

Her boss's voice broke into her concerns. "You know what? I'm going to take you up on that. I promise you, Tuesday it will be business as usual. We'll turn everything around. I'd like to write a piece to honor Vernon. We'll include the last story he was working on. Leave a spot for that in next week's issue, okay?"

"Of course," Molly said, her pitch rising with another tug of emotion. Tigger picked up on it and hopped off the couch where he'd curled up. "Cute little guy. I don't recognize him."

Alan picked up a stack of papers from his desk and shoved them into his open briefcase, closed it and picked it up.

"You're sure you're okay here alone today? I think I'll tell Elizabeth to stay home as well. She's quite emotional over the whole thing." He paused and fixed a curious glance at Molly. "You're the one who found him and you're holding up better than any of us."

Molly picked up Tigger, held him tight. "I'm the outsider. The one least impacted by his loss, though I won't say seeing him that way…it's something I won't forget, unfortunately."

Alan put a hand on her shoulder and squeezed. "If you're not up to staying, it's perfectly fine."

Unlike the rest of them, her distraction from life was right here in this office. Knowing so few people in town meant that she'd spend her day mostly alone. Might as well spend it working.

"I'm good. Really. Go. I'll call if I need anything."

He nodded and walked out of the office, leaving Molly to wonder what would have happened if she hadn't taken the job. Would Vernon be alive?

The thought threatened to bring her to tears again. *It's not your fault. Look at how many others had reason to want him dead.* She shivered. The thought wasn't really that comforting. The best thing she could do was distract herself with work. Letting Tigger go back to sleep on the couch, she went to search up story ideas for the coming weeks. It was time to bring a little more of the outside world to the not-so-sleepy town of Britton Bay.

* * * *

By late afternoon, both Molly and Tigger were hungry. At least, she assumed he was hungry because when was a dog not down with eating? She closed up the layout she was working on, pleased with her progress. She'd managed to keep her mind busy gathering story ideas for Elizabeth and…

"Hmm. Who will take over Vernon's position? We'll need another writer," Molly said to an uninterested Tigger as she locked the back door.

It still felt so odd to Molly that Vernon was gone. Leaving the Jeep, she walked around the side of the building to the sidewalk that lined the shops of Main Street. Walking along the storefronts would let her window-shop, give Tigger a chance to be seen, and clear her head. Hopefully. Eventually, she wanted to check out each of the little shops along the main drag. The Candy Boutique caught her eye, but with Tigger, she couldn't go in. She passed the Sip & Sit. Callan was behind the counter, laughing with a co-worker while mixing up a shake.

Morning Muffins was quieter, being late afternoon, but a few people sat in the fold-up chairs Bella kept outside. The awning over all of the shops would keep them dry if the rain hit. She smiled at an older couple who cooed at Tigger, who sniffed at positively everything. Continuing on, she passed a gift shop, a small bookshop, a teashop, a pet store—which she'd be checking out on the way back, and an empty unit. Prime real estate.

She wondered who owned the shop. Perhaps they'd like to advertise in the *Bulletin*.

Molly waited at the crosswalk that led to the beach, seeing heads turn as she walked past. The new girl always drew interest. The new girl who found a dead body? That was small-town gold. Which, she admitted, was another reason to just walk along the beach rather than go into one of the shops. Not only was she tired of asking herself questions, she didn't feel like answering any right at this moment, either.

There were several families hanging out on the sand. A group of teens close to the water tossed a bright green Frisbee around a circle. Tigger tugged on his leash and sand fluttered up.

"We should get you a couple toys when we pick up food," Molly said.

She stopped and smiled at a couple holding hands. They smiled back as they crossed her path. Music thumped from someone's docking station and laughter rippled through the shore. It was a good place, but like everywhere else in the world, it wasn't safe from tragedy or danger. From the often scary truths of life.

She and Tigger walked along the water, listening to the waves. He was curious but didn't go in, which was probably a good thing. He might be cute, but wet dog was not a great smell. When her stomach rumbled, she realized she hadn't grabbed food. Heading back, she stopped at the pet store. A broody teen with several piercings helped her choose some kibble, a dish, and a couple of toys. With that done, Molly decided she couldn't put off her final chore of the day any longer.

She got Tigger into the Jeep, made a quick stop at home to drop him off, and then headed to the police station. Hopefully by the time she got there, she'd figure out a way to get some more information on where the police were at with the case.

On the way, she passed a small convenience store and decided to pop in for a long overdue lunch. She grabbed a delicious-looking pastry from their small selection of baked goods. Looking at the chocolate chip cookies, Molly decided they might make sweet-talking some details out of Officer Beatty or the sheriff a little easier. And if not, they were a nice gesture. As she placed the individual cookies in a box, a flash of messy blond hair caught her eye. Heading out the door was a man who looked too much like Clay to not be him. Molly's heart pounded. He wasn't supposed to be here. It could have been someone who just looked like him. *With what looked like a pen cap between his teeth?*

A teen wearing a green apron, pushing a cart of boxed apples, smiled at her. "Finding everything all right, ma'am?"

Molly nodded. She hadn't seen the man's face. It could have been anyone. Clay wasn't the only scruffy looking, shaggy-haired blond in town. But maybe she'd mention it at the station.

Gobbling her own pastry on the ride, she walked toward the station carrying her purse and a box of cookies. It was a faded red, mostly brick building. Unless there was a basement, it looked to only be one floor, but it was wide. Glass doors read *Britton Bay Police Station*. Inside, there was a small, rectangular foyer with scuffed, but remarkably shiny, white tile. Straight ahead was the front desk and to either side were wide hallways.

A tall woman with her hair pulled back in a tight bun sat at the long counter that separated the lobby from the…what was it called? *Bullpen! Ha. Thank you,* Veronica Mars*!* Several officers walked, talked, or sat at desks in the wide open area behind the counter. The receptionist wasn't wearing a police uniform and Molly briefly wondered how many non-officers worked at the station. She might edit more than she wrote, but she was curious by nature. The woman looked up and smiled.

"Hi there. How can I help you?" Her name tag read *Priscilla*.

"Hi. My name is Molly Owens. Sheriff Saron asked that I stop by the station today. Is he or Officer Beatty available?"

Priscilla typed something into her computer, then looked back at Molly with a tight grimace. Her voice was lowered when she said, "You found Vernon East's body."

Nausea rolled into Molly's stomach like a wave. She nodded. "Unfortunately."

The receptionist shook her head, leaning closer. "You poor thing. I read your article online. Very tasteful. Just give me a minute and I'll grab Officer Beatty, all right? Sheriff isn't in right now."

"Thank you." It was probably selfish that she felt pleased about the *Bulletin* being read online.

Some of the desks were pushed together, front to front, while others were separated by gray partitions. At the very back of the room were closed doors. Priscilla walked behind one of the partitions and came out a moment later with Officer Beatty. He waved at Molly and nodded at something Priscilla said.

Despite being dressed in full uniform, his eyes had a kindness that made him seem approachable. He was tall and lanky, built kind of like a runner. Molly could see him chasing down a suspect with ease.

"How are you doing, Ms. Owens?" he greeted.

Priscilla went back to the computer as Officer Beatty unlatched the small gate at the end of the counter and came around.

"It's Molly. Please. And I'm okay."

She walked beside him as he gestured down one of the wide hallways she'd passed on the way in.

"Fingerprinting is this way. Molly," he said, giving her a small smile.

She passed over the box, then froze. "I brought cookies, but it's not like a bribe or anything." Or was it? She wanted information, didn't she?

Officer Beatty laughed. "I'm not sure what I could give you in exchange anyway, but I'll happily take cookies. Wasn't necessary, but thank you all the same."

He had a nice laugh—hearty and deep. If he'd gone to school with Sam, they were close to the same age. Having moved around so often, Molly couldn't imagine growing up in one place, but she liked the idea of settling in for the long haul. They continued walking past more closed doors to one that was open. Inside was…different than Molly expected. It was a small, windowless room with a table along one side wall. The back wall had height measurements in large black numbers along one side. A tall, dark cabinet rested against the wall across from the table.

Officer Beatty put the cookies down and started arranging the tools to fingerprint her. She'd never been fingerprinted before. Glancing at the box, she wondered if she'd left viable prints there. It was horrible to be there because someone had died. But, she couldn't stop herself from being oddly fascinated by the behind-the-scenes process.

"Come on over, Molly. How are you settling into Britton Bay? Other than…" he said, his voice trailing off.

She gave a gruff laugh. "*Other than,* I'm doing well. I really like it here. The people are great. Well, except for whoever murdered Vernon."

She froze again and closed her eyes, covering her face with her hands. In a muffled voice she apologized. "I don't know what's wrong with me. I don't why I said that. I'm sorry."

With a gentle laugh, he nudged her shoulder, making her lower her hands. "No reason to be sorry. You're not wrong. I need to print each finger. It'll stain, but it's painless."

She stepped over to the table, appreciating the kind way he'd let her off the hook. Letting him move her hand, she felt like a life-size doll, her finger being dabbed, rolled, and pressed onto an off-white piece of card stock. In just a few minutes, he handed her a wet wipe for the ink.

"That's it?"

"That's it."

He was good-looking in an all-American kind of way. He had the small-town charm and manners that seemed inherent in Britton Bay. He didn't make her stomach do pirouettes like a certain mechanic, but he was nice and Molly found herself grateful trustworthy people were looking into this serious crime.

"Any word?" she asked as he picked up the cookies and led her out of the room.

"On the case? No. These things take time. There's the autopsy, questioning people, following up on what we know of his last two days alive. And with every step comes paperwork. I don't want you to worry, though. Britton Bay is a safe place. We take care of our community. I'm sorry Vernon's gone, but he's the kind of man who thrives on making enemies. This isn't the norm for our town."

"I know. Still…it's unnerving to think the person you're sitting next to could be the murderer, you know?"

They reached the lobby and stopped walking. Officer Beatty pulled out a card.

"I do know and that's understandable. Listen, if you need anything or get a bad feeling about something, give me a call. I don't think you're in any danger at all, but I trust my gut, so I expect others to follow theirs."

She accepted the card. *Tell him.* "I know this might be unrelated or unimportant, but when I came home last night and let my dog out, the flowers under my window were trampled. I took a picture because it kind of freaked me out. And today, on the way over, I was almost positive I saw Clay Reynolds at the Stop and Shop. But he said he was going out of town."

Officer Beatty pulled out a notebook. "That is curious. Mind sending me those photos? You can text them to me or send them to the email on my card. I can stop by and take a look in person, if that would make you feel better. Did you see anyone on the property?"

She felt foolish now, but also relieved she'd said something. "No. But it was dark when I got back."

He glanced up from his notebook. "You were coming home from…?"

Molly's cheeks heated. "Uh…I had a date with Sam Alderich."

Flames of embarrassment licked at Molly's skin. It wasn't untrue.

Officer Beatty grinned. "Sam's a good guy. I'll look into whether Clay is still in town. He did say he was going to Portland."

"Do you think the two things are connected?"

He finished writing and closed the notebook. "Can't say. But I'll look into it. You have my word."

"Thank you. I appreciate that."

He held up the cookies. "I appreciate these. Take care of yourself, Molly."

"Thanks. You too."

The sun was slipping when she left the station and headed for home. Other than the emails, which she still didn't feel were her business to mention, she'd told them everything. Officer Beatty didn't seem to think she was in any danger and though he'd taken her seriously when she mentioned Clay, he didn't seem bothered by the information. Did that mean they weren't considering him a suspect, despite knowing he lied about being at the scene? *At the scene? You aren't actually a cop, you know. Heck. You're not even a good Veronica Mars.* She'd have chased after Clay and cornered him until he answered her questions without even meaning to.

She should be taking comfort in the fact that it was looking more and more like Vernon's death had nothing to do with the Phillips interview. That would absolve her of guilt. But if she was truly unconnected, why would someone want to peek through her window? *You convinced yourself last night it was a guest. Stick with that until the cops say differently.* She nearly slammed the brakes when she realized that if Vernon was killed over something to do with the Phillips interview, she was now the one in possession of those same items. Had she just put a target on her own back?

Chapter 10

A good night's sleep and an early-morning walk with Tigger cleared Molly's head and lessened some of the worries she'd dragged to bed with her. She took the now-familiar trail to the ocean, laughing at how Tigger seemed almost frightened of the water. Falling asleep early had them up with the sun. When she rounded the bend that led back to the sprawling Victorian home, Katherine was putting out muffins for the couple Molly had seen the other day.

She waved at Molly. "You're up early!"

Molly waved back. "Couldn't sleep any longer."

Tigger tugged on the leash, trying to close the distance between them and Sam's mom.

"Come have some breakfast," Katherine said.

"Oh, that's okay. I'm good."

The pup continued to fight her hold as Katherine put her hands to her hips. "Don't be silly. Meet me on the front porch in five minutes."

Leaving no room for argument, the woman turned and spoke with her guests. Molly chuckled and took the path to her place.

"I bet no one says *no* to her," she told Tigger.

Her furry companion did not appreciate going from the bright outdoors to the kennel. Maybe she should try leaving him out. He was really well behaved—which made her think he'd been someone's pet. But, what if she left him out and he tore things up? Katherine had been so gracious about him being there, Molly didn't want to risk it.

Not yet. Grabbing her cell phone, she made it to the front porch with about thirteen seconds to spare. Katherine came through the front door, a basket of muffins in her hand.

"What do you like in your coffee? Mine is already out here. You take these and I'll grab you a cup," she said, passing over the basket.

"Please don't go to any trouble," Molly insisted, knowing her landlord wouldn't listen to her.

"Hush. How do you take it?"

Molly laughed. "Cream and sugar. Thank you."

When Katherine went inside, Molly took a seat at the cozy bistro set nestled into the corner of the wraparound porch. In the other corner was a gorgeous wooden swing. She'd have to see about reading a book in that spot one day soon, if Katherine didn't mind. Looking around, Molly noted that the other homes on the street were similar in style, but the bed-and-breakfast—aptly named Creekside—stood out in a dozen tiny ways: The path from the street to the porch paved with intricately carved stones, the clusters of flowers adorning the adorable window boxes, the miniature birdhouses that were barely noticeable. It was the tiny touches that set it apart. No doubt all because of Katherine Alderich.

The front door opened and Katherine came through, her smile and outfit matching the shine of the sun.

"Here we go. I'm sorry I haven't had a chance to sit with you yet. How are you doing? Honestly. Don't use the words *fine* or *okay*."

Again, Molly found herself laughing. She had a feeling that her mom and Sam's mom would get along well. "I'm enjoying the day off. But, *honestly,* I feel out of sorts. Like my skin doesn't fit right. I'll be feeling happy and carefree and then realize a man died and I feel terrible and even a little scared."

That was as honest as she'd been with anyone, including herself. Picking up the brightly colored mug, she took a welcome sip of really good coffee. So good, she sighed in pleasure.

"That's a lot of weight to carry. What you saw...most people go a long time without seeing."

She passed Molly a still-warm muffin. After removing the wrapper, she broke a piece off and put it in her mouth. The delicious mixture of cinnamon and apple assaulted her taste buds. If all of the food in Britton Bay was going to be mouthwatering, Molly was going to have to up her workout routine.

"These are indescribably delicious," Molly said when she'd swallowed.

"Aren't they? I'd love to take credit, but Bella made them. You've met her, right? She owns Morning Muffins."

Molly broke off another piece. "I have met her. I thought her scones were a thing of beauty, but these. Wow."

"She's a talented girl, just like her mama was," Katherine said, taking a bite of her own.

"This town is full of good food, nice people, and interesting stories," Molly said. She looked at her coffee cup and her throat tightened. *And one murderer.*

A woodpecker rapped at one of the large trees that stood like pillars to the path of the house.

"That's the truth. What's your story?" Katherine picked up her coffee and leaned back in the chair.

What was her story? Most days, she wasn't entirely sure. "I think I'm still searching for it," Molly said, dabbing at the muffin crumbs on her plate with her index finger.

"Don't spend so much time searching that you miss out on what's right in front of you," Katherine warned.

Looking up, she met the woman's gaze. "Wouldn't be the first time I didn't pay attention to what I should have seen all along. I promise, I'm paying closer attention now."

Katherine nodded, looking pleased with Molly's answer. They sat, enjoying their coffees, listening to the birdsong, the smell of magnolia blooms curling around them. Molly was thinking about the best way to spend her day off when her cell phone buzzed.

Picking it up, she saw Alan's name on the screen. "Hi Alan."

"Molly, I know it's your first day off and it's been a heck of a week, but can you come in? Hannah's going to come in for a few hours as well," Alan said. His voice was thin, on the cusp of panic.

Sitting upright, she nodded even though he couldn't see. "Of course. What's wrong?"

"The police are bringing Elizabeth in for further questioning. As an actual suspect. I can't let her go through that alone. I'm sorry to ask—"

"Don't be silly. I'll be there shortly."

She hung up and shared what Alan had told her.

"Poor dear. She's been through enough," Katherine said.

Molly squashed her immediate curiosity about the statement and started to pick up her plate and cup.

Sam's mom waved her hands away. "I'll take care of that. You go on and get ready."

"Thank you," Molly said.

As she whipped through her routine to get ready, she couldn't believe the chain of events. If anyone she worked with was going to be considered a suspect, she really thought it'd be Clay.

Chapter 11

The office was empty when Molly arrived. She didn't mind, as she'd brought Tigger. She wasn't sure how Alan felt about having a pet in the building, but she didn't want the little guy in the kennel all day. Before she got much more attached, she should consider putting an ad out describing him. With the newspaper being at the end of the street, her sign in the window wasn't getting much foot traffic.

As Tigger bounced through the door, Molly smirked. "An ad. That's just silly. In a town like this, I just need to get the *word* out."

Tigger ran back to her and jumped on her shins. She bent her knees and told him "down," but couldn't help crouching to give him a scratch behind the ears.

"We shouldn't get attached, bud." She leaned closer and whispered, "Too late, isn't it?"

She knew it and so did the dog. But it could be their little secret for now. Setting him up with his kennel door open in case he wanted to sleep, some water, and some toys in her office, Molly got to work. As summer tiptoed closer, Britton Bay had a host of regular activities and it was time to focus on some of those. The police would focus on the murder.

There was the night market, midweek, where vendors sold their wares and food trucks came in from other areas. On weekends, live music played on a makeshift stage at the park kitty-corner to the newspaper office. Toward the edge of town, an old drive-in was being resurrected. There were plenty of things to share with the townspeople.

Molly started a list of similar activities in neighboring towns because it was a great way to increase their readership. She changed the layout to include a list of movies at the theater about thirty minutes outside of the Bay. What she really wanted to get done was the website. Now that she knew people actually used it, they needed to be sure it was updated regularly. She took a quick break to take Tigger out and toss his ball a few times before digging in. She was pleased with her progress by the time Hannah showed up after school.

"Hey," Hannah greeted.

Molly turned from her laptop to say hi. "Hi. How are you?"

Hannah's blond hair was tucked back in a braid. She wore yoga pants and a hoodie. She tossed her bag on the floor near the desk she used. Molly had a quick flashback to her own high school days. At Hannah's age, she'd also worked on the school newspaper, but she'd been much shier and definitely not as graceful.

"Okay. School wasn't great. All anyone is talking about is the murder. Did you really see his body? Was it horrible? I can't stop thinking about how much I disliked him and now he's dead and I feel so guilty for that."

When the teen sniffled, Molly stood and gave her a hug. "Don't beat yourself up. From what I've heard, he wasn't pleasant to anyone. He didn't deserve to die for that, but people can't live their lives tearing others down and expecting them to feel good about it. You only disliked him because he gave you reasons."

Hannah returned the hug. Before letting go, she whispered, "I can't believe they think Elizabeth could have done it."

Molly pulled back and gestured to the work counter. They each took a stool.

"Do you know Elizabeth well?"

Hannah nodded. "Sure. She and my aunt Vicky are best friends. After Elizabeth's husband left her, she often joined us for family events."

Was that what Katherine had been referring to earlier? Elizabeth's husband leaving her? Molly was forming more questions when Hannah continued.

"My dad and uncle Alan are brothers. They have one other brother and two sisters. Family get-togethers are a pretty lively—sort of a bigger-is-better type of thing."

That sounded wonderful to Molly. "Of course. That's nice that your family included her. Are you close to your aunt and your uncle?"

A stitch of guilt lodged in Molly's side. She shouldn't be questioning a teenager to get the inside scoop on her boss's marriage. But, if Vernon had been killed by one of them because of an affair, then Molly was off the hook. *Selfish much?* She didn't mean to be, but the idea that her pushing had led Vernon to his death made Molly feel like her airway was closing.

She wondered how Hannah knew Elizabeth was in for questioning. As a suspect. Maybe she'd overheard a conversation. It didn't seem like the sort of thing Alan would just outright tell the teenager.

"I am. With Auntie being sick, she doesn't join us as much, though. What do you think will happen now? Do you think Clay will come back and work here? I guess a new writer needs to be hired."

Alan's wife was sick? With what? Molly didn't get a chance to answer—or ask anything— as Hannah's sentences were one long stream, even when she jumped off her stool.

"Oh, I forgot, I did a few interviews. I played around with the questions we worked on together and changed some of them to fit who I was interviewing. I spoke with our quarterback, our coach, and our principal about different things."

Pleasure knocked the stitch clear. "That's wonderful, Hannah. What great initiative."

Hannah brought a binder over and sat beside Molly again. She flipped it open, showing Molly the interviews. There were ways to deepen the questions to elicit more emotional and thought-provoking answers, but overall, Hannah had a gift for writing. Her style was similar to her personality—approachable, kind, and invested.

"When do you get out of school?" Molly asked.

She made a note on one of the pages to look into the long-term winning and losing record of the high school team. Adults were a more likely demographic for the website, but if they wanted to pull younger readers in, Twitter or Instagram were better avenues. Posting updates on the teams was an easy way to get the attention of local teens.

"Middle of June," Hannah replied.

"I'm just thinking out loud here, but you're right, we're going to have to hire another writer," Molly began.

Possibly two, she thought, but didn't voice the concern. "What if I talk to your uncle about a paid internship over the summer? You've got talent and whether it's your youth or just intrinsic nature, you have an excitement that transfers to your words."

The look of disbelief on Hannah's face had her wondering if she'd misspoken. Until the teen threw her arms around Molly's neck and squealed; right in her ear.

Molly laughed. "I'm a little rusty on my teenager-speak, but I think that's a yes."

Hannah nodded. Molly had returned the hug and was about to drop her arms when she felt the shift in Hannah's embrace. A very soblike sound was accompanied by shaking shoulders and it took Molly a second to realize the teen was crying.

Pulling back, brows scrunched, curious if it was just emotion, Molly smiled. "Hey. What's going on? You okay?"

Hannah sniffled and muttered "yes," but clearly it was a lie. She got off the stool and grabbed a Kleenex from Elizabeth's desk. Leaning her hip against it, she spoke to Molly from there.

"Dusty—the quarterback?" Hannah gestured to the interviews. "He asked me out. I've liked him for the last four years and he finally asked me out."

Oh dear. Molly hadn't been joking about her rustiness with teens. She hadn't been around them since she was one.

"Isn't that a good thing?"

Nodding, she wiped her nose, then tossed the Kleenex in the trash bin. "It would be if I was allowed to say yes. My mom says football players can't be trusted and if I want any kind of future, it's best I keep my eyes on the prize."

Molly's own eyes widened. *Tread lightly.* "What's the prize?"

A wry smile played on Hannah's lips. "Anything I want. As long as I don't get distracted by hormones and boys."

Slipping off the stool, Molly measured her words. Part of her was touched that Hannah would open up to her, but she didn't want to steer the teen in the wrong direction.

"My mom worried about me hooking up with boys too. The thing is, when you fall for someone, it's natural to kind of be all about them for a while. The newness and excitement of relationships is invigorating. Maybe your mom is just worried about you getting caught up in that. You're in your last year of school. All parents want their kids to have the best chance possible, right?"

Not always. There was a chance that Vernon cared so little about what his son wanted that he'd been killed over it. Wondering if the police had followed up on whether he was in town or not nearly distracted her, but Hannah huffed out a breath, bringing her back to the subject.

Hannah nodded, but her gloomy eyes suggested she did not agree. Molly remembered her own heartaches when she had to leave a town and all the friends she'd made there. It would be easy to tell Hannah that everything would work out in the end and time would pass faster than she could imagine. But in this moment, the teen could only see the here and now.

"If it helps, I can keep you busy enough to take your mind off things," Molly said.

Hannah laughed. "Not exactly what I had in mind, but sure."

"Why don't you grab us a couple of waters from the fridge and I'll show you how to do part of the formatting?"

As easy as flipping a switch, Hannah's mood changed and she went to grab drinks. Molly used the time to take Tigger out and they all wasted some time playing behind the *Bulletin* before getting back to work. Or sleep, in Tigger's case.

Chapter 12

If the teen's phone hadn't buzzed a few hours later, they probably would have carried on working. Like most teens, Hannah had an ease and comfort level with technology and picked up the photo program Molly showed her with little trouble.

"Oops, that's Savannah," Hannah said, swiping her hand over the phone to answer.

"Hey. No, I'm pretty much done. Can't you drop your mom off and then come get me? We'll go to my house." The teen turned, lowered her voice. "Sav. We always go to your house. No. Okay, but come in. I want you to meet Molly. Please. 'Kay." She hung up and slid her phone into her pocket.

Molly stretched, going up on her tiptoes and rolling her neck from one side to the other.

"Everything okay?"

"Yeah. Savannah and I were supposed to hang at my house today. I wanted to tell her about Dusty and…stuff."

Molly gave a tight smile. She knew from what she'd overheard they weren't heading to Hannah's.

"Can't you dish in Savannah's room?"

Hannah snorted with laughter. "No. Not so much. Her mom is too busy serving us cookies and milk like we're still in third grade."

Molly didn't push her for more, but realized she was showing her age when she could understand why both girls' parents wanted to keep them young. Life had a way of whipping by quicker than the teen could imagine.

Molly logged off the computer. "I'm going to shut it down too. I didn't think we were at it for so long. You did great."

"Thanks. It was fun."

They cleaned up the workstation and Molly was just about to grab Tigger when the front door opened. Savannah Black waved a timid hello as she came in.

"Hey," Hannah greeted.

"Hey."

Molly laughed at the quiet exchange between the friends. "Hey," she added.

"Sav, this is Molly. This is my best friend, Savannah," Hannah introduced.

Savannah was nearly the opposite of Hannah—though every bit as lovely—with dark, short hair that sat just under her ears in a stylish bob. She was short, despite the thick heels she wore, and while Hannah suited both casual and dressy styles, Savannah seemed made for the designer dress she wore.

"Welcome to Britton Bay," Savannah said.

"Thanks," Molly replied. Truthfully, she wasn't sure what to say to the teen, but meeting her brought all of her concerns back. Was it the interview with this girl's grandmother that had led to Vernon's death? She was a strange contrast to the woman Molly had met in the diner. She hadn't gone through the box yet, but it was time. She'd been sidetracked, but tonight, she'd look through and maybe see what Vernon saw. Though, if he saw anything of consequence, Molly wondered why he'd leave the box in the car. Guilt bubbled up in her chest. Rightfully, the box should be with Savannah's family or the police. But not before Molly had a chance to look through it.

And how did Elizabeth factor in? The teen broke eye contact and looked around the office. Despite the gracefulness of her posture and the obvious polish, there was an air of uncertainty in her mannerisms.

"You okay, Molly?" Hannah asked as she slung her backpack over her shoulder.

Molly pasted a smile on her face, but inside, her stomach clenched as questions piled up in her brain.

"Fine. Just tired. I think I'm going to go get something to eat. Thanks for all your help today."

"It was fun."

Not ready to stop surveying the other girl yet, Molly blurted, "Savannah, your family has a long history in the community."

The teen's gaze met hers again. "Yes. We're very proud of our legacy."

"I enjoyed reading your interview with Hannah," she said. *Can you tell me more about your grandmother or maybe some family secrets that would lead to a man's death? Yeah, that'd be real subtle, Molly.*

Savannah looked down for a moment, then back up. The way her lips curled up seemed practiced. The smile she gave was pleasant, but…odd. "We're always happy to share our family history. The Phillips name is something we're very proud of. Especially my parents."

Molly didn't know much about teens anymore, but she knew they didn't talk in such stilted, rehearsed ways. Before Molly could reply, the teen's mom, Clara, walked through the door looking every bit as lovely as Molly remembered. With a wide smile, she glanced at the girls.

"Savannah, honey, we need to get going. Hello, Hannah," the woman greeted.

With her dark hair in a perfect bob, similar to her daughter's, it was easy to see where Savannah got her proper posture and classic looks.

She gave Molly a warm smile, with just a hint of sadness. "Hi Molly. How are you doing? I should have found time to come and see you after the ordeal you've faced. What an awful thing." She held out her hand.

Molly appreciated the concern, but wanted a break from talking about it. She accepted Clara's hand. The woman's palm was like silk against her own rough one. She dropped her hand, held Molly's gaze. Molly considered the word *ordeal* and didn't think it adequately described finding a dead body. An ordeal was working through City Hall red tape. Finding a dead body was…was…horrific.

"I'm fine. Thank you. How are you?"

Clara beamed. "Oh, I'm good. It's a busy time of year for us, planning for the tourists and all. Thomas—my husband— is giving the eulogy for Vernon on Thursday, so I'll introduce you then. It's just so shocking that he's gone. He was such a good reporter and Thomas will be sure to mention what he gave back to the community."

Hannah and Savannah chatted quietly by the door, heads bent together. Clara sent them a quick glance. Molly tipped her head, curious.

It was honestly the first time she'd discussed Vernon with anyone and had them say anything positive. "Oh. That's very kind of you. I'm sure your husband will be too busy to worry about meeting me, though. It's not necessary." Molly wasn't sure a funeral was a great place for a meet and greet. Especially with the mayor.

Clara's smile was tighter this time, more forced. "I feel like it is. I just can't stop thinking about how awful Vernon's passing is. He was interviewing my mama just the other day and now he's… gone." She snapped her fingers. "Just like that. Such a shame."

Guilt dug sharp claws into Molly's chest, deflating her lungs. Clara ignored Molly's silence.

"Mama was just so sad to hear of Vernon's death. She really enjoyed the interview. They had a wonderful chat. Will you still be printing it?"

Confusion warred with guilt. Vernon certainly hadn't enjoyed the meeting. "You don't mind?"

Clara's perfectly sculpted brows arched. "Not at all. No reason not to, right?"

Other than not actually having the interview, probably not. Molly had been so worried about being the catalyst for Vernon's death, but if Clara and her mother still wanted the interview to go forward, maybe she really was digging under the wrong rock. She'd need to get her hands on the interview to honor this woman's request, but if the meeting was as straightforward as Clara suggested, there was no reason to believe Vernon had uncovered anything unsavory about the family. Which let Molly off the proverbial hook, didn't it?

"Mom, can we go?" Savannah called from the door.

Clara rolled her eyes a little, making Molly laugh. In a whispered voice she told Molly, "I'm not allowed to socialize if it interrupts her time."

Glancing over her shoulder, she answered her daughter. "In a second, sweetheart."

Clara turned back to Molly. "Please let me know if you need anything. We really are a community here in Britton Bay."

"Thank you. I appreciate that."

"I mean it. Anything you need. Let's go, girls."

"See you later, Molly," Hannah said.

"Yeah. Nice to meet you, Savannah, and to see you again, Mrs. Black," Molly replied.

Clara turned. "It's Phillips. And it was really nice to see you too."

Right. Molly watched them go, more confused than ever. She locked the front door behind them. After grabbing her laptop, her purse, and what was really starting to feel like her dog, she loaded up her Jeep. Uncertainty swirled around a pool of curiosity in her gut during the short ride home. Tigger kept his paws on the door, staring out the window as the trees and people whipped by.

Molly reached over and gave his back a pet. "Best thing about you is you stop me from eating out too much."

And gave her company she hadn't even realized she was craving. There was parking for the bed-and-breakfast guests near the front of the house, but like Molly, Katherine parked her vehicle around the back. Molly had her own gravel pad, but could easily see Katherine's parking spot closer to the house. At the moment, there were two vehicles in that drive: Katherine's—with the hood open—and a silver Chevy.

As she rounded the hood of the Jeep, Sam did the same to his mom's car. She saw his smile even from a distance. Fortunately for her, he couldn't see or feel how her heart decided to tap-dance at the sight of that smile. *Oh man.* There was no denying that seeing him lifted her spirits and her day in general. She might as well accept that and see where it went.

He was wearing coveralls again and Molly decided she was headed for murky waters if that got her heart pumping. With a wave, he called out, "How's it going?"

She opened her passenger door and let Tigger out. He squirmed out of her arms and over to Sam.

"Good. Doing some side work?" Molly walked, making sure her pace did not reflect the excitement Tigger wasn't too proud to share.

Sam crouched and rubbed behind Tigger's floppy ears. "Hey, you. You still here? Don't blame you. It's a good place to be."

Molly's lips tipped up even as her heart fluttered. She pushed her hands into her pockets. "I haven't found his owner. Or rather, the owner hasn't found me."

Sam stood, which prompted Tigger to flop down across Sam's large shoe. "Make yourself cozy," he laughed before looking up at Molly. "Just changing some spark plugs and the oil for my mom. If I don't remind her, she'll let it go. Easier to come here than nag her down to the station."

Molly smiled. They took care of each other. It'd been a long time since anyone had taken care of her. *Which is fine, because you can take care of yourself.*

"You're a good son."

His shoulders lifted in a humble shrug. "She seems to think so. How was your day?"

Molly sighed. She didn't mean to. It just came out. "Good. Mostly. It was my day off, but I had to work. Elizabeth got called down to the station for further questioning and Alan wanted to be with her."

Darkness clouded Sam's eyes. "My mom mentioned that. You think it has something to do with the emails?"

That was exactly what she'd thought and it was really nice to have someone to discuss the idea with. "Possibly. Alan didn't say they wanted to question him, but he insisted on needing to be there for her."

His eyes cleared—clouds shifting to reveal a lighter shade of blue. "Because he's a good man. They'll get it all cleared up, I'm sure."

"I hope so. Not to seem selfish, but the *Bulletin* can't survive with me running it on my own and I moved here for the job."

What was it about this man and his mother that made her voice things she hadn't really even admitted to herself yet? Her job security had already been in question when Alan told Vernon it was time to save the newspaper or shut it down. Now, with Clay out of town—or not—Vernon gone, and the other two tied up in questioning, Molly didn't know how long she could make it work with just her and Hannah.

"Don't worry just yet. Hopefully, things with Elizabeth will get cleared up quick and she and Alan will both be back tomorrow. If you're looking for staff writers, my cousin just moved back from college and does some writing. Her degree is in business communications."

Tigger woke up just to chase his tail, making Molly laugh. She crouched down as she answered Sam. "If she's interested, I'd love to chat with her. Soon, if she's got time."

"I'll text her later."

"Thanks." She should go in and make something for dinner. Take a shower and do some research. She wanted to dig through the box and see what was there. If she couldn't get Vernon's interview, maybe she could piece some things together for herself and just allude to the story he was writing. Or, perhaps she could get ahold of Vanessa Phillips and redo the interview.

Sam ran a hand through his hair and glanced back at his mom's car. "I have to finish this up, but won't be long. You want to meet up for dinner at Come 'n Get It in a while?"

Yes! She bit her lip and looked down at Tigger. When her eyes met Sam's again, she felt like she was the one chasing her own tail—running in circles. *Beats standing still.*

"That sounds good. I have a few things I need to do, but I can meet you in just over an hour?"

Sam's smile made her feel like she'd just snuggled into a warm jacket on a cold day. "Perfect."

As if she wasn't already in danger of acting like a silly teen, he kneeled down and clicked his tongue. Tigger bounded over to him. "Sorry, pal. No pets at Calliope's."

Molly laughed. "He'll have to settle for kibble. I think he'll survive, seeing as earlier he tried to eat paper."

Sam gave the pup one last rub and stood up. Taking a couple steps backward, he continued to shoot that easygoing-sexy smile. "See you in a while."

"Crocodile," Molly said, then realized she'd actually said it out loud. Heat slapped at her cheeks. Could she be more of a dork?

Luckily for her, Sam appeared to like dorks, because his hearty chuckle carried through the air as she turned and walked away, shaking her head at herself.

Chapter 13

To avoid obsessing over what felt like an actual date with a guy who seemed as sweet as he was good-looking, Molly cleared her countertop and brought over the box she and Sam had taken from Vernon's car. Carefully, she placed photos and newspaper articles on the smooth surface. Unfortunately for her, she could multitask, so thoughts of Sam and whether or not she should have agreed to dinner kept popping into her brain.

"Focus," Molly said.

Tigger, thinking she was talking to him, yipped in agreement. She looked down at him. "You're seconding the motion? Thanks, mister."

He plopped his butt on the floor, waited a few seconds, then wandered over to grab one of his toys and nibble on it. "Some sidekick you are."

There was a mix of items in the shoe-sized box. As she pulled it out of the backpack, the Post-it note Sam had grabbed from the car slipped. Grabbing it, she wondered if it had anything to do with the box. Knowing Vernon's need to scribble his thoughts down, it could be nothing—just a scrap of paper he'd made a note on in his car. Macintosh…maybe he was looking for a new computer. Like her, he had a PC. Molly set it aside on the countertop and pulled the lid off of the box. There were several photographs of Vanessa as a teen—as Vernon had mentioned. She'd married into the Phillips family. Molly had already learned quite a bit about them.

The Phillips family was something of an institution in Britton Bay—which, aptly, had once been called Phillips Cove. In the early 1800s, while other men were settling in other areas along the Oregon coast, three brothers and their wives arrived in the small town just south of Astoria. From a wealthy family in London, the Phillips brothers decided that the small chunk of land overlooking the sea was a perfect spot to build the lives they wanted.

Molly picked up a faded and worn journal page and squinted to make out the words. One of the brothers' wives was pregnant and all three of them had built homes beside each other. One of the brothers was working on a hotel, while another was building a saloon.

She was, quite literally, holding history in her hand. Setting the page down, she smiled as she picked up a grainy shot of two men outside of a building site, shovels in hand, smiling. There were a few letters between Vanessa and her husband, Charleston, but there were also fading photographs of Charleston's father and grandfather. *Quite the mix. Like a bunch of drawers were cleaned out and shoved into one box.* She wasn't even sure how to sort her findings. Remembering what she read online helped her fill in some gaps.

In the late 1800s, trading was happening further down the coast between indigenous people and European settlers. With that came the arrival of more families to the swatch of land the brothers had claimed for their own. Over time, the Phillips broods grew along with the town's population. At one time, the library, town hall, general store, and schoolhouse had been named after the brothers. When one of the grandsons of the oldest brother, Britton, died of unknown causes at a young age, the town was renamed by the family as Britton Bay.

Molly found it both sad and incredibly heartwarming that they named it after the boy. The box was nearly overflowing with a seemingly random collection of memories. Molly checked the time and decided she could pour over things at a later time. For now, she wanted to empty the box and see what was there. By the time she'd emptied it, she knew there were many stories to be told right there, but she wasn't sure that any of them would have incited murder.

She'd dig in more when she got home from her da—*dinner* with a friend. While she styled her hair, choosing to flatiron it, she wondered if she was grasping at straws—or photographs. Was there anything in what Vernon found that led him to something he had no right to dig into? She knew that he liked to poke at peoples' weaknesses. Had he found one with this family? Or maybe he'd stumbled across something that had nothing to do with the Phillipses at all. She often found items in places they had no business being, so what if there'd been a link to something else randomly tucked away in this old family treasure trove? Vernon would capitalize on anything he could—regardless of who it hurt.

Pleased that she managed to get ready with twenty minutes to spare, Molly picked up her phone and dialed Elizabeth's number. As it rang, she sat down on the couch, her hip touching a curled up, sleepy Tigger.

"Hello," Elizabeth said.

"Hi Elizabeth. It's Molly. I wanted to check on you and see how you're doing."

She put her feet up on the table and scratched Tigger's back absentmindedly. If Elizabeth had been arrested and locked up, she wouldn't be answering her phone, so Molly took that as a good sign.

"Oh. That's sweet of you. I was just making some tea and then heading to bed. The day has been exhausting. I'm so sorry that we left you with everything today. And on your day off too."

Molly closed her eyes. She just didn't see this woman as a murderer, regardless of her secrets or the veiled threat in the email. *But it doesn't make sense that she'd have an affair, either. You don't really know her. How well can you really know anyone?* As her ex had proven, even living with someone didn't translate to really seeing them.

"You have nothing to apologize for. I've been worried about you. Alan said they wanted to question you?"

Molly thought about circling around the topic and waiting for Elizabeth to open up, but she didn't want to wait.

"They did. It was awful. It felt like being on trial. They had the completely wrong idea," Elizabeth said.

Molly heard the woman's voice break and her own heart clenched. "Do the police know that now? That it was all a misunderstanding?"

Please tell me what the misunderstanding was.

Elizabeth sniffled into the phone. "As if his father wasn't a nasty enough man, Clay decided to pick up where Vernon left off. He told the police that Vernon was blackmailing me. He told them I had motive to want him dead." She paused and Molly's heart hammered against her rib cage. So Clay knew about the emails too. When had he told this to the police? There was a very real possibility that he hadn't left town or at the very least, had returned sooner than anyone had expected him to. In time to leave prints outside her window? She wondered if Officer Beatty had taken a closer look at the photos or Clay's story.

"He was right in that Vernon was blackmailing me, but I didn't hurt him over it. They said they had to follow through on any threats. Which is pretty ironic, considering the threat Vernon posed. It was...humiliating."

They'd let her go, so they must have been satisfied. Elizabeth didn't mention the emails, but she didn't know Molly knew. Molly bit back her frustrated groan and stood up. Opening the back door, she let Tigger run out in the yard.

"I'm sorry you had to go through all of this. Where did they leave things?" A deep, breathy sigh came through the phone. "Vernon and I had exchanged some emails. When Clay let them know I'd warned him to stop blackmailing me, they brought in his laptop and printed out the exchange. They went through the entire thing with me. Point by exhausting point. Eventually, they let me go. They said they're satisfied, for *now*. But I didn't kill him, Molly. Can't they see it makes no sense?"

Nothing made any sense. Molly leaned against the open doorframe, being careful to avoid looking down at the crushed flowers. Instead, she watched Tigger dance across the lawn. The sun was still high in the sky, but the breeze cooled the early evening. Nothing made sense to her—not Alan and Elizabeth, Clay's lies, Callan's temper—none of it. She didn't see how it all fit. Maybe Elizabeth had told the police the truth and just didn't feel comfortable telling Molly? *She doesn't really know you, so why would she open up?* Maybe she had told the police everything and if they let her go, it was because they'd cleared her as a suspect.

"I'm sorry that all of this is happening," Molly said.

She wasn't exactly sure what was happening, since Elizabeth's explanation only led to more questions. But they weren't questions she felt comfortable asking.

"Thank you. You're such a sweet girl. What a terrible thing you've walked into. Don't let it scare you off. We need you," Elizabeth said.

The sentiment was like a good bear hug. It was nice to be needed. Plus, she liked the job and wanted to stay.

"It takes more than that to scare me," Molly said. In truth, what really scared her was the idea that the items lying on her counter could be clues to Vernon's death. Clues he wouldn't have had if she hadn't forced him to go to the house. With Elizabeth cleared as a suspect—if that was true— that was one less person to focus on. She glanced over at the papers and pictures. *It's not your fault.* She still didn't know why he died and clearly, neither did the police. All the more reason to keep digging. She might not have swung the cup, but if the cause of his death had been in that box, she owed it to Vernon to find the killer.

Chapter 14

Molly parked beside Sam's truck, but he was already inside. Nerves crested like waves in her stomach. Even though they were showing up separately, they'd be eating a meal together. In a small town, dining together at the local hot spot was the equivalent of having a date broadcast over the jumbotron at a sporting event.

Sam waved from a booth near the kitchen, which was far more private than the spot she'd chosen the other night in front of the window. Being a Monday, there weren't that many customers. Molly made her way back to Sam as Calliope came out of the swinging door that led to the kitchen. She carried an oval platter piled with delicious-looking fried foods in one hand and two plates in the other.

"Hey doll. How you doing?" Calliope paused briefly and Molly couldn't imagine standing there balancing all that weight.

The smell of the food she carried made Molly's mouth water. "I'm good."

"Back in a sec," the perky redhead promised.

Sam stood when Molly reached the side of the table. She sat across from him and he took his seat. They stared at each other a moment. Under the table, Molly ran her thumb over her jean-clad thigh, telling herself not to be nervous. It had been a long time since she'd had a date and an even longer time since she'd wanted—so badly—for one to go well.

"You look like you might bolt," Sam said. One side of his mouth quirked up.

"I won't. Doesn't mean it didn't cross my mind. But I won't." Might as well be honest.

Sam folded his hands together and stretched them out on the table. Molly kept hers where they were, on her lap, but maintained eye contact.

I'm no chicken. Just a crocodile? Mortification made her want to squirm as she recalled her words.

Sam pulled his right hand from his left, turned his wrist and gestured with his index finger to lean closer. Molly leaned her upper body in.

"How about if I promise to work hard not to give you a reason to bolt. Would that relax you a bit?"

Hmm. Mr. Mechanic was perceptive. She knew she couldn't base her future on her past and not every man—heck, not every person—was out to rip her to shreds. But a girl had to at least attempt to protect her slightly dented heart.

"That sounds…doable." She put her hands on the table.

Country music pumped through the speakers just loud enough to hear over the talking and laughing. Dean was hollering to someone in the kitchen. When he saw Molly through the pass, he lifted his spatula and winked.

Molly looked back at Sam. "Sorry. I'm being weird. I guess I was just a little nervous."

Sam's smile didn't help with that. "It's all right. Nothing to be nervous about. Just two friends having a bite to eat."

Right. She could tell by the way his gaze was nearly lighting her on fire that both of them felt something a little bigger than friendship. But it was a nice start.

Molly picked up a menu, glancing up when she heard Calliope's laugh bounce through the place. It made her smile and finally, she exhaled a deep breath.

"What's your favorite?" Molly asked.

Sam was looking at his menu. His eyes met hers over the top of it. "Well, they don't serve crocodile, so that's out."

Oh. My. God. She could *feel* the red on her cheeks. She pulled the menu closer to her face so Sam couldn't see her. But she could hear him laughing his handsome butt off. She giggled despite the bone-deep embarrassment.

"You're terrible," Molly said around a laugh from behind the menu.

"Aw, come on. That was the cutest thing," Sam said, tugging at her menu.

"Nope. Go away. We're eating like this."

"You're gonna need both those hands if you get another burger, doll," Calliope said.

Molly lowered the menu. Great. More witnesses to her dorkitude. "Hi Calliope."

The waitress tucked a strand of hair behind her ear and tipped her head. "Hi Molly. How you doing? I heard you walked into something awful. You holding up okay?"

Closing the menu, realizing that the switch in topic had doused both her embarrassment and her smile, she nodded. "I'm okay. I'll feel better—like everyone else, I'm sure—when the police know who did it and why."

Sam lowered his menu, his expression serious. "They will. They'll get it sorted."

Calliope clucked her tongue. "I sure hope you're right, Sam." She waved a hand dismissively and then pulled a notepad from her apron. Her bright green T-shirt read *Waitress Power.* "Enough of this sad talk. What can I get you two?"

Sam glanced at Molly, waiting. "I'll start with a cola, but I need another minute with the menu."

"Same," Sam said.

"Back in a sec," Calliope said.

Molly started to pick up her menu, but Sam's long fingers pressed it down. She looked up through lowered lashes, feeling her face warm again.

"You know I was just teasing you, right? I like the way your cheeks flush pink when I do."

She bit the inside of her cheek. "That's fine. Just be warned that as soon as you do something silly, I'm going to tease you mercilessly over it."

Sam chuckled and removed his hand. "Duly noted and may I just say, you spend any amount of time with me, I'm positive I'll give you a reason to do just that."

The idea of spending more time with him certainly appealed. They decided to order the appetizer platter and share. It had looked so good going by, Molly wanted to give it a try and it was something she'd never get on her own.

Calliope took their order when she brought their sodas and to Molly's surprise, didn't say anything about the two of them being together. *Just wait 'til she catches you alone and she'll mention it.* Molly smiled, knowing she was right.

Sam told her about his day, doing a couple of brake jobs and some office work.

"I hate that part of it, but I can't see paying someone for what I know how to do," he said. He took a drink of his cola.

"I guess not, but if you dislike it and can afford to have someone else do it, it'll free up your time for doing more of what you love. Which I'm guessing is the working-on-cars part."

"It is. I'm going to give it the summer and see where I'm at. If things just keep getting busier, I'm going to have to hire someone to take over that part."

"Did you text your cousin?" Molly asked.

Sam snapped his fingers and pointed at her as he dug his phone out of his pocket with his other hand. "I did. Let me see your phone; I'll put her number in there for you. You can call her whenever you want. I don't know if you need to talk to Alan or if you want to talk to her first and then him, but I told her you'd be in touch."

Molly slid her phone over, trying to think of a way to subtly suggest he put his own number in with his cousin's. She didn't realize how out of practice she was at the whole dating thing.

"What's your cousin's name?"

Sam's thumbs were tapping over Molly's screen, but he glanced up with a smile. "Jill. You'll like her."

As he slid her phone back to her, his own buzzed. Molly tried to hide her disappointment. *Why didn't you just ask for his number?* He looked down at his screen with a smile and she tried not to let that irritate her. *It's fine. Lots of people text during dinner. On dates.* When he started tapping a response to whatever had come through on his phone, Molly bit her lip, tilting her chin down so Sam couldn't see her frown. Maybe she was misreading his signals. Maybe they weren't signals at all. Could be they really were just two friends grabbing a bite to eat. Molly slid her own into the side of her purse, but it chimed loudly, signaling an incoming text. She ignored it because that was the polite thing to do.

"You going to answer that?" Sam asked, lowering his phone.

With a tight smile, Molly shook her head. "It can wait."

Sam's brows furrowed together. "What if it can't? What if it's important?"

She doubted it was, but now she also doubted it wasn't. She pulled her phone out with a huff. Molly was grateful she didn't have a mirror in front of her, because if she did, she'd be staring at a reflection of herself grinning like a smitten idiot.

Sam: I'm glad you said yes to dinner. I have your number now and it won't be the last time I ask, just so you know.

Molly glanced up and met his playful gaze. "You think you're funny."

He nodded and picked up his soda. "Sort of."

He was right, but no way would she admit it. *Now you have his number and from the sounds of it, the promise of another date.* She slipped her phone into her purse as Calliope brought their food.

"I'll come back in a minute and top up your drinks," she said, bending to set the tray down.

"Mmm, this looks delicious, Calliope," Molly said.

The waitress straightened and took a deep breath, letting it whoosh out. "I am overheating like oysters in the fryer. So, when did this happen?" she asked, waving between them.

Molly was happy she hadn't taken a bite of food or she might have choked on it. Sam was clearly more used to Calliope's nature. He winked at Molly, putting both of his feet on the outside of her crossed ones. The gestures sent ripples of excitement up her spine. Deep trouble. As if she didn't already have enough on her plate.

"Settle down, Calli. Molly and I are just having a bite to eat. It's not hot in here. You feeling okay?" Sam asked. He set an appetizer plate in front of Molly and then himself.

"Nothing hiring a little summer help won't cure," she said. She put a hand on her shapely hip and gave Molly a pointed stare.

"You've had more happen in a week than most of us do in six months. Next day off you have, you and me? We're having a full-out gossip session."

Cornered, Molly could only nod. "Yes, ma'am."

Calliope laughed and grabbed their glasses. Molly looked at Sam, who was waiting patiently to dig in.

Molly picked up a crisply breaded chicken strip and broke it in half. "I get the impression not many people say *no* to Calliope or your mom."

Sam's laugh was warm. He picked up a mozzarella stick. "I've never met any who would."

Once Calliope brought back their drinks, they dug into their food a bit. Molly didn't want to keep bringing Vernon up, but his murder was always in the back of her mind. She was surprised when Sam brought it up first.

"So, you got me thinking about Callan and Vernon's argument. The one you said Calli told you about?"

Pulse picking up, Molly nodded around a mouthful of potato popper.

"Callan brought his car in yesterday and I asked him about it. Like I thought, it was about Vernon cheating him out of money a few games ago. I wasn't at that one and I didn't see it go down. He was miffed, but he didn't seem all that angry about it."

Because he'd extracted his revenge? "Do you think he's telling the truth?" Molly asked.

Sam shrugged. "No reason not to. He's not being looked at by police."

Yet. But that didn't mean they wouldn't be interested in finding out the two men had been at odds or that Callan had quite the temper. But would anyone kill over some poker winnings? It scared her that she knew the answer was *yes*.

"So if they fought because Vernon did steal or cheat, do you think that would wind Callan up enough to actually kill him?"

Molly leaned in. The restaurant was quiet with just a few other couples scattered throughout, but still, she didn't feel right about everyone knowing their topic of conversation.

Sam leaned back, wiped his mouth with a napkin. "I don't. I really don't. But… I was trying to think like a suspicious newspaper editor," he said, pausing for a smile.

Molly's heart flipped over like Tigger when he wanted rubs. "Cute."

"I asked him, casually, what he'd gotten up to after poker the other night. The one Vernon skipped out on."

"And?" Molly's heart tripled its pace.

Sam's cheeks brightened slightly. "He didn't do it."

Frowning, Molly put down the chicken wing she'd chosen. "How do you know?"

Sam picked up his soda and took a long sip, stirring the ice in the bottom with his straw. His eyes darted over her head, but she waited patiently.

"He was otherwise occupied," he answered when he set the glass down.

Molly snorted, then slapped a hand across her mouth. Sam's grin widened and he laughed. Taking deep breaths, Molly removed her hand.

"I'm sorry, but it wouldn't be the first time a man has fabricated that sort of information. You can't possibly know."

The twinkle in Sam's eye kept the conversation amusing enough that Molly was able to push Vernon to the back of her mind for a moment. Just while she teased Sam about having absolute faith in his friend's tall tales.

Sam pointed at her, wagging his finger jokingly. "Jaded city girl. But, I did think the same. Then I popped by to grab some muffins from Bella. I said something about Callan and she turned about twelve shades of pink. I wasn't looking to embarrass her—I don't even remember why I brought up his name. But all of a sudden it was like we were back in high school and she asked if he'd said anything about her. Then she told me they'd met up the other night after poker and she had a real good feeling about things."

Molly leaned back, not sure whether to laugh at Sam's high school comment. She wasn't purposely trying to pull him into a he said-she said situation. Especially with people he'd known most of his life.

"I wasn't trying to pull you into anything," she said in a quiet voice.

Sam pushed the mostly empty platter to the side of the table. "You didn't. You just made me curious. So I asked some questions. But, you have to admit, it does clear Callan from the list. One less worry, right?"

Why didn't he think she was crazy for even having a list of people?

Still. She wasn't entirely convinced. Molly wondered if there was any way to find out Vernon's time of death. Would Callan have had time to go to Vernon's after poker, before meeting up with Bella?

Sam frowned. "You're thinking somethin' unpleasant."

She forced a smile. This was his friend. And sort of their first date. She didn't want to wreck the evening. "No. Sorry. You're right. Callan probably had other things on his mind if he was on his way to meet up with Bella. I spoke to Elizabeth tonight before I came here."

"How is she?" Sam asked.

"She's home." Biting the inside of her cheek, she decided to take a leap of faith. He'd trusted in her enough to question his friend. She could return the favor and share her thoughts. She leaned forward and told him about the conversation.

"Why wouldn't she just be open about the emails? She said the police found them on Vernon's computer. Even when she told me that, she wouldn't say what the cops suspected Vernon of blackmailing her for—but she and Alan must know how their relationship looks to an outsider. How it obviously looked to Vernon."

Sam rubbed his hand across his mouth and then folded his arms on the table. "Maybe she's embarrassed? I mean, whatever it is, and I don't think it's cheating, it's enough to make her look suspicious to the police. That can't be an easy thing for her or for Alan."

Molly sighed. "There's just so many unanswered questions."

Sam's lips quirked. "Good thing there are police officers trying to answer them, huh?"

Calliope brought their check over and though Molly attempted to pay, Sam wouldn't let her.

As he shifted to put his wallet back in his pocket, he arched a brow. "Though I wouldn't turn down having you stop by my work with a box of cookies some time."

Small. Towns. Molly rolled her eyes. He was teasing her again and it was working. She bit her lip, but it didn't hide her smile.

"I see you've been talking to Officer Beatty."

"One of the brake jobs I did today was his. He may have mentioned it."

"They were just cookies," she said. Regardless of what they were doing, Molly only danced with one partner at a time.

"How many?" Sam slid out of the booth and offered her his hand.

"How many what?" she asked, sliding her own into his and acknowledging to herself how good it felt.

"Cookies?"

Molly laughed. "Six."

Sam squeezed her hand, lacing their fingers together. He leaned in, close enough she could smell the crisp scent of his cologne. "I want twelve."

"You two on your way?" Calliope came back over, looking like she'd cooled off some. Her red hair was no longer trying to escape her ponytail and her cheeks weren't as flushed as they'd been when she was dropping off food. Molly saw her glance at their clasped hands, saw the smile tweak her lips, and appreciated the woman's restraint from saying a word about it.

She only pointed at Molly. "Gossip session. Soon. I might just come by your little carriage home for a visit."

The idea thrilled Molly. "Any time. I mean it."

They said good night and walked out of the diner. Sam released her hand when they got to their vehicles. He leaned against the driver's door of his and she did the same on the passenger side of her Jeep.

"So? Find anything in those photos?"

"Not yet. I don't know if I should pass it over to the police, but from what I can tell, there's nothing in there anyone would kill over. Maybe it has nothing to do with the Phillips family after all, but the timing…I just can't stop feeling like it isn't a coincidence." Molly tugged her purse up on her shoulder.

"Maybe the killer took it."

That was her fear. "I thought about that, but why leave everything else in the car? It didn't look like anyone had been in there before us. Other than Vernon. But if you're right, and you could be, then it is likely it was related to the interview or at least the family."

Sam straightened and stepped closer so Molly had to crane her neck. "It's not your fault, Molly. Not one bit."

She nodded, but her eyes watered. She had to keep telling herself that.

"There's a good chance—if something was in there—it has nothing to do with the family. You just can't know. I'm worried you're going to make yourself crazy trying to sort it out."

She just might. Sam ran a hand down her hair just before he stepped back and the gesture tugged at Molly's heart like an anchor. Or a buoy.

"Watch out for yourself, okay?"

"I will. Thank you for dinner."

"My pleasure."

He waited until she was in her Jeep, belted, and backing out before he got in his own truck. Streetlights lit the darkness like the stars that were popping out in the sky. Happy feelings—despite recent events—swamped Molly. She was settling in, making friends. She liked her job and the town felt like home. Take murder out of the equation and it was almost too good to be true.

Don't look for negatives. Be happy. She was. But as she pulled up to her carriage home, she wondered, How long could it last? Everything ended. Some things sooner than they should, some long after they should.

Molly couldn't shake the feeling that the interview and Vernon's death were tied. But what evidence did she have? Clara had no issues with the interview going to print, so clearly she wasn't hiding anything. There'd been nothing in the box to suggest dark secrets. Savannah had given Molly a strange vibe, but maybe she was just an awkward teen. Sam could be right about Callan, though she hadn't told him about seeing his anger that day. She trusted the police enough to think that if Elizabeth was guilty of anything, they'd have held her at the station.

Which left her...where, exactly? *Go back to the start.* In Molly's mind, that was still the interview. If she took out all of the little bits in between— the suspects—what she knew was Vernon hated her, she'd forced him to go somewhere he hadn't wanted to go, he'd been strange that night on the phone, after the interview, and then he'd wound up dead. Without all of the people clouding the timeline, the connection between his death and his job shouted at her.

She needed to go and meet with Vanessa Phillips face-to-face. Maybe then she'd be able to stop obsessing about a possible link. If she could prove that she hadn't sent a man to his death by being overzealous and demanding, the happiness she wanted to grab hold of like a lifeline had a better chance of sticking around.

Chapter 15

Even though Molly agreed that Callan's alibi was probably airtight, the need to be sure—along with a hard-core love of Bella's scones—had her dropping by Morning Muffins on her way to work the next day.

She'd walked from the carriage house, figuring it was a good way to counterbalance all of the delicious food she'd been packing away. Morning Muffins had a small lineup of customers and a few people sitting at the bistro-style tables scattered throughout the small space.

Bella handed a coffee and a small bakery box to the customer in front of her and caught Molly's eye. She waved and Molly waved back, getting in line. The woman in front of her turned and looked up at Molly. Snow-white curly hair fell to her shoulders and beneath the lines time had left, she was still quite attractive. Except that she was frowning at Molly quite severely.

"You're the new girl from California, aren't you?" the woman asked.

It seemed safe to assume there was only one recent California transplant in Britton Bay, so Molly nodded. "Yes, ma'am."

The woman shook a gnarled finger. "Don't try your slick manners on me. It won't work. My Shannon has had her eyes set on Sam Alderich for years now. Don't need no big-city girl stepping on her toes."

Eyes turned their way and amusement warred with embarrassment. Molly cringed and gave a rough laugh. "Um. Okay?"

Who was Shannon? Who was *this* woman?

"Leave the girl alone, Cora," the man in front of them said. Also older, he gave Molly a weathered smile and beneath the brim of his ball cap, his eyes crinkled.

Cora turned to the man. "Never you mind, Henry. Your grandchildren are all married off. You got great-grandbabies on the way."

Henry chuckled and put a hand on Cora's arm. Molly glanced ahead and saw Bella had her bottom lip between her teeth. She gave a small shrug and lifted her hands in a *what can I say* gesture.

Molly sighed. She'd known the risk of having dinner at the restaurant last night, but so few people had been there, she'd forgotten the way things worked. Someone always knew someone else to pass information on to. *Then why can't you get any information on Vernon and the night he was killed?*

Would the question ever stop haunting her, she wondered as a conversation swelled around her. From the bits and pieces she listened to while she waited her turn, the older crowd—Molly realized everyone in the small bakery was elderly—was debating whether Sam would be better off with Shannon or Molly.

When it was finally Molly's turn, Bella leaned forward and covered the hand Molly had placed on the counter.

"I'm so sorry. Tuesdays are twenty-percent off for seniors, so there's always a pile of them in here. Usually, it's the best gossip session around and pretty fun to listen to, but I'm sorry you got dragged into it." The baker leaned in further still.

"Cora's been trying to marry Shannon off to Sam or any man who'll have her since she graduated from high school."

Molly couldn't help but chuckle and lean close. "Is there something wrong with Shannon that she can't get a date without her grandma's help?"

Bella leaned back and straightened her shoulders, a sassy grin lighting her face. "Not if you ask her. That girl is more full of herself than a hot-air balloon."

She didn't mean to laugh, but it felt good and the tension in her shoulders eased. "I wasn't looking to steal the town bachelor. We're just friends," Molly said.

Bella winked at her. "That's the best way to start."

It was like the conversation gods were laying out the red carpet for her. *Play it cool.* In her mind, Molly rolled her eyes at herself. She wasn't great with subterfuge.

"I'll take six of your blueberry scones," she said. "And a large coffee."

"You got it. How are you settling in?" Bella asked as she pulled a flattened box from beneath the counter. With a few quick twists, it was ready to be filled.

"Pretty well. I really love the carriage house and…well, work has been… good in spite of everything."

Using tongs to grab the scones, Bella looked back over her shoulder. "What an awful thing for you to see. You're holding up?"

"I am."

Bringing the box over as she closed the top, Bella's gaze was serious. "Are the police getting anywhere?"

"I'm not sure. Last I heard, the suspect list had shrunk."

The bell chimed and a few more seniors shuffled in. Molly needed to hear Bella's answer for herself. Before the woman could turn and grab Molly's coffee, she practically blurted, "So, speaking of starting as friends, you and Callan? Over at the Sit and Sip?"

Way to be subtle. Bella's skin flushed and her eyes nearly glazed over. Molly couldn't help but smile. Regardless of anything else, there was no hiding the fact that Bella was smitten.

"Yeah. Finally. Been waiting long enough, I'll tell you that."

The seniors chatted loudly behind Molly as they waited their turn. Molly leaned in.

"It's pretty recent, though?"

"Yeah. Takes men twice as long as it does us to figure out what's been there the whole time, right?"

Molly wasn't sure about that, as she didn't have the best track record with relationships, but she was willing to take the baker's word on it.

The seniors were crowding her a little, trying to see what yumminess Bella's shelves held.

"You guys met up after his last poker game, right? The other night?" The night Vernon was killed.

Bella's eyes narrowed slightly and a different flush washed over her cheeks. *You're just being intrusive now.* But she had to know. Sam trusted his friend, but as Molly knew all too well, men lied.

"We did. Listen, Molly, it's getting a bit busy again. I'm going to grab your coffee," Bella said.

Regret lodged itself in Molly's stomach. She'd crossed the line being so forward and more than that, she'd been rude. Putting money on the counter, Molly waited until Bella came back with her to-go cup.

"Bella, I'm sorry. I didn't mean to be rude or cross a line."

The baker studied her for a moment. "It's okay."

Molly didn't feel like it was, though, but with seniors at her back, needing to get to work, and Bella shut down, she knew it was time to go. She could fix this later, she hoped.

"I think it's nice that you're happy. I love when things work out for good people," Molly said. She hoped Bella could see she meant it.

Though it had only a percentage of its usual glow, Bella smiled. "Thanks. Me too."

Molly caught Cora's glare on her way out the door. Without meaning to, she'd made herself an enemy there. She had a feeling it would be easier to get Bella to forgive her misstep than it would be Cora.

When she showed up at work with scones, Alan and Elizabeth pounced on them immediately.

"Bless you, sweet girl," Elizabeth said, taking a bite.

Her hair was down today, making her look younger, but the dark circles under her eyes suggested she'd had a restless night. Molly didn't exactly want a long list of people disliking her, so she didn't ask any questions about the day before. If the police were satisfied with her answers, she should let it go.

Alan leaned on the work counter, polishing off his scone without a word. Wiping his hands with the napkins Bella had included, he made a sound of satisfaction.

"That was exactly what I needed. Thank you, Molly."

"No problem." She broke off another piece of her own.

The elephant in the room was starting to toss his trunk around, but she held firm. No more nosy questions. For now, anyway. If the police were satisfied, so was she. Besides, she'd sense something if she were working alongside someone capable of murder, wouldn't she? Had Vernon sensed something that night?

"I should be thanking you for a lot more than just scones. The layout for the next paper looks fantastic. The story ideas you want to run with are high quality. With only the three of us for now, we won't be able to follow up on all of them right now. Which is fine, because with all that's happened, the town isn't going to be too focused on the paper."

"That's understandable," Molly said. She popped the last bit of scone in her mouth and grabbed a napkin.

He and Elizabeth shared a glance. If Molly hadn't been looking right at Elizabeth, she'd have missed the subtle nod she gave to her employer.

"I was wondering if you'd like to come for dinner at my house tonight. Elizabeth will be joining us as well."

Looking back and forth between them, Molly pushed down the feeling that there was more being left unsaid, than said. "That sounds nice."

"I'd like you to meet my wife. We've been telling her about you and I think you'll get along great."

The sickly wife who didn't attend dinner parties or family events, according to Hannah. *Hannah!*

Molly nodded. "That's great, I'd love to. I wanted to talk to you about Hannah. It's clear we're going to need to hire someone and with her break coming up, we could utilize both her time and talent. Instead of being a volunteer, we could train her to be a staff writer. I don't mind putting in the time to help her. I think she's got a great style."

Alan's smile spread slowly, until it took up his entire face. It was the youngest she'd seen her boss look. "That is a wonderful idea. Something tells me you're going to be good for a lot of people in this town, Molly. It's our good fortune we found you."

She appreciated the accolades, but could think of a few people who didn't share the sentiment.

"Thank you. That's a nice thing to say. On another note, the police haven't returned Vernon's computer, have they?"

Elizabeth frowned. "Why would they give it to us?"

Cleaning up the napkins and closing the box of scones so they could get to work, Molly glanced at Elizabeth. "I was hoping they would because his work for the paper is on there. But if they haven't, I'd like to still go forward with the Phillips interview. I spoke with Clara and she said her mother was fine with it. Which means, I should do a follow-up, since we don't have her answers."

And then maybe she'd get some of her own.

Alan rubbed a hand over his chin. "All right. That's a good idea. In fact, you get that arranged and I'll work on the write-up for Vernon. Once we do get whatever was on his computer, maybe we could compile it, sort of a way to honor him and the last story he was working on?"

Molly's stomach cramped. "Okay. Sure."

Heading to her office, she told herself that the sooner she connected some dots, the sooner she could figure out why that had been his last story. Ever.

Chapter 16

Molly wasn't sure what she hoped to gain—other than answers—by stopping at the police station before heading to Alan's house. She'd tried to contact Vanessa Phillips, but ended up leaving a message. When she left work, she went through the photographs and notes, some letters, and a few journal pages again. There was nothing in it—that she could see—which would push someone to murder. Though she probably shouldn't have, she'd taken pictures of everything before packing it up.

As she carried the box into the station, she hoped she wouldn't get in trouble after the fact. Officer Beatty, wearing plainclothes, was just coming through the gate as she walked toward the front counter.

"Hey. More cookies?" He smiled at her.

Little coils of tension tightened along her shoulder blades. "Not exactly. Can we talk for a minute?"

He glanced at the box again and gestured to the hallway she'd gone down with him the other day. "Sure."

"You look like you're finished for the day. I'm sorry to keep you. I just wanted to follow up on things." She didn't mean to ramble and yet she couldn't stop herself.

"No worries. Everyone knows everyone's business here, so I'm sure you're well aware we had Elizabeth in here yesterday," he said when they walked into a room across from the fingerprinting one.

Molly walked to the long, rectangular table that took up most of the room and set the box down. She took a deep breath in and out before turning to face him.

He closed the door, leaving it open a crack and leaned against the wall. Easy and calm. Those qualities probably made him a very good cop.

"What's up, Molly?"

"Officer Beatty—"

"You can call me Chris," he said. He gestured to his clothes. "Off duty and all."

"Right. Okay. Chris." She took a deep breath and noticed his frown. He pushed off the wall and walked toward her.

"Why don't you sit down? You okay?"

She sat, grateful for the suggestion. He sat down beside her and she put her hand on the lid of the box.

The way he leaned forward a little made it seem like he was still relaxed. Easy. But the serious gaze changed the tone.

"I took this from Vernon's car. I'm sorry. There's nothing in it, not that I can see. But, I wasn't sure if I should return it to the family or bring it here, so I brought it to you."

He straightened, looked at the box. "You took this from his car after his death?"

She nodded.

"I drove you to the newspaper office. You didn't take it with you."

Molly looked at her lap. "No. I went back later."

"Was his car locked?"

Staring at her jeans as if they were the most fascinating thing on earth, she nodded with her head down. "Yes."

The quiet made her stomach roll, but she kept her gaze down. Breaking and entering didn't look good on anyone's record.

"And you knew how to break into a car?"

Molly's gaze snapped up to his. There was a slight quirk to his lips. It matched the arch of his brow. Molly cleared her throat.

"Y—y—yes?"

He closed his eyes and pinched the bridge of his nose with two fingers. When he lowered them, opening his eyes, his stare pinned her, making her heart skip a beat.

"Lying to an officer of the law isn't a great idea, Molly."

Nope. Definitely hadn't been on her to-do list, but throwing the cute mechanic, who did no more than help her, under the bus wasn't on that list, either.

"I know."

She pulled her hands onto her lap and clasped them. He glanced at the box, then back at her.

"But you're still saying you broke into the car on your own to get this box?"

She stretched her lips upward into what she hoped looked like a smile. "Yes. That's my final answer."

His lips twitched. "It's not a game show, Molly. Why'd you take it? What is it?"

"It's the story Vernon was working on. He'd gone out to interview Vanessa Phillips and she gave him a box of photos and such."

Officer Beatty—Chris—pulled the box toward him and lifted the lid. "Can't imagine he got much from the woman. Never can tell which days she'll be lucid."

Molly's heart clutched like a giant had stepped on it. "I'm sorry? What do you mean?"

Chris frowned. "It's only a rumor, mind you, but I heard she's in the early stages of dementia."

Molly felt like she'd been punched in the chest. Her breath caught painfully. If Vanessa Phillips was ill, would Clara have been fine with the interview being published? She'd said her mother was saddened by Vernon's passing, but hadn't mentioned anything else. *Savannah had such a strange vibe. Like she'd been groomed to say and do the right things. Because image matters.* But if image mattered that much and the elder Phillips was losing her memory…

Was *that* what got Vernon killed? "Oh." Molly couldn't think of what else to say.

He shifted through the contents, flipped through a couple of pictures. "You keep anything?"

"No!" She breathed through her nose. Photos on her own phone didn't count. "Of course not. I just wanted to look through it. I…I couldn't help feeling somewhat responsible for Vernon's death."

Chris leaned back in his chair. "Why's that?"

She worried he was going to grab a notepad or quickly put his uniform back on and make this official, so she rushed through her answer. "I pushed him to be more thorough with the Phillips story. He didn't want to interview her and even after he agreed, he didn't want to go out to her house. Then I make him do it and he hates me for that and for being basically his new boss and then all of a sudden he's dead."

Chris digested this. She could see him doing it—moving her words around in his head to sort them out.

Finally, he leaned forward. "It's not your fault, Molly."

Her throat thickened. "But you let Elizabeth go home despite the emails, so you obviously think she's no longer a suspect. I haven't seen Clay again, but I'm guessing if you were worried, you'd have arrested him. And Callan didn't do it because he was with Bella." She slapped a hand over her mouth.

Officer Beatty—he was definitely in officer mode, even without the uniform—stiffened. "You trying to do our jobs, Ms. Owens?"

She cringed. "No. Of course not. I think you and Sheriff Saron are wonderful. Very kind and certainly thorough, but like I said, I felt a certain...weight of responsibility and couldn't just let it go."

He shook his head. "Callan Blair? Why'd you suspect him?"

Molly felt her neck warm. "He argued with Vernon."

Chris chuckled. "Everyone who knew him argued with Vernon."

He sighed and put the lid back on the box. "Let us do our jobs, Molly. It's not your fault and certainly not on you to find the killer."

"But who do you even have as suspects? I was thinking, if Vernon felt like he was onto something—which is why I thought whatever it was might be in that box—maybe his phone records would be worth looking at."

Once again, he shook his head, but this time he stood. He pulled a small, square leather folder from his back pocket and flipped it open. A gold and blue police badge sparkled even in the dimly-lit room. "You have one of these?"

Molly lowered her gaze. "No. Of course not."

"Then let us handle things."

It wasn't a request. She nodded and pointed at the box. "Am I in trouble for the box?"

He picked it up. "Not this time, but I'm going to advise you to find a better hobby than breaking into cars. I'll take a look through this and then return it to Mrs. Phillips."

"Okay." She felt like a scolded child.

Chris walked her to the lobby. "Trust us, Molly. We may not get a lot of this sort of thing, but we're taking it seriously. We're following every lead. Just because we don't post it on Twitter, doesn't mean we're not doing it."

Ouch. "I didn't mean to imply otherwise," she said, hoping he could see—hear—that she meant it.

"I know. You're new in town and this is about the worst welcome anyone could have had. But we got this covered. All you need to do is work on making Britton Bay your home. It's a good one."

She could only nod, knowing she was trying to do just that. Still, as she drove to Alan's home, which was on the upper bluff of the bay, Molly couldn't shake the feeling she was missing something. Something right in front of her.

Chapter 17

Molly arrived at the adorable cottage-style home with a clutch of flowers and a bottle of what she was assured was good red. The home was smaller than she'd expected, given Alan's family's long history of success in the town. But as she pulled her Jeep over to the side, where an area had been paved for extra vehicles, she saw the view. Getting out of her Jeep, she grabbed the flowers and wine and took a deep breath. Elizabeth was already there. Molly had parked beside her. *Everything is fine. You would know if you couldn't trust these people.* Molly froze. That was her biggest problem. She didn't trust herself to *know*.

The air coming in off of the ocean was vitalizing. Waves crashed loudly below, welcoming her to this secluded, little piece of heaven. Alan's Mercedes was parked in the carport behind a bright red sports car. The front yard was a grass mound leading to the cliffs and Molly fought the urge to go to them and just stand there, looking out at the water.

It overwhelmed her sometimes, how insignificant they all were in comparison to the world around them. Would anyone miss her if she wasn't here the next day? *Of course they would. Get out of your mood!* She couldn't help it. Handing over the box to Officer Beatty had felt akin to giving up. Though he assured her they were looking into everything, she got the impression it wasn't their biggest priority. Vernon might not have been a nice man, but no one deserved to die at the hands of someone else. She pulled out her phone. She trusted these people, but she wasn't going to be the babysitter walking back into the house in a slasher film.

Sam

Hey. It's Molly. I know we trust everyone in this town, but just in case, I'm at Alan's home having dinner with him, his wife, and Elizabeth. I'm wearing a pair of dark blue capris and a pink and white striped top. If it should come up. You know, like if you have to say what I was last seen wearing.

She pressed *send*, feeling like an idiot. But a smart one. Her phone rang a second later and Sam's laughter came through the speaker.

She whispered over the sound of the water. "It's not funny."

"You're right. It's not." But he was still laughing. "I'm sorry. But that has to be the most unique text I've ever read. It sounds like you look very cute, though."

"You'll feel bad if something happens to me."

The laughter stopped. "You're absolutely right. I'd feel terrible if something happened to you, Molly. So if you really feel like you're in any jeopardy, get in your Jeep right now. I'll meet you somewhere."

Tears stung her eyes. His willingness to take her seriously even when she was being ridiculous was making her fall for him, even more than his smile.

"I'm being stupid. I'm sorry. I don't know what's wrong with me. I'm fine."

"What's wrong with you is you had to see something no one should have to see. I know you have reason to suspect just about everyone, honey, but I'm telling you, I grew up with a lot of these people. When my dad died, Alan stepped in, made sure my mom and I had everything we needed. He helped my mom with the funeral arrangements when I was useless to her."

Sadness dug a hole right under her heart, just big enough for it to sink down into. Even through that, the endearment sent sparks along her skin, making her wish he was with her for dinner tonight.

"You're right. I guess I just don't trust my own judgement. I've thought people were trustworthy before and I've been wrong."

She looked back at the house, then at the water. She needed to get inside.

"We've all been wrong before. Maybe you should forgive yourself for believing in someone so you don't second-guess yourself when you're ready to do it again."

Like the waves did to the rocks below, happiness pushed against her, nearly knocking her back a step.

Deep breath. "Okay. I'm going inside before I'm late."

"Night, Molly. Maybe you could text me when you get home?"

She owed him that much and she liked that he wanted her to. "I can do that."

"Probably too much to hope you'll tell me what you're wearing later?"

Molly laughed and all of her unease dissipated, trickling away so she could breathe.

"Good night, Sam."

With the last of her moroseness gone, she walked the cobblestone path to the arched doorway that led to a small porch. The front door was painted a bright burgundy.

Shifting the wine under one arm, she knocked. Within seconds she heard footsteps. Alan answered, looking freshly shaven and…relaxed. He wore a pair of jeans and a T-shirt, which made Molly smile. He looked different out of his suit.

"You made it. Come on in," he said, stepping back and opening the door wider.

When Molly crossed the threshold, the warm colors and charming decor immediately made her feel at home. This was not just a house. It was where a family lived. Loved. Counted on each other. As Alan shut the door, she slipped off her shoes, looking at the dozens of frames lining the wall of the entryway. His family and him—a timeline of happiness. She couldn't equate the man she knew, the man in these photos, with a cheater.

When she turned, he had his hands in his pockets, waiting patiently.

"Sorry. I love photographs."

"No worries. We do too. Vicky was a professional photographer for a while. She used to help with the paper."

His voice trailed off and Molly wondered if he'd stopped before the word *until*. She'd helped with the paper…until.

She stood facing him, meeting his gaze. It was a warm and kind one. One she knew she could trust. She handed the wine over. He gave a little start and pulled his hands from his pockets to accept it.

"Thank you. You didn't need to do that."

"My mom and dad would be appalled if I hadn't," Molly said.

Following him along the light hardwood floors, Molly was charmed by the arched doorways and huge windows. If she ever bought a house, she'd want great big windows with a view of the ocean like they had. The hallway led to a quaint little kitchen that, while modern, seemed like a throwback to another time. Sitting at a round table was Elizabeth and Alan's wife. She was every bit as pretty in person as she was in photographs. She stood, an easy smile making her dark eyes seem bigger.

"You must be Molly," she said, walking toward her and pulling her into an unexpected hug.

Molly returned it lightly, but when her hand pressed to the woman's back, she felt the outline of bones. Her features suggested she'd always been a small woman, but clearly, she'd lost some weight. From her illness? Molly pulled back, brought the flowers around. "It's a pleasure to meet you, Vicky. These are for you."

Her eyes lit up and Molly saw the subtle shadows below them. "They're beautiful. Thank you."

The scent of spices made Molly's stomach growl. Someone knew how to cook.

"How are you, Molly?" Elizabeth greeted. She'd stood as well.

"I'm good. This place is so beautiful. Do you live around here as well, Elizabeth?"

Vicky got a vase from beneath the old farm-style sink. "Just down the road. Thank God. Don't know what I'd do without her."

The affection in Elizabeth's eyes for her friend was undeniable. Sam was right. Whatever else may have happened, these people were trustworthy. She didn't know what the story was, but it wasn't anything like Vernon had hinted at in his emails.

"I have a little cottage further down the bluff. Doesn't have as great a view, but I do love it," Elizabeth said.

"Molly brought wine, sweetheart. Anyone want a glass?" Alan set it on the countertop and went to a cabinet by the table to retrieve wineglasses.

"I'll have a small glass," Molly said.

"I'd better not," Vicky said.

Alan glanced at her and Molly wondered if she'd made a mistake bringing the wine. "I'll grab you a ginger ale. Elizabeth?"

"Absolutely. After the last few days, I'm likely to polish off the bottle."

The three of them laughed and Molly took that as another positive sign. There was nothing funny about being accused of murder, so clearly none of them were worried. She hoped that, aside from being a nice evening, tonight proved informative.

"Please, sit. Tell me about yourself," Vicky said as Alan poured wine.

Molly set her purse on the counter, keeping her phone in her back pocket. She sat across from Elizabeth at the table, noting it'd already been set.

"Well, I've figured out the way things work in a small town remarkably quick, so I'd say you probably already know a few things about me," Molly said.

Alan passed her a half glass of wine before giving Elizabeth her quite full glass. He poured one for himself as well.

"You have learned quickly," Vicky said, arranging the flowers. "Let me see. You're from California. Living in the carriage home behind the bed-and-breakfast. Dating the very cute Sam and you have a new puppy."

Molly's mouth hung open a little. Wow. How was it that no one knew who killed Vernon? This town was like walking around in a glass house. She sipped her wine, enjoying the crisp sweetness of the berry flavor on her tongue.

"I feel like I'm being filmed. All right, except Sam and I are just friends," she said.

Elizabeth tried to hide the twitching of her lips but lost the battle. "I heard Cora asked you not to be so friendly."

This time her mouth did drop open. "Is someone following me with a camera?"

Alan laughed as he opened a can of soda for his wife and poured it into a tall glass. "You'd think, right?"

Elizabeth sipped her wine and set it down. "I ran into Henry while I was filling up my car. He said to tell you not to listen to what Cora said. And I quote, 'If Shannon thought less of herself, she wouldn't need her grandmother trying to marry her off.'"

Pressing her lips together, Molly wasn't sure what to say. Despite trying not to, she laughed. "This is like some strange reality show. I'm not sure if I love it or fear it."

Alan pressed a kiss to Vicky's cheek as he set the soda beside her. They exchanged a look that could only be described as loving. Molly's heartstrings tightened. She could definitely see why Sam believed good things about this man. *Then focus on what you actually see. Not speculation or rumors.* Or emails that didn't make sense.

Vicky joined them at the table with her soda, setting the bright spray of flowers in the center of the table. "So, tell me the parts I missed."

"Nothing to tell, really. I was looking for a change of pace and location when I stumbled across Alan's ad for the editor job. I'm one of those 'things happen for a reason' believers, so I took it as a sign. Packed up my Jeep and headed here. If it weren't for everything that's happened with Vernon, it would be almost too good to be true."

"Nasty business. And scary," Vicky said, shuddering visibly.

While Alan checked on dinner and readied a salad, Molly became more comfortable with both Elizabeth and Vicky. By the time they actually started their meal—a delicious spread of roasted chicken, baked potatoes, and a green salad—Molly felt as if she'd known them for much longer than she had.

"This is delicious," Molly said, swallowing another bite of chicken.

"We take turns cooking, but I can admit Alan is better at it than me. But I'm the baker in the family," Vicky said.

"How about you, Elizabeth? Do you like to cook?" Molly stabbed her last piece of chicken, not sure if she could handle even one more bite.

"I can, but cooking for one has a certain element of loneliness to it. Don't you think? More often than not, I end up nuking one of those packaged dinners. I'd stop if they didn't taste so good."

Setting her fork down, Molly put a hand on her stomach. "With all the great food in this town, it'll almost be disappointing to cook for myself."

"What do you like to do when you aren't working, Molly?" Vicky asked. *Try to come up with a reason for Vernon's death.* "I like to be in the water, but it's a little cool yet. I don't mind hiking, but mostly, I've been entertaining Tigger. That's the pup I found. I didn't mean to keep him, but no one's claimed him yet."

Alan tossed his napkin on his plate and leaned back in his chair. "Could be he's a stray. We had some trouble a while back with stray cats and dogs. Turned out there was a puppy mill not far from here. A few escaped and they ended up getting closed down, thank goodness. But there's some pretty big pieces of property out this way. People might not even know they've got a few strays around and before you know it, there's a litter of pups wandering around."

"At first, I hoped someone would claim him right away. But now, I'm attached. I don't know what I'll do if someone says he's theirs."

"Even in a town this size, you can't know everyone, but I still think someone would have passed word along and if he belonged to someone, you'd know by now," Elizabeth chimed in.

She hoped so. Especially since she wasn't the only one getting attached. Katherine had insisted on puppy-sitting this evening, rather than Tigger being put in his kennel. She had new guests who'd brought their preschool-aged child. Tigger and the little boy had become fast friends and Katherine had insisted the pup stay out to play while Molly went for dinner.

"Thank you again for dinner. It was delicious. Truly," Molly said.

Alan stood and picked up his and Vicky's plates. "Our pleasure. This is a much nicer way to welcome you to the *Bulletin* than what's happened so far."

Molly stood, intending to help clear the table.

"No you don't. We'll take care of this, you sit. Would you like some coffee or tea?" Vicky asked, picking up Molly and Elizabeth's plates.

"I couldn't. I'm stuffed. Thank you, though."

"I was telling Vicky about your idea of Hannah writing more actively for the paper," Elizabeth commented.

"It's a great idea. That girl certainly has more passion and drive than I had at her age. She's very serious about her future," Vicky said.

Molly smiled. Her future and…Dusty. She truly hoped the teen found happiness—and balance—in both areas.

Unable to just sit there, Molly picked up the salt and pepper shakers and brought them to the counter. "Speaking of writers, Sam's cousin, Jill, is back from college and would be interested in working for the paper. I haven't spoken to her yet, but I wondered if you'd be okay with me bringing her in for an interview?"

Alan pressed his lips together like he was trying to remember. "Don't know if I know her, but any recommendation of Sam's is solid in my book. Maybe have her come in with some samples next week?"

"That's what I was thinking."

Drumming her fingers on the counter, Molly realized she hadn't learned anything tonight, but had still enjoyed the evening. If anything, she was more certain than ever that Elizabeth was no killer and whatever was happening between her and Alan, it just couldn't be an affair.

"I like to take a walk after dinner. Helps clear my head. Would you like to join me?" Vicky asked.

Molly glanced at the others. Alan was filling the sink with water and Elizabeth was clearing the table. "Okay. Sure."

"There's a bit of a chill, so I'll grab you a sweater."

While she did that, Molly waited for Alan or Elizabeth to say they'd be joining in. Neither of them did. Nerves tickled the inside of Molly's stomach.

Vicky came back with two zip-up hoodies. Molly pulled it on and they left through the back door in the kitchen that led to a porch with a few steps going down to the yard.

The wind had picked up, but it felt great washing over her, the slight dampness in it from carrying up the ocean spray. They headed toward the edge of the bluffs where a clear path was worn.

"I love it here. Always have. When Alan and I bought this house, I don't even know that I saw much of the actual building. All I saw was this and I thought, I need to look at this every day for the rest of my life," Vicky said.

Molly smiled as she walked alongside her. In the distance, she could see a few other houses, but there was a significant sense of isolation.

"It's an incredible spot. Did you raise your children here? You have a son and daughter, right?"

Vicky tucked her hands in the pockets of the sweater. "Yes. Jessica is in her first year of college at University of Oregon and Trevor is in his third year. It's been a lonely transition."

Molly pressed her lips together. She was an editor, not a reporter, but her skin tingled, knowing her boss's wife was on the verge of telling her something.

The sky had darkened with night, but there was still enough light shining from the moon to see the path. Vicky stopped and picked up a few rocks from the gravel path. She tossed them into the water. Molly stood at her side, listening to the waves.

"When Jessica left...I started thinking I had no purpose. I'd spent the last eighteen years raising my babies and loving every minute of it. Every day was something new and then one day, she was off to college and I woke up and thought, Now what?"

Molly knew what it was like to feel left behind. She'd hated when her father had to go away, but she'd had her mother and the naive security that her dad would always return.

"I can't imagine that was easy," she said.

"Harder than I expected it to be. I'd let a lot of who I was go, over time. I mean, it happens. There's only room for so much and I wrapped myself up in being a mom and a wife. The paper was struggling, meaning Alan was putting in more hours. Trevor was already away at school. When Jessica decided she didn't want to live at home while she studied, I thought, Well, what now? What about me?"

Molly had never spent much time thinking about how her mom felt when she had moved to L.A. Or to Britton Bay.

"It came on so slowly, so subtly, that I didn't realize what was happening at first."

Molly stared at Vicky's profile, confused.

"I started sleeping in. Why not? Nothing to get up for. By the time I realized that I was spending more time in bed than out of it, I was too deep to pull myself out. Alan came home one day and asked if I was feeling okay. It was after seven in the evening and I hadn't gotten out of bed all day."

Molly pressed her lips together, seeing where this was going. "You were depressed."

A sad smile tilted her lips. She glanced at Molly. "What on earth did I have to be depressed about? That's what I worried people would say. I have this wonderful husband and home. Two children in college. Which we can afford to pay for. I'm healthy. I mean, I'd just watched my best friend go through a bitter, life-altering divorce. I had no right to be depressed." Sadness tugged at her heart. "Depression doesn't care much about any of that."

Vicky shook her head. "No. It really doesn't. It just got worse."

Her heart squeezed tight, bracing for impact.

"Elizabeth found me one afternoon. I'd had a small surgery a couple of years back and hadn't used all of my pain relievers. I figured pain was pain, so I washed them down with about two quarts of wine."

Molly closed her eyes and breathed through her nose. "I'm sorry."

Vicky started walking again. Molly, numb from more than the wind, followed.

"Town this size, word is going to travel fast. But Alan managed to keep a lid on things. He's good friends with the doctor who pumped my stomach and recommended counseling. It's helped. A lot. So has the medication he started me on. Which I take only as prescribed," she said, shooting Molly a wry smile.

"Thank God neither of the kids know. Once I got past feeling mortified, all I could feel was guilt. Even now, Alan or Elizabeth or both check on me once a day. I hate knowing I did that to them."

"I can't imagine feeling how you felt, but I don't think either of them blame you for anything or resent checking on you. You clearly matter to them."

Her smile was bigger now, more genuine. "I do. I wish I could have seen how much before I put them through this. All of this. I don't know if I would have believed it, though. Not in the state I was in. We managed to keep my news quiet, but in exchange, the two of them face the whispers of cheating and adultery constantly."

She knew. They all knew. Except Vernon, who'd believed the absolute worst. *Like you didn't have your doubts.* She pushed back the shame—she didn't have the benefit of knowing them the way Vernon should have.

"For what it's worth, the people who know Alan believe him to be faithful and completely in love with you," she said, thinking of Sam and his mom.

"That helps. It does. But I know it's still hard on them."

The waves crashed harder and a chill wracked Molly's body. They were a ways from the house now. As if just realizing, it, Vicky turned and they walked in the opposite direction.

"My best friend in the world, other than my husband, was questioned about a murder because of me."

"Not because of you," Molly said more forcefully than she'd intended.

"Vernon was trying to blackmail them. He was positive they were cheating."

"And he was wrong. Elizabeth warned him to let it go. He chose not to listen to her."

Vicky stopped walking and Molly shut her eyes, realizing what she'd said. "You knew what was in their emails?"

Opening her eyes, she met Vicky's. "Yes. I saw a printout on Alan's desk."

"That had to make you wonder."

Molly shrugged, stuffing her hands in the lined pockets of the sweater. "Sure it did. But it didn't jibe with what I've seen of either Alan or Elizabeth. It just didn't sit right. Thank you for sharing your story with me."

"I hope one day I'll be brave enough to share it with others. I've thought of it. Especially the first time the cashier at Stop and Shop and Cora—you met her, so you'd know that evil glare she can give—whispered behind my back and gave me pitying looks. I hate the thought of Alan's good name being dragged through the mud. Or Elizabeth's. They're two of the best people I know."

Molly could understand the torment, but she also knew it wasn't fair for Vicky to have to share something that was still so painful and private to her. "Anyone who really knows Alan and Elizabeth will already know the truth."

"That's nice of you to say."

"It's true. There may be a lot of gossip in small towns, but the people you want on your side know how to weed through it."

Vicky linked an arm through Molly's as they approached the back of the house. The porch light was shining and she could see Elizabeth and Alan on the patio. Alan waved.

"I like you, Molly. I'm glad you're here. I like how you think—the whole, everything-happens-for-a-reason idea. I wish I had a little more insight to the reasoning of things, but it gives me comfort thinking it."

Molly laughed. "I hear you. I don't always know the reason, either. Sometimes it's pretty hard to figure out."

All in all, it had been a lovely, if not slightly sad, evening. All three of them stood on the tiny front porch when Molly said good-bye. They watched her walk to her car and she looked up at them, waving back. Grateful for the motion light that had come on over the carport, Molly looked down to put her key in the lock. Her eyes widened and filled with tears. Blue, painted letters were scrawled on the side of her Jeep's smooth polish, spelling the word *LEAVE!*

"Drive safe," Vicky called.

"Thanks for coming," Alan added.

"See you tomorrow," Elizabeth said.

Molly looked up again, biting the inside of her cheek so hard she tasted blood. She gave another half-hearted wave and let herself into the Jeep. Holding her breath, she started the engine and backed up, hoping they wouldn't see anything when she pulled away. She made it to the end of the driveway before the first of her tears fell.

Chapter 18

Molly ended up pulling over, knowing the tears and the way her hands shook weren't conducive to a safe drive. On the side of the freeway that had led her to Alan's home, she dialed Sheriff Saron's number. When she got his voicemail, she dialed Officer Beatty's.

"'Lo?" His voice was thick with sleep.

"Officer Beatty? It's Molly."

She heard some shuffling. "I already told you to call me Chris. What's wrong?"

Molly forced herself to breathe evenly and told him what had happened. "I'm sorry. I should have just called the police station, but it has to be connected to…everything."

"Don't apologize. Head home. I'll meet you there."

Molly nodded, forgetting he couldn't see her. When she hung up, she'd stopped crying, but she had to grip the steering wheel tightly to keep her hands steady.

By the time she pulled up to the carriage house, there were two vehicles parked behind Katherine's: Sam's and a police cruiser. Maybe Sam had been visiting his mom, but seeing as he was standing near her house talking to Chris, she doubted it.

Getting out of the vehicle, she grabbed her purse. Sam reached her first and pulled her into a hug. She hadn't expected it, but she welcomed it like chocolate on a sundae. Wrapping her arms around his middle, she rested her head on his solid chest, letting the slow, steady thump of his heartbeat soothe her nerves.

One hand stroked down her hair. "Are you okay?"

Steadier and working her way toward mad over the damage to her Jeep, she pushed back. "I'm fine."

"Evening, Molly," Officer Beatty said. He was in plainclothes, but held a notepad and pen in his hand. He tapped them against his thigh as he wandered over to the driver's side.

"What are you doing here?" Molly asked Sam quietly while Chris inspected the Jeep.

"Chris called me. Said you'd had some trouble and thought I might want to know." Sam stared at her, then bent his knees so they were eye level. "He was right. I wanted to know. Just like I would have wanted to know about you thinking someone had been peering in your windows."

Molly pinched the bridge of her nose, then looked up at him. She hadn't wanted to bother him with that. She didn't want to bother him with any of this.

"You don't need this kind of trouble. I'm not sure who would have done this, but you don't have to be concerned about me."

The last thing she needed was him or his mother getting pulled into something because she was causing problems. Though she couldn't figure out who would have reason to do this. Even more reason to keep Sam and his mom out of the fray.

"Door's already open there. It's too late if you want to close it. Doesn't mean I won't leave if you ask me to, but you don't get to say what I worry about or don't."

She hadn't heard that tone from him and realized that she was not only still shaky, she was being ungrateful.

"I'm sorry," she whispered. "I just don't want you and your mom getting dragged into something because of me. I have no idea why anyone would have done this."

Sam's expression softened and he took her hand, linked their fingers in a way that made her feel grounded. Connected. Cared for.

"It's messy. Looks like they worked quickly. Might have been done like that on purpose. Paint looks nearly dry," Officer Beatty said. He was taking pictures with his phone. "Sam, I'm going to try and get some prints off this. Need you to hold a flashlight. Molly, why don't you go on inside. I'll come talk to you in a few minutes."

She started to argue. She didn't want everyone doing everything for her. She could hold the flashlight. She could clean up her own mess. Tears filled her eyes again. She hadn't *done* anything. Why would someone do this? Sam squeezed her hand.

"Tigger was whining a minute ago. I think he can sense you're home. Why don't you go let him out?"

She nodded. Letting the dog out and giving him a cuddle sounded better than holding a flashlight on the damage someone had inflicted on her pretty paint job.

Tigger was, literally, bouncing off the walls of his kennel in his effort to see her. She laughed, despite the tearstains on her cheeks and let him out, going straight to the back door. He ran out into the yard, back to her, then back out to the yard.

"Calm down, you silly fool," she said. Inside, she was grateful for the happiness the affectionate dog felt at seeing her. When he finished in the yard, he came over, half-hopping, half-running and launched himself at her. She crouched down and gave him rubs on his back and his belly. When he'd settled a bit, she brought him in and locked the back door behind her.

Keeping herself busy, she got him some fresh water and practiced making him sit for a treat. He was getting it some of the time. Mostly, he was too excited for his own good and Molly couldn't fault him for it. Sam and Chris came into the carriage house about fifteen minutes later. She offered them both a drink.

Passing Sam a soda, she took a seat on the couch, beside him, while Chris sat on the chair.

"You were at Alan Benedict's house? For dinner?"

"Yes."

She fidgeted with the label on the bottle of water she'd grabbed for herself.

"How'd that go?"

Molly looked up. "Go? It was fine. It was really nice, actually. We had roast chicken and potatoes. What does this have to do with my Jeep?"

"Who knew you'd be there tonight?" Chris asked, ignoring her question and her tone.

Molly glanced at Sam and he gave her an intimate smile. She thought back to their conversation only a few hours ago and her cheeks warmed at the memory.

"Sam. Katherine. Elizabeth. Alan and his wife. Though I'm guessing if they wanted to, anyone in town could have found out. Seems to be the way things work here. Everyone knows everything, except who committed a murder or painted my Jeep."

Molly groaned and covered her face with her hands. Sam's hand came to her back, rubbing gently. Huffing out a breath, she looked up at Chris.

"I'm sorry. That wasn't a nice thing to say."

Chris smiled and gave Sam a look. "No problem. You've blocked every punch so far. Just keep your chin up and we'll figure this out. I'm thinking we can rule out Sam and his mom. Probably the others too. Unless they weren't with you the whole time? Did any of them have a chance to sneak off alone and do something like that?"

Molly frowned. She and Vicky had walked for a while. But...*no*. Why would Alan or Elizabeth do such a thing? Her head swam with questions and Molly felt like she was drowning.

"Why would they do that?"

Chris shrugged. "Why would anyone? Have you made anyone mad?"

Molly thought through the events of her day and stiffened. Sam clearly noticed.

"What?" he asked.

She looked at him and gave a weak, one-sided smile. "I, um...well. I know Cora—not sure of her last name—is not a fan of mine, since I apparently stole Sam from her granddaughter, Shannon."

Sam snorted with laughter and after a second, Chris joined in. "Cora Lester. She's been trying to marry Shannon off to Sam since high school."

"So I hear," Molly grumbled.

Sam laughed and his hand moved again, rubbing slow circles on her back. "Probably not Cora, though I'll ask her whereabouts. Anyone else?"

"Uh...Bella might not be all that happy with me," Molly admitted.

Sam's hand stilled again. She heard him sigh, but kept her gaze on Chris. "Why's that?"

"I may have gotten a little nosy about her...um...relationship with Callan?"

Chris closed his eyes and rubbed his hand across his face. When he looked at her again, there was a warning in his eyes.

"Didn't I tell you to let me do my job?"

She was almost sure she heard Sam mutter "Good luck with that."

"Yes. But that was after I'd already asked her," Molly said, knowing she sounded defensive.

Heat traveled up her spine—a strange combination of embarrassment and the feel of Sam's hand on her back.

"I'll ask around. I'll question Cora and Bella, though I don't think it was them. We'll connect the dots, Molly. You just need to give us a chance."

Despite wanting to, she didn't censor her next question. "Is Clay back in town? He could have been the one in my backyard. It could have been him tonight. Unless he's not in town. But he was the one who told you about the emails, right? He gave you Vernon's computer?"

ne absolutely should not ask for at this moment. Officer Beatty
her, like he was trying to decide how to proceed. "We're still
ng up on all of those things. Please trust us."
d be easier if he'd give her something to hang onto. She wanted to
ieve they'd solve things. But she needed them to do it before it was too
late. Before someone vandalized more than her Jeep.

* * * *

When Chris left, Molly found it hard to meet Sam's eyes. Would he think she didn't trust him? *You didn't trust him enough to let it go.* She regretted asking Bella about Callan and not just because of Sam, but because she'd hated the way the friendly baker had shut down. She should be trying to make friends, not push people away.

"You doing okay?" Sam asked from where he still sat on the couch. Tigger had nestled into his side. Sam stroked him with one hand, earning the dog's everlasting affection.

"Other than making people mad at every turn, pretty good."

Sam's laugh was quiet. "Not everyone."

When he pushed to his feet, Tigger lifted his head and whimpered in protest. Sam smiled, but walked over to where Molly stood, leaning against the counter. Sam stopped in front of her.

"Sorry I didn't take your word for it with Callan and Bella."

"It's okay. You haven't been given a whole lot of reason to trust people in this town so far."

It was true, but certainly not of him or his mother. "I trust you," she said. It was true. She did. Regardless of the mistakes she'd made, they'd led her here. Even with everything that had happened—was still happening—she liked where she was; in general and right this moment.

"Do you?" Sam asked.

Staring at his chest, she nodded slowly. "I do."

She heard the smile in his voice. "Might be more convincing if you were to look at me."

She was afraid if she did, he'd see how very much she wanted to lean on him. To have him just wrap his arms around her again like he had earlier. She was tired, mad, and just on the edge of tears. It would be far too easy to get lost in him.

"Molly?"

"Hmm?" She put a hand on his chest, let her finger trace along the patterned line of his T-shirt.

His hand closed over hers. His other hand nudged her chin up and he gaze met his. She was close enough to see she wasn't the only one feeling something.

"I trust you," she repeated, her voice barely above a whisper.

Sam's green eyes crinkled at the sides when he smiled. "I'm glad."

It was hard to say who moved first, but they met somewhere in the middle, his mouth brushing over hers with a sweet softness that stole her breath. His hand tightened around hers and the other went to her waist. She let her free hand wander up, over his chest, to his shoulders and around his neck. When he changed the angle of the kiss, pressing her back against the countertop, she figured she didn't really need to breathe all that badly. Not if it meant he'd keep kissing her.

But slowly, in tiny, measurable degrees, he pulled back until they were still in each other's space, but his lips were no longer touching hers. His nose brushed against hers, his breathing uneven. Her heart galloped in her chest. She closed her eyes and gave herself the extra moment to breathe him in. To appreciate the moment and tuck it away.

"Bring your Jeep into the shop tomorrow. I'll take care of it," he said.

She opened her eyes and smiled up into his. He kissed the tip of her nose and then backed up, out of her space, putting his hands in his pockets.

"Thank you for being here tonight," she said. She hadn't shown much appreciation for it earlier.

He nodded. "I should go. I'll see you tomorrow. Stay out of trouble until then?"

She laughed. Tigger came running, as though worried he was missing out on the fun. Sam crouched down to pet him. "See that she does, okay, pal?"

"Very funny," she said as she walked him to the door.

Sam looked down at her again and reached out, brushing his thumb over her cheek. "Sort of. But I also mean it. Watch yourself, okay?"

When she bit her bottom lip and nodded agreement, he leaned forward and kissed her again, just brushing his lips over hers. She watched him walk to his truck, then locked the door behind her. Leaning against it, she smiled when Tigger flopped down over her feet.

Officer Beatty was right when he'd said she'd taken a few hits. But she wasn't going to let them knock her down. She'd focus on the good and hopefully, they'd figure out who was behind the murder and the damage to her truck. The memory of Sam's lips on hers warmed her from inside out. Maybe it was time to focus on something other than solving this puzzle. Sam had certainly given her more pleasant thoughts to dwell on. Maybe if she did that, she really would be able to keep herself out of trouble.

Chapter 19

Thursday marked its presence with rain. The first Molly had experienced since arriving in Britton Bay. The cloudy sky and cool drizzle seemed apt, given the circumstances. With the *Bulletin* being closed for the day due to Vernon's funeral, Molly managed to sleep in later than usual. When Tigger had decided enough was enough, he'd barked until she let him outside. Once he came back in, there was no going back to bed. She felt unusually sluggish. Gloomy, like the day.

Once she'd downed a cup of coffee, she puttered around in the carriage house, did some laundry and a bit of cleaning, remembering she didn't enjoy either task. She thought of wandering the grounds with Tigger, just to get outside, but didn't relish the idea of coming back in and being stuck with the smell of wet dog.

Instead, she phoned Vanessa Phillips again, leaving yet another message. She couldn't get the inconsistency of what Chris had told her compared to what Clara had said out of her mind. What had Vernon really seen when he'd interviewed her? Had she been of sound mind? Vernon and Clay had both thought she'd had a few drinks. She really wished she could get her hands on his computer so that she could see the interview. Tapping her fingers restlessly on the counter, she wondered what Officer Beatty would say if she called and asked about it.

The funeral wasn't until two. She could swing by the station, pick up the computer if Chris agreed. But he wouldn't. Molly knew that without even asking. Personal effects would go to relatives. Not nosy editors. Relatives. Clay had been at the interview, but she hadn't had the chance to ask him anything about it. She hadn't seen him—for certain— since the day he found out about his father's death.

"You cannot go ask him about the interview, today of all days," she told herself.

But why not? If she was asking as a way of getting the information to honor his father in the coming week's newspaper, would it be so wrong? Besides, she could go by and offer condolences. Maybe even ask him if he'd come by to see her the other night. *And accidentally smashed all your flowers while he was peering in your window?* Grabbing her notebook, she opened it up. She'd forgotten to keep track of dates. If anyone found the notebook, they'd consider the notes the ramblings of a madwoman.

Which, at the moment, didn't feel far off. She was going a little stir-crazy, the need to move or do something making her blood rush.

Tigger whined and she looked down at him. He was sitting beside her stool, staring up at her. "I know, bud. It's no fun when it rains. We'll go out later, though, okay?"

He turned his head at the tone of her voice, making her laugh. "Do you think Officer Beatty or Sheriff Saron ever followed up with Clay about the pen cap?" Molly asked the dog.

As if he were tired of her fixation, Tigger padded off, circling a few times before curling into himself under the coffee table to snooze.

"Right. None of my business. Because I'm staying out of it. But, I can do my job. Which means I need to know about the interview."

Telling herself she had good intentions, Molly dressed for the funeral in case she didn't have time to return home. She swung by Morning Muffins to pick up a treat to bring to Clay—an offering of sorts. Disappointed that Bella wasn't at the counter, she was in and out quickly.

Driving the rental car Sam had arranged for her while he had her Jeep painted felt different. She didn't like the ride nearly as much, but was grateful she'd have her own vehicle back soon enough. Thanks to a sweet mechanic who'd given her one more enticingly sweet kiss yesterday when she'd dropped the Jeep off.

Clay lived further from Main Street than his father, in a more run-down area than she expected to find in Britton Bay. The homes along Clay's street may have held charm at some point, but it had faded long ago. At the end of the bedraggled lane, Molly found Clay's home. It matched the others, but had the added eyesore of a poorly tended, overgrown lawn.

Alongside his older vehicle, was one similar, darker in color and also poorly maintained. Armed with a box of muffins, she noted the large rust marks along the car's passenger side. She was about to turn toward the house, to walk along the broken concrete path that led to the door, when the dashboard of the car caught her eye.

Or more specifically, the items cluttering the dashboard stopped her short. From the driver's side to the passenger side, the entire windshield showed a line of little teddy bears. All different colors, but all approximately the same size. Molly had a fleeting thought that it'd be difficult to warm the car with all of them in the way, before realizing why they'd stopped her in her tracks. Her pulse raced even as her breath halted.

One of the little bears had fallen to his side. Molly stepped closer. If there'd been another bear in the spot beside the tipped one, that little guy would have sat up like all the others. Molly's stomach flipped like an overcooked pancake. Heavy and with a thud. She knew where the missing bear had gone. He'd been tossed near a dumpster behind the *Bulletin*, where he'd gotten the best of Tigger by coming apart at the seams.

Unable to swallow, Molly told herself to calm down. This was absolutely nothing. At all. *What would you say to the police? Oh, there was this bear that Tigger was playing with and I think it belongs to whoever is parked in Clay's driveway. There you go. Murder solved.* Ridiculous. She didn't understand how or why it was connected, but it was a piece of the whole. Whoever drove this car had been at the newspaper office. She was sure of it. To see Vernon? To see Clay? It could be nothing. A girlfriend? *Then why does your stomach feel like you've been punched?* Chris had said to trust her gut. *Nope. He said he trusted his own gut.*

"Molly?"

She spun around at the sound of Clay's voice. He was walking toward her. Wearing a collared shirt and a pair of dress pants, he was as well dressed as she'd ever seen him. As he got closer, she noted the dark circles under his eyes. His hair was a mess and a mild scent of beer wafted over her, but he'd lost some of the cocky attitude she'd come to expect. Butterflies battled it out in her stomach.

Without even the hint of a sneer, he looked down at her and asked, "What are you doing here?"

Right. She had a purpose. She thrust the muffins toward him. "I... uh, wanted to see how you're doing. I haven't seen you since...well, since and I know today is going to be a hard day. I just wanted to make sure you were okay."

The smile he gave her was so genuine that guilt immediately set in.

"Thanks, Molly. That's really nice. I'm okay. I'll be glad when all this sh—stuff is over. Tired of company. Tired of answering questions about how I'm doing. I'm tired of talking to insurance companies and cops. Really tired of talking to cops."

Molly's skin prickled. At least the cops were questioning him. She hooked her thumb over her shoulder at the car. "Who's visiting you?"

He frowned. "My mom. She and my dad divorced when I was like three, but she's been crying like a maniac since I told her."

"Oh? Had she seen your father recently?"

He shrugged and looked back at the house. Molly's eyes scanned down and it was then she noticed the red scraping on his knuckles. Like he'd hit something? Returning his vacant gaze to Molly, he replied without feeling. "Doubt it. They hated each other. Which makes it even weirder that she's his beneficiary in his will. Dealing with *that* has been almost as much of a nightmare as having her sleeping in my room while I bunk on the couch."

Insurance. Molly felt like she might throw up. "I'm sorry. That sounds difficult." And possibly lucrative for Vernon's ex? But he didn't have anything. His house wasn't anything special, nor was his car. Didn't mean he was broke, though.

She'd apologized more in the last couple weeks than she had in her entire life. She couldn't make sense of the thoughts ricocheting through her brain—they were firing too fast.

"It's not my favorite. Anyway, I should get back in. Are you coming to the funeral?"

She could only nod. He held up the pastry box. "Thanks for these. I'll see you later."

Watching him walk away, thoughts still bouncing, Molly went back to her car once he'd gone in. Vernon's ex-wife *had* been at the *Bulletin*. Either Clay didn't know his mom had seen his dad or he was lying. Again. Molly might not have a badge, but she knew, deep down in her gut, that the same teddy bear she'd found Tigger arguing with was the one missing from that dashboard.

But she had absolutely no idea what to do with that information.

* * * *

Molly barely spoke on the ride to the funeral. Sam held her hand in his as he drove his truck and hummed along to the radio. She hadn't told him anything yet. Mostly because she really *did* like him and wanted to appear somewhat sane in his presence. But she couldn't push away her thoughts. Somehow everything was connected. Why couldn't she see how?

"You okay?" Sam asked as he parked the truck.

She looked over at him. His freshly-shaven face was so handsome it made her heart sigh. He wore a dark suit with the same ease as he did jeans or coveralls. He was a really good man. *So don't screw it up with your theories.*

"I'm good. It's just…sad."

He nodded. "It is. This whole process is sad, but I think it does provide families some closure. So let's hope it gives them that."

He stared out the windshield as he spoke and Molly's heart pinched. She was wrapped up in all of her nagging questions and had totally missed that this might be hard on Sam—being at a funeral. It was a small town and likely, his father was buried in the same place.

Putting a hand on his thigh, she leaned in. He turned toward her, his eyes widening a little as she initiated the kiss. His hand cupped her cheek and she pushed everything else away. When he pulled back, he rested his forehead against hers.

"We should go."

They got out of the car and walked toward the small building that would house the funeral. Behind the building was a large cemetery. Molly didn't think much about death or dying usually, but lately, she couldn't escape the thoughts. Hopefully, Sam was right and this would provide everyone with some measure of closure. Including her.

Molly was surprised by the number of people filling the pews when they walked inside. Sam took her hand and she stayed close to his side. Inside the double glass doors was a small lobby area. Another set of doors were propped open, showing a large room packed with people.

A huge picture of a much younger Vernon sat on an easel. At the door, Clay stood, greeting people, looking like he'd rather be anywhere other than there. A heavyset woman dressed in black stood at his side, wiping her nose with a crumpled tissue.

"Thank you for coming," she sobbed to the people ahead of Molly and Sam.

"That's Gretta," Sam whispered.

"I figured."

The offered condolences as they passed through the doors. "Let's sit at the back," Sam said quietly, putting a hand to the small of her back.

She couldn't argue with that idea, especially when she saw Hannah and what had to be her family sitting in the back pew. Hannah smiled when she saw Molly and stood to hug her.

Molly returned the hug. "You okay?"

Hannah pulled back and nodded. She took Molly's hand and pulled her forward. Molly sent Sam a "what do I do" look and followed. It was when

Hannah started to introduce Molly to her parents, Leslie and Graham, that Molly noticed the little flecks of paint on Hannah's arm.

Without thinking about it, Molly touched her arm, her stomach clutching when she recognized the shade of blue. Hannah turned, looked down at her arm and laughed.

"Oops. Savannah and I were painting signs for the pep rally at her house. Guess I didn't get it all off. Mom, Dad, this is Molly."

They both shook Molly's hand and she knew she smiled and spoke, but her mind had gone utterly blank.

"Thank you for encouraging Hannah with her writing," the girl's mom said.

Molly blinked. "Sure. No problem. If you'll excuse me."

She hurried back to Sam, feeling winded. He took her hand as she sat and looked at her, his brows furrowing.

"What's wrong?"

Molly clenched her teeth, then looked at him, forcing herself to remain calm. She leaned into him.

"Please don't think I'm crazy. But Hannah has paint on her arm and it's the same color as the painted words on my Jeep."

Sam pulled back, his frown deeper. "Hannah?"

Molly nodded. "She said she was painting at Savannah's house."

Squeezing her hand, Sam glanced over, then back at Molly. "I'm sure it was just a coincidence, honey."

Her heart melted, distracting her. "Don't do that," she whispered.

His eyes widened. "Do what?"

"Be all charming and call me sweet names when I'm freaking out a little. It's distracting."

Sam's smile spread slowly, like the warmth in her belly. He leaned closer so she could feel his breath on her skin. "Sorry, honey. Carry on."

She narrowed her eyes and tried to glare at him, failing miserably. His fingers tightened around hers again.

"We'll figure it out. I'm sure there's a reason. Let's just get through this, okay?"

She agreed and gave into the temptation of just leaning her head on his shoulder.

The funeral itself was tasteful and quick. Other than Gretta taking the podium to express an undying love for the one she let get away. Clay ended up coming to her side, urging her to go back to her seat.

Molly hadn't even noticed Clara Phillips until her husband took the podium. Thomas Black was the perfect match for his wife's Kennedyesque style, with his wavy dark hair, dimpled cheek, and polished exterior. He smiled out at everyone.

"I'm not sure how many of you are familiar with Idowu Koyenikan, but in one of his books, he says: *There is no denying that there is evil in this world but the light will always conquer the darkness.*"

The mayor let those words settle over the crowd before he continued.

"It's difficult to lose anyone and we've lost one of our own in a terrible way. But as I look out at a sea of people, I think, you are all the light in the darkness of this situation. The proof that goodness exists. It's no secret that Vernon wasn't the friendliest guy any of us had ever met, but he was, at heart, a good man. He was a father. A former husband. A citizen of our town. A storyteller. You don't have to get along with someone for them to matter. You've all shown that today by showing up, by offering your condolences and support to Clay and to Gretta. Yes, there is darkness in the world. But it is what makes the light seem so bright and we have to hold onto that."

Gretta sobbed in the front pew. Molly's eyes scanned the crowd. Clara looked like she wanted to applaud her husband's speech. Her hands were clasped in front of her, almost like she was praying. She continued to survey the room while Thomas spoke. Alan gave her a grim smile, as did Vicky, who was at his side. Elizabeth sat on her other side, staring straight ahead.

Molly couldn't read the tone of the room and truthfully, she didn't want to. She'd never been to a funeral, but could now say, with authority, that she hoped not to attend another. She had an overwhelming urge to see her parents. *I'll call them tonight and invite them for a visit. They'll love that.* They'd like her new home very much and they'd been stationary for a bit, so no doubt her dad would welcome the opportunity for a road trip.

The only ray of light Molly could see in all of what had happened was she now knew how very grateful she was to be alive. And safe.

Chapter 20

The Come 'n Get It was packed with people. Calliope and Dean had set out a buffet-style spread and closed down the kitchen. It was kind of them to offer their space and made Molly like them even more.

Sam and Molly found a spot near the window, close to where she'd sat when she'd come on her own. Sam leaned against the wall, a small plate of appetizers in his hand. He'd let Molly take the stool. She picked up one of the crackers she'd put on her plate, but set it down.

Sam nudged her and she looked up. "We should do something fun this weekend. Do you like to camp?"

Molly scrunched her nose up. "Only when I'm pretending I can't afford a night in a hotel."

Sam rolled his eyes dramatically, pulling her out of her funk. "Oh, man. I should have asked you that before I ever put air in your tires. How can you have that awesome Jeep and not like to camp?"

Molly took a small bite of the cracker. "I didn't know the two went hand in hand."

"City girl."

She smiled. "Guilty. Especially when it comes to not wanting to sleep in the great outdoors."

"Fine. We'll leave it for now, but we've got summer coming, so plan on me trying to convert you."

"Good luck with that," she said.

He chuckled and popped a cheese-covered cracker in his mouth. The noise of so many people was giving Molly a headache at the base of her skull. She gave up on the cracker and massaged the spot, tucking her hand under the loose ponytail she wore.

Sam set his plate down and put both hands on her shoulders, letting his fingers dig in. Molly dropped her hand and sighed, nearly giving into the desire to lean her head on his chest. The rain had stopped, but the sky was still dark and unfriendly, making it difficult to turn her mood around.

Sam leaned closer. "How about a picnic and a movie? Sunday. We'll drive out of town to a real theater, one of the big ones with seats I actually fit in."

Molly smiled up at him. "That sounds perfect." Something to look forward to.

Calliope was working her way through the crowd, carrying a jug of water. While she had a smile on her face, it wasn't the full one Molly had gotten used to.

"How are you two doin'?" she asked, setting the jug down.

Sam dropped his hands and leaned back against the wall. "Not bad. How are you? Packed house today."

"Yup. Everyone paying their respects. Glad Dean suggested we just put out a spread instead of trying to keep up with orders." She sighed and sent Molly a frustrated glance. "I hate things like this. Makes me feel like a hypocrite. Not one of these people got along with Vernon and yet here they all are."

Molly couldn't disagree and had, in fact, had the same thought. "It's just what people do, I guess."

Calliope nodded. "I guess so. Anyways, that's not why I came over. The sheriff and Chris are in the kitchen. They came in through the back. They want to talk to you, Molly."

Sam looked at her and she put her palms up. "I didn't do anything. I've been staying out of it, I swear."

Calliope looked back and forth between them and laughed. "I won't ask. At least not now. Go on back."

Molly slid off the stool, looking at Sam. "You going to come with me?"

He straightened immediately. "Absolutely. Just didn't want to overstep."

She grinned, despite the butterflies in her stomach. "Liar."

They wove through the crowd and pushed through the swinging door. Both men were dressed in uniform.

"Molly. Sam," Sheriff Saron greeted.

After they'd all exchanged hellos, the sheriff got right to it.

"We wanted to let you know we've confirmed that it was Clay who was outside of your house. Didn't want you worrying or thinking we didn't look into it. Though we aren't certain yet, I think it's safe to say it was him who vandalized your Jeep as well. Since we think so, thought it'd be best to tell you so you wouldn't keep speculating about it."

"As you tend to do," Officer Beatty added. His lips were tipped up in a smile when he said it, though, so Molly didn't take offense.

"Why would Clay want Molly gone?" Sam asked, reaching out and taking her hand. His tone darkened protectively.

Molly couldn't reconcile the snarky young man she'd originally met with the subdued one she'd seen earlier today. He'd looked relieved to see her, so Sam's question was more than valid. He'd lied again that morning, though, about his mother and Vernon talking.

"It doesn't make sense," Molly said.

"Don't know the why of it yet, but we'll find out. We know it was him, so we're hoping that's enough to assure you we don't think you're in any danger."

Molly sucked in a breath and looked at Sam. He looked as confused as she felt. But what about the paint she'd *just* seen on Hannah? It matched the color of the paint on her Jeep and all she'd seen on Clay was…bruised knuckles. Who or what had he hit? The police had hoped to stop her wondering, but they'd only propelled it forward.

"He told you about the emails between Elizabeth and Vernon on purpose. To distract you?" Her brain felt cloudy as she tried to fit all of the pieces together.

Both officers looked at her and *not* with happy expressions. "We aren't here to talk about emails. Just wanted you to feel safe in your new town," the sheriff said, his tone clearly a warning.

Molly's mouth moved before she thought it through. "Gretta must have visited Vernon at work. I saw the teddy bear."

Sam stared at her, brows scrunched, but it was Officer Beatty who spoke. "Teddy bear?"

Her cheeks warmed, but she had no choice but to explain herself now. "When I found Tigger—my pup—he was wrestling with this weird-looking stuffed bear. It didn't mean anything at the time, but when I stopped by Clay's house this morning, I saw Gretta's car in the driveway. The whole dash was filled with these same type of bears, only one was missing. You could see that there was a spot where one had been."

All three men stared at her. Sam sighed. "You were at Clay's house this morning?"

Molly rushed on. "I just wanted to ask him about the interview. If Vanessa Phillips had seemed strange or anything like that." Molly pointed at Officer Beatty. "I was going to phone you and see if I could get Vernon's laptop to finish the interview he started. Clara Phillips said her mother was happy with how things had gone, but you'd told me there was a rumor going around that Vanessa was losing her mind and Vernon seemed to think she had a drinking problem. I just wanted answers."

"What?" the sheriff chimed in, staring at Chris.

"I don't believe I used the phrase *losing her mind*. And it was a rumor, Molly. That typically means *not true*."

She huffed out a breath and let go of Sam's hand. Music and voices carried through the swinging door and the pass. Fortunately, they were out of the line of sight. "I know what it means. But I didn't think you'd let me have his laptop and I want to print the interview. We're doing a feature on her family and their heritage. On top of that, it was the last thing Vernon was working on. Alan wants to proceed as a way of honoring his career."

"Well, you were right about one part, anyway. I would not have given you the laptop, as it isn't your property."

"No, but the story belongs to the *Bulletin* and I was just looking for that. Either way, Clay told me this morning that his mother is the beneficiary of Vernon's will."

The sheriff rolled his hand, meaning for her to go on. "So?"

Her thoughts merged, getting tangled together and she tried to sift through them. "So that means she could be a suspect and maybe that's why Clay wants me gone. To protect his mom?"

"Molly," Sam said.

She looked up at him.

"What?"

"Let them do their job. They'll sort it out."

"We will. You seem like a nice girl, Molly. But you're getting close to stepping on my toes and I can't say I like it," the sheriff said.

Molly was reminded of the time she'd snuck out to meet a boyfriend in senior year. Her father had been waiting for her in the kitchen when she'd snuck back in. He hadn't said a word at first. Just looked at her in that way that made her spill her guts and promise never to do it again.

"I'm sorry. I'll stop. But I have one more thing," she said.

"Sweet Lord, help us," Chris muttered.

When Molly glanced at Sam, she could see he was trying not to smile.

"Out with it then," the sheriff said, no longer sounding so indulgent.

"My Jeep. You said you *think* he did it, but I just saw Hannah with the same color paint on her arm that was on my vehicle. I can't imagine her doing something like that—we get along well. She said she and Savannah were painting signs, so I thought maybe they got the paint from school or something. Maybe it was just a dumb prank, but it's too coincidental to see the exact color on her arm. What if Clay didn't do that?"

Molly crossed her arms over her chest and stuck her chin up, trying to hold herself steady as she faced off with the two officers. "Thought I should tell you, rather than looking into it myself."

A slight smile lit the edges of the sheriff's mouth. "I appreciate that and can promise you, we'll look into it."

They left through the back entrance, leaving Sam and Molly alone in the quiet of an empty kitchen. The dimly-lit room was spotlessly clean.

"I like you, Sam," Molly admitted quietly, running her hand along the edge of the counter.

Since she was looking down, she saw him cross his legs at the ankle as he leaned on the counter across from her. She looked up. He was almost smiling.

"I like you too, Molly." She recognized the amusement in his tone.

"I swear I am not trying to act like a crazy person or some detective. From your side, it must look like I'm doing everything I can to make you run in the opposite direction."

She worried that was exactly what getting tangled up in this whole mess would do.

Sam uncrossed his feet and stepped over to her, stopping her hand from moving. He tipped her chin up and the look in his eyes made her stomach feel like it was the spin cycle of a washing machine.

"You're going to have to try harder than that if you want to get rid of me. From my side, what I see is a smart, beautiful woman with enough interesting quirks to label her cute, but not quite enough to call her crazy. You make me laugh and when I think of you, I smile without even meaning to."

A shuddery breath escaped and Molly threw her arms around his neck. He hugged her tight, his arms closing around her back. There in the dark, stainless steel kitchen, Molly's heart opened just a little—just enough to make room for some hope. Enough room to stop being too scared to let Sam in.

If everything happened for a reason, Molly was more than happy to accept that Sam was hers for coming to Britton Bay.

Chapter 21

Molly's phone rang about an hour after she'd fallen asleep. Tigger, the spoiled pup that he was, lifted his head from her second pillow, then flopped it back down.

Molly groaned. "Sure. Make me get it."

She reached for it, pulling it off the docking station. Alan's number flashed in front of her blurry vision. "What's wrong?"

"Clay was arrested for murdering his father."

Molly bolted upright. From leaving footprints to murder! A heavy weight sank in Molly's stomach again. She should be relieved, but she was also sad. "I spoke with the sheriff earlier tonight. He didn't say anything."

Because he'd wanted her to stay out of it. Blinking as her eyes adjusted to the darkness, Molly shoved back the covers.

"I'm on my way into the office. This is news. It needs to be printed. We're going to do a special edition and have it out by seven a.m."

Molly looked at the clock. It was just past midnight. "You want me to come in."

She heard the sound of keys and a door opening.

"I'll meet you there. It's been a long time since there was something controversial to put in the paper. Clay confessed. I can't even wrap my head around it, but it's our news and we need to print it before someone in a neighboring county picks it up. This is our story and we're going to share it the way we want it. You in?"

He confessed? After lying about even being at the scene, he'd admitted to murdering his dad. Her mouth hung open, but she was already moving. Molly wasn't sure why Alan would offer her a choice on coming in, but there was only one in her mind. "Be there in twenty."

Wearing sweats and an oversized hoodie, she grabbed Tigger's leash and one of his toys and they were at the *Bulletin* with a few minutes to spare. She parked in the front because the streetlights lit the sidewalks. Alan was already at the worktable. He wore a ball cap, sweater, and a pair of shorts. Molly smiled, despite their reason for being there.

"Nice outfit," she said, letting Tigger go say hello.

Alan crouched down to greet the pup. "Back at you. Hey fella. You're turning out to be a keeper."

He definitely was. Molly shrugged off her laptop and purse and took a look at the layout Alan had started.

CLAY REYNOLDS CONFESSES TO MURDERING HIS FATHER. Well, Molly thought, cringing, it was a headline.

"Too much?" Alan asked, standing behind her.

"It's true, whether it's harsh or not."

"Did you talk to the sheriff?"

Alan nodded, all but buzzing like a man who'd had too much caffeine and too little sleep. "On the record. They have Clay's DNA at the scene. Apparently, he and Vernon had argued and Clay punched his father in the face. He admitted to lying about being at the scene and apparently they'd already known he was at your house. Which you didn't tell me, by the way. Their fighting got out of hand and the result was Vernon's death."

"What were they fighting about? What would have made Clay so mad, he'd kill over it?" Molly said.

Alan frowned. "Right now, we don't need why. We just need to be the source people go to for the right information."

She knew that. Of course she knew that. But things getting out of hand meant another punch or harsh words. Not a steel mug to the head.

As they worked together, Alan on Photoshop and Molly on the actual story, Tigger snored at her feet.

"How did you find out?" Molly asked, covering her yawn.

"Gretta called Elizabeth in a panic. She called me. I guess Gretta figured I'd post bail for him, but truthfully, she ought to do that. The woman cut and run years ago. Least she can do is stand by her son now."

Molly thought about that as she typed up the story, including the quotes from the sheriff and what was known of Clay and Vernon's relationship. She summarized the events surrounding Vernon's death.

"Do we want to add anything else about Vernon and his career or are we doing that in another issue?" Molly asked.

Alan cracked open a can of cola. "Let's save it. We can run our regular edition on Sunday. I just don't want everyone running around speculating.

I know they will, but at least this way, everyone is starting from the same point. There's no way to limit the gossip, but with both the death and the arrest happening to two of my employees, I feel like we should be the ones to lead the conversation."

It made sense, as much as anything could, going on three in the morning.

"You spoke with Vicky," Alan said as they worked.

"I did. Your wife is lovely. And very brave."

Alan glanced over and their eyes met. Molly saw the gratitude in his. "She's my whole world. If I felt even a fraction of what I feel for her for this paper, I probably would have taken better care of it. Mind you, I didn't do such a great job taking care of her, either, did I?"

Molly stopped typing. "You can't do that to yourself. You're giving her everything she needs." She didn't know what else to say, as she couldn't fathom how hard the entire thing had been on him and his family.

They finished up just before five and Alan said he'd take care of getting the couriers to drop papers off at the bins and stores. It was the first time in many years that the *Bulletin* had done a midweek run. Molly was both sad—for the reason behind it—and happy—to be part of it.

Alan locked up behind Molly, a tired smile on his face when he waved. As she pulled out onto Main Street, the sun was lifting itself from the depths of the ocean. Even with her eyes heavy and her body weighted down by the need for sleep, she couldn't help but pull into the parking lot closest to the pier.

"Come on. Let's watch the sunrise," she said to Tigger.

The empty beach offered a kind of peace Molly hadn't expected. So much had happened over the last several days and she felt like she'd been stuck in one of those human-size rotating balls. Constantly spinning. Now it was over, but nothing felt still. The breeze kicked up bits of sand, but Molly didn't mind. She and Tigger found a spot, close to the water, and settled in, sitting side by side to watch the sun bleed several shades of orange and yellow across the sky.

When she felt as if she could fall asleep, right there in the sand, she tugged on Tigger's leash and they headed back to the car. By the time she got into the carriage house, she barely managed to slip off her hoodie and sweats before she crawled into bed. Even in her tired state, she knew she didn't want sand between her sheets.

* * * *

Tigger's bark snapped Molly out of a sound sleep and had her shooting out of the bed before she even realized where she was. He ran back and forth between her bedroom and the front door like he didn't understand her lack of enthusiasm over having a visitor. A knock sounded—probably not the first, if Tigger's excitement was anything to go by. Molly grabbed her robe and swung it over her body as she shuffled her feet to the door.

When she pulled it open, the last person she expected to see was standing on the other side. Bearing gifts. Molly practically drooled.

"Did I wake you?" Bella asked, her tone raising a bit in surprise.

Molly ran a hand through her hair, got it tangled halfway, and gave up. She stepped back. "Yeah. I have the day off. I was at the paper most of the night."

Bella nodded. "Right. I saw it. It's a good article. Disturbing and shocking, but well written."

Molly shut the door behind Bella, her stomach growling at the sight of the square, white box with little muffin imprints on it.

"Thank you. It was a hard one to write, but Alan wanted it out first thing."

She led Bella into the kitchen area and started the coffee. Her unexpected visitor sat on one of the stools. Molly needed to be a tad more awake to figure out what it was Bella was doing at her house at—

"Holy goodness! It's noon?" Molly said, looking at the time on her stove.

Bella laughed. "Yes. Hence the surprise when I realized I woke you."

Turning, her mouth watered as the coffee began to drip and she tried again to smooth her hair. "It's nice to see you. I wanted to apologize again for the other day. I was out of line."

Bella glanced down at the pastry box and busied herself with opening it. "That's actually why I came by." Her eyes popped back up to meet Molly's.

"When the news came out this morning, it kind of hit me that not only did you work with both the...victim and the killer, but you found Vernon and you had to write about Clay. I was embarrassed the other morning when you were so...inquisitive about Callan and me, but you've had so much going on. The last thing you need is someone holding a grudge over something so small. I'm sorry I overreacted."

Relief rushed out of Molly's lungs in one fast breath. "You didn't. Like I said, I was out of line. Finding Vernon's body was horrible. I felt like I had to find answers and I'd heard he and Callan fought and it's ridiculous, I know now, but I just wanted to rule him out. I'm sorry if that makes things worse, but I want to be honest so you know why I was asking. The very last thing I want is to have any animosity with anyone, really. But most of all with the very best baker I've ever met. I have a near-obsessive love for your scones," Molly said.

Bella's laughter chimed through the room and Tigger joined in, jumping up on her leg for attention.

"You're in luck. That's exactly what I brought," Bella said, sliding the box over.

"You are a magician with flour and sugar. Thank you. For those and for taking the chance and coming over here. I was going to swing by your shop and try to apologize again."

Molly avoided looking at the scones on her way by the counter to let Tigger outside. When she came back, she grabbed a couple of plates and two mugs.

"No more apologies. I'd heard about the fight between Callan and Vernon too, but I've known them both for so long that it didn't mean anything to me. Both of them loved to rile each other up." There was a sadness in Bella's tone that reminded Molly how much death could shake people up. Change them and make them look at things differently.

Pouring two cups of coffee, Molly joined Bella at the counter. It was hard to say which was better, the company or the baked goods. Happiness helped wake Molly up. Maybe now that things were getting resolved, she could start building a quote-unquote normal life. She already had a great guy and a good job. She loved where she lived. Adding a few girlfriends to the mix felt like one more brick in the new path she was paving for herself.

Tigger came bouncing back in through the open back door and attacked his food bowl.

"Gosh, he's just the cutest," Bella said. She picked up her mug with both hands and took a sip.

Molly had already finished half her cup and was ready for more. Bella had probably been up for hours, though. "He is. I really did not mean to keep him, but honestly, if someone claimed him now, I don't know what I'd do."

Bella's light blue eyes twinkled. "Not the only cutie you have in your life."

Feeling her cheeks heat, Molly set down her cup and broke off another bite of scone, popping it in her mouth and pointed to her cheek.

Bella laughed. "I can wait until you finish."

Once she did, Molly figured if she was going to have girlfriends, this was a good way to start. "I came here pretty certain I wanted nothing to do with men for a long time. Things are still new, but it feels…different. I try to think that things happen the way they're supposed to, so I'll just hope it goes somewhere good."

The sweet smile on Bella's face matched the warm feeling Molly had in her chest. "I can understand that. Especially lately. I want to hang onto anything good I can. Be honest: Do you think Clay did it?"

Unease fluttered restlessly in her stomach. "He confessed. I knew he lied about being at the scene, but if I'm being completely truthful, murdering someone— even in the heat of the moment—seems like it would take far more effort than I've seen him exert." It bothered her that she still didn't know the why of it. The article she'd typed up this morning simply said that Clay's DNA was found at the scene, he'd admitted to arguing with his father, and they had a contentious relationship. His claim was things went too far and the death, while he may have caused it, was accidental.

Bella rose and made herself comfortable on the couch, which was all the invitation Tigger needed to join her. Molly filled her coffee and sat in the chair, curling her legs under her.

Bella spoke the thoughts Molly had been pondering. "I wonder if it was an accident. You know? He got all mad at his dad and just punched him one time too many. Or too hard. Or in the wrong spot. Things happen like that."

Pausing before her cup made it to her mouth, Molly's lips tightened. Vernon had died from being hit with the stainless steel mug. It had his blood on it and Molly knew the autopsy listed blunt force trauma as cause of death. Alan had been able to get more detailed facts from the sheriff than Molly had from Officer Beatty.

"I don't know," she said truthfully. She tried to picture Clay punching his dad and then just picking up the travel mug and smashing him with it. Why wouldn't he just keep using his fists as most men were apt to do?

Okay. You're barely on your second cup and you think you can make sense of why he did what he did? The mug did seem like a spur-of-the-moment sort of weapon.

"I'm just grateful he's locked up. It's so strange to think of how many times I've sold him muffins or scones. And the whole time, he was a murderer."

Molly took a long swallow of coffee, then set the mug down on the short table in front of her. "Well, it's not as if he plotted to kill Vernon. I'd say, from the scene and the way it happened, that it was an escalation of temper and the violence came from that."

"Hmm. I guess you're right. I just couldn't imagine living with myself if I'd hurt someone. I couldn't even stand the thought of you thinking I was still mad at you," Bella said. She gave Tigger some rubs and smiled at him affectionately.

"Yeah. Hard to say what pushes anyone to the breaking point." Everyone had their own version of a last straw. That didn't make it okay. In fact, in Molly's mind, it just made the world a scarier, more unpredictable place.

"I should get back," Bella said, nudging Tigger's head off of her lap.

Molly walked her to the door, thanking her again for the gesture of friendship. Tigger whined as they watched Bella walk back to her car. Shutting the door behind her, Molly prioritized her day in her mind. Grabbing her notebook on the way back to the couch, she opened it up, intent on writing a to-do list.

She flipped past the first pages, the ones with circles and lines leading from Vernon's name to the people who knew him. She placed several circles around Clay's name. There was an arrow pointing from Vernon to the interview, with question marks around it. She still needed the transcript. Especially if Vanessa wasn't going to return her calls. Why had there been such an eclectic mix of items in that box? It didn't matter anymore, she supposed. Putting the book aside, she picked up her phone and went to her contacts list.

She nudged Tigger with her foot while listening to the unanswered ring of Vanessa Phillips's number. She hung up and picked up her book again.

1. Drop by Mrs. Phillips's.
2. Schedule meeting with Jill to talk about a position at the Bulletin.

Molly felt the childish urge to draw Sam's name in a heart. She may have had faulty judgment in the past, but she had good feelings about Sam. There was something about his easy smile and the way he looked at her like he really *saw* her, which made this feel different than her other relationships. Of course, it didn't hurt that she adored his mother and everyone spoke so highly of him. She smirked at her own thought that he was a man who came highly recommended.

"Focus."

3. Stop by police station to ask if Hannah and Savannah were questioned about damage to the Jeep.
4. Stop by and get the Jeep. :-)

With her day mostly set, she went for a shower and got ready to make the most of her first full day off.

Chapter 22

Sometimes, Molly wondered why she made lists. Or at least, why she put numbers beside the items. Instead of heading to Vanessa Phillips's home first, she stopped by Sam's shop. She hadn't been inside of the actual building yet, but it was bigger than she expected.

The lobby was a square, highly functional space. One door led out to the different work bays. Another led to *Offices*, according to the sign on it. There was a long, tall countertop that stretched across the room. Around the side of it, where employees exited, there was a small hallway that led to the bathroom, which was *not* for public use.

Though it smelled of motor oil and air freshener, it was unexpectedly modern. The dark gray tile gave the light gray room warmth and the black-and- white vintage posters of different vehicles made the space seem like a home garage rather than a shop. Molly was about to ring the small silver bell to announce her arrival, as the sign advised—Sam appeared to be very big on signs—when the office door swung open.

His eyes smiled nearly as much as his mouth when he saw her.

"Hey. How are you doing?" Coveralls again. How could he look so good in everything?

"I'm good. I was hoping maybe I could sweet-talk my way into getting my Jeep. I miss it."

Sam chuckled and set the papers he was carrying on the counter. He leaned against it, resting an elbow on the top. "Hmm. Give it a try."

Her brows came together. "What?"

"The sweet-talk. Let's see what you've got."

When she just stared at him, he arched his brows expectantly.

Molly's eyes widened, but she refused to look away. Even with the heat crawling up her neck. "Uh...please?"

Sam's laugh took away some of her embarrassment, but she still pulled her bottom lip between her teeth, trying to think of something better to say. She hadn't expected him to take her literally.

Reaching out, he tugged gently on a strand of her hair. "That's weak. You'll need to work on that."

"Ha. I'm operating on less sleep than usual." She told him about the night, writing up the paper, and Bella's visit.

The phone rang, but someone else must have answered it, as it cut off on the third ring.

"I'm glad you sorted things with her. Not that it was a big deal. It's crazy to think Clay did this."

Crazy, indeed. "Anyway, that means we definitely have an opening at the paper, so I'm going to call Jill on my way over to Vanessa Phillips's house."

Sam frowned. Before he could say what he was thinking, the side door opened and another mechanic poked his head through.

"Hey, boss? Can you take a quick look at something for me?"

The guy didn't look old enough to be a mechanic.

Sam smiled his way. "Sure, Mac. Be right there." Sam turned back to Molly. "Work placement through the high school. Why are you heading to Vanessa's?"

"We still want to run the interview, but Vernon never emailed it. I'm going to go speak to her myself. Her daughter said she enjoyed chatting, so I figured it wouldn't be a big deal. But I can't get ahold of her. I've left four messages."

His lips tilted down. "Maybe she's out of town? Did you try phoning Clara?"

Molly had thought about it, but since she hoped the sheriff would be following through on asking Savannah about blue paint, she didn't want to risk getting in the way. The officers of Britton Bay already thought she was developing a habit.

"No reason to. She told me when she stopped by that she and her husband are busy getting the town ready for tourist season. I'll just swing by Vanessa's and see if I can catch her."

The phone rang again. Molly smiled. "I'll let you get back to work."

Sam reached over the countertop and grabbed her keys. "You want to grab a pizza later or something?" They walked out of the shop together, around the side of the building, where her Jeep—freshly coated—was parked.

"I'd like that. Oh! It looks fantastic. Thank you," Molly said, rushing forward. Her insurance had taken care of the cost, minus the deductible, which still stung, but the shine made it look brand new.

"No problem." He put his hands in the pockets of his coveralls and rocked back on his heels.

"It looks like it just rolled off the showroom floor," Molly said.

"Nothing a little backwoods camping trip wouldn't fix," Sam teased.

Molly's smile was quick, like the spark of heat that trailed over her skin. "Not in this lifetime. Even if we come to some sort of glamping compromise, there'll be no backwoods involved."

Sam laughed and leaned in to kiss her cheek. "See you later, city girl."

She watched him walk away and then slid behind the wheel, gripping it in her excitement to finally have it back. Vanessa Phillips lived on the outer edge of town, where more land separated each home. The further Molly drove from Main Street, the larger the homes got. Unlike Alan's area of town, however, the upper point of Britton Bay was set back, more in the hills, without the view of the water.

At one time, it had probably been farmland, but now, it was where the more established residents of the area resided. Even if Molly could afford one of the stately homes, she preferred the view of the water and the easy access to all of the shops. As she took the winding road that led to the Phillips home, she could admit that there was a different kind of peace and serenity in this area than the ocean offered; like they were removed from the frenzy of life.

As Molly parked the Jeep in the circular driveway, she saw a woman in a wide-brimmed sun hat kneeling in front of one of the many flower gardens. Color blossomed everywhere, a rainbow of blooms that Molly couldn't even begin to name. She got out of her Jeep and strolled over. The woman turned, tipping her head up to greet Molly. In the shade of her hat, Molly could see the striking resemblance to Clara and a classic kind of beauty that only grew more with age.

"Hi there," the woman—who had to be Vanessa—greeted with an inviting smile.

Around her knees, which Molly saw were covered with pads, weeds were tossed in small piles.

"Hi. Are you Mrs. Phillips?" Molly greeted.

Small creases formed on the woman's mostly smooth skin. "I am." She stood, brushed off her dark, linen pants. Trim, with thick, dark hair that trailed out from under the hat, Vanessa Phillips did not look like she was suffering from dementia. *Looks can be deceiving.*

Still, she decided to tread lightly. "I'm sorry to bother you at home. My name is Molly Owens," she said, extending her hand.

Vanessa's eyes widened and she took a step back. "The reporter. You've been leaving messages."

Nerves clanged in Molly's chest like cymbals. Had she truly been that annoying? "I'm actually an editor for the *Britton Bay Bulletin*. I wasn't trying to pester you, Mrs. Phillips."

The woman waved her hand, cutting off Molly's intent to apologize. "No. Stop. It doesn't matter. You need to go. If I'd wanted to talk to you, I'd have answered or returned your call."

Pressing her lips together, Molly held both hands up. Was paranoia a sign of dementia? "I mean no harm. Honestly. I just wanted to follow up on Mr. East's interview with you."

Vanessa shook her head, almost frantically. "No. Stop. I shouldn't have done the interview. I need you to leave."

Words flooded Molly's head, but she couldn't get any of them out in coherent sentences. Her pulse raced as Vanessa walked a wide berth around her and headed for the stairs that led up to the columned porch. She opened the huge wooden door and turned before going inside.

"Don't come back. And stop calling."

She slammed the door, leaving Molly with absolutely no clue what had just happened.

Irritation and nerves took turns nagging Molly as she got back in her Jeep. *What on earth? Officer Beatty said it was just a rumor, but if that reaction is anything to go by, Vanessa Phillips is certainly suffering from something. She looked almost...scared. The last person who interviewed her ended up dead. Maybe she's developed an aversion.*

It didn't sit right and on top of not understanding, Molly felt badly for upsetting the woman. Turning back in the direction of town, she saw the sign for the Greedy Grocer and remembered Calliope telling her it was the best place to shop. Maybe instead of pizza, she could make Sam dinner. She was an editor, for goodness sakes—surely she could follow a recipe well enough to make up for her ineptitude with sweet-talk. She tried to think of what she could make instead of rolling the conversation—or lack thereof—with Vanessa. The grocery store was tucked back from the street. It shared a large parking lot with a gelato shop, an antique store, and a liquor store.

Molly got out, thinking more about Vernon's thoughts that Vanessa was a drinker, than of what she could make for dinner. The inside of the store was much like any chain store, but smaller. An older gentleman was behind the counter, scratching a lottery ticket. He nodded hello when she stepped inside. The cool air sent goose bumps up her arms. Heading away from the check-out area, Molly combed the aisles with a basket, paying little attention to the food, even though that's what she was there for.

In the end, she grabbed some soda, beer, cereal, and a delicious-looking chocolate torte cake. They could have pizza and cake. She saw the headline of the newspaper before she reached the counter. She'd helped print it and it still surprised her to see it there.

"Sure is a shame, isn't it?" The man who'd greeted her gestured to the copy of the *Bulletin* he had sitting in front of him.

Molly nodded. She set her basket on the counter and unloaded the items.

"You're new around here. I'm Archie," he said as he tapped on the register.

"Molly. I work at the *Bulletin*, actually. We printed the story for today's edition."

Archie's weathered face scrunched up. "Not the best time to start a job there, now is it? Been no trouble of this sort in this town for as long as I can remember. Sad to see, I'll tell you that. Where you from, Molly?"

She shared the basics as he rang her up.

"California. Well, I'd say we're a lot quieter and friendlier than a big city, recent circumstances aside. He was in here just last week complaining about my prices."

Molly froze as she was putting the basket into the stack of them. "Who was? Vernon?"

Archie nodded, placing her items in a paper bag. "Who else? Hadn't seen him in a while. He was dating a woman out this way last year. Didn't last long, but he used to come in once a week, Wednesday nights, grab a bottle of wine."

Molly couldn't even begin to think of Vernon grabbing a bottle of anything to share with a date. He'd have to be civil to be on one and she'd never had a chance to see him that way.

"What did he buy?"

Archie pushed the bag over to her. "Hmm?"

Feeling an unusual amount of impatience, she forced her tone to stay steady. "What did Vernon buy? When he came in?"

"Oh. Nothing. Came in and asked if I had a landline. Checked the price of bananas on his way out and told me they were cheaper at the Stop and Shop. Some people are born complainers."

Molly was only partially listening to Archie by this point. "Who did he phone?" More importantly, why didn't he use his cell phone? *Maybe it died.*

The old guy stared at her as if she'd grown feathers. "Gosh, girl. I don't know. Didn't ask him. Costs nothing to make a local call. I let him use the phone, he told someone to meet him at his house and hung up on 'em. His cell was chiming away in his pocket, so he answered that as he wandered around checking out my prices. That's twelve forty-seven." Archie was clearly done with their conversation or Molly's questioning.

She handed him a twenty and waited for the change. She didn't want to ask more questions and irritate someone else in town, but there were dozens brewing in her head.

"It was nice to meet you, Archie," Molly said.

He frowned, like he wasn't entirely sure he could say the same. "You too, girl. Have a good day."

She loaded her things in the Jeep and forced herself to take a few steadying breaths before she started the engine. Something wasn't right. The puzzle pieces might fit, but they were being jammed into open spaces. Molly had a feeling that the pieces needed—the ones that actually went with this puzzle—were still missing.

Putting the Jeep in *drive*, she headed toward town. She crossed a couple of items off of her to-do list, but she'd sure put a lot more on her mind. Clay might have confessed—heck, he may well have done it, but Molly firmly believed there was more to the story. *What am I missing?* She wasn't sure, but she couldn't ignore the nagging feeling that she really needed to see Vernon's laptop.

Chapter 23

Who had he called and why hadn't he used his cell phone? The questions slapped at Molly like pesky mosquitos. She pulled into the driveway of Vernon's home, her stomach clenching at the sight of his car. Gretta's car, with its trove of teddy bears, was parked behind it.

Molly got out of her Jeep and walked to the door. It was opened seconds after she knocked. Gretta's face was red and blotchy. She could have been a human version of a puffer fish.

"Hi," Gretta said, her voice scratchy.

"Hi. I'm not sure if you remember me. I'm Molly Owens. I worked with Vernon and Clay at the *Bulletin*."

The teary-eyed woman inhaled a bumpy breath. "Okay. What can I do for you, Molly?"

Beyond Gretta, she saw boxes scattered, but didn't hear anyone moving around.

"You packing up Vernon's things?"

Gretta wiped her nose as she nodded. "I am. It's gotta be done. Clay was supposed to help me." Her voice trailed off and she turned, her shoulders shaking as she walked away.

Molly stepped inside and closed the door behind her, unsure of how to proceed. Setting her purse on the coat hook by the door, Molly followed Gretta down the hall and into the living room.

"Is there anything I can do?" she asked. Molly had no idea what she could do for this woman, but she was willing to try.

Gretta sank into the couch, still sniffling. "Can you bring back the man I love? Get my boy out of jail?"

Frowning, Molly watched her step as she went into the sunken living room. She took a seat on the edge of a chair, her eyes drawn to the desk; to the spot beside the desk on the floor, where Vernon's body had lain lifeless. Her pulse slowed and her breathing felt thick. *You're fine. You're fine.* She hadn't considered how it would feel to come back here.

"I'm sorry to say I can't do either of those things. But I can listen if you need to talk or help you pack if you'd like."

"Were you friends with Clay or Vernon?"

Molly figured honesty was the best route. "No. I've only known both of them just over a week. I'm the new editor at the *Bulletin*. Vernon and I didn't get off to a great start, because I'd assigned an addition to the story he was working on."

Gretta gave a rough laugh. "Yeah, he didn't care much for being told what to do."

Molly glanced at the laptop sitting on the desk. "No. I wish we'd gotten off on better footing, though. Actually, the reason I'm here is because the story Vernon was supposed to send to me, he never did. The police had to check the laptop, but I see they've given it back."

Glancing over, Gretta shrugged. "Yeah. I'm not much good with computers."

"Is there any chance I could take a look at it? I could pull up the interview he was working on and email it to myself. Alan—he owns the paper—wanted to do a special tribute to Vernon in the next few weeks, so we'd really like to have the last piece he was working on."

Gretta nodded. "Sure. That sounds nice. I'm probably just going to sell it anyway. I've got all of this stuff to sell. I don't want it. He left me everything. Why would he do that?"

Molly eased back in the chair. "I don't know. Maybe he was still in love with you? You're the mother of his son."

Tears started flowing again. "The son that killed him. I just can't believe it. I don't understand. When I got here last week and found out Vernon was dead, Clay said he thought it was some Elizabeth woman that they worked with."

He wouldn't likely point the finger at himself. "The police did suspect her, but they found nothing when they looked."

Gretta stood abruptly. "I don't believe my boy has it in him to kill."

Speaking over the heavy pounding of her heart, Molly tried to keep her tone neutral. "It sounds like things just got out of control. An argument that led to blows and it just got pushed too far. Have you talked to Clay since he confessed?"

Pacing, she shook her head. "Doesn't want to see me."

Because he's ashamed? Gretta's earlier words registered. "You were already here when Vernon was killed?" Clay had said he was going to go visit his mother. Presumably at her house. He'd said Portland.

The woman stopped, her breathing ragged. Her back-and-forth motion on top of the crying was wearing her out. "I'd gotten here the day before he died. Wanted to surprise Vernon. We'd started keeping in touch through texts. Should have known I was reading too much into them. I showed up on Clay's doorstep Wednesday night. I tried to go talk to Vernon at his work Thursday. Couldn't believe how angry he was I'd just shown up. Said he'd texted cause he was bored, but it was a mistake. He didn't want nothing to do with me. We argued some, but I thought, Why bother? I was going to just go home. Spend a few days with my boy and head back to my own life. But then Clay came home and told me they'd found his dad dead."

The timeline flashed like cue cards in Molly's head. "You saw Vernon on Thursday? Behind the *Bulletin?*"

Gretta started up her pacing again. "I did. There's a lot of history between us and I know a lot of the bad things that have happened are my fault. I owned that. But I told him I was ready to start fresh. Gave him my favorite teddy in my collection and that jerk threw it as I was driving away. God. Why'd I ever love that man? He was born with poison in his veins."

Once more, she flopped to the couch, displacing one of the cushions. "And even knowing that, I loved him."

Molly was trying to focus on staying compassionate, but questions fired like missiles in her head. "Vernon was killed Friday night sometime. Was Clay home at all that night?"

"Sure. We ordered in and watched some television. One of those fix-it shows. I was telling him he could stand to fix up his little dump of a house. Must have made him mad because he said he had to go out. I was in bed before he came home."

Clay had left his house, with his mother there, to kill his father? But *why?* "Do you know what Clay and his dad argued about?"

Closing her eyes and resting her head back on the couch, Gretta shook her head again. "What didn't they argue about? I know Clay was mad at his dad for treating me like dirt and telling me to get lost. But they've always fought. Never had two nice words to say about each other. But I still can't believe my boy would hurt someone. Especially not his own family. Heck, half the time he was spitting mad at us because we didn't act enough like a family."

The sad, lonely boy who wanted his parents back together, even as an adult? It didn't seem like much of a motive to Molly, but she didn't mind not being able to understand how a killer's thought process worked.

Gretta was staring at her, most of her tears dry now. "When the sheriff came to arrest him, I tried to stop them, but they had one of those warrants. There was nothing I could do. Clay looked like he was going to cry. He just kept looking at me, like he couldn't believe it was happening, you know? And he told me that it was about time one of us did something for the other. Then he told the officers he did it."

Molly's phone buzzed and she pulled it from her pocket. Wincing, she apologized to Gretta for the interruption and answered. "Hello?"

"Hi Molly, its Officer Beatty. I wanted to talk to you about your Jeep. You at home?"

"Uh...no. But I will be in a little while."

"Okay. I'll swing by after my shift."

"All right. Thanks."

She hung up and noticed that Gretta had pulled herself together. She waved a hand around at the furniture and boxes. "I should just send it all to the Salvation Army. Don't need none of it. That's for sure. I'll sell the house. I can't stay in it if Vernon isn't here. Guess I'll have to go take care of Clay's house too."

Molly scooted forward on the chair and leaned in. "I'm really sorry for everything you're going through, Gretta."

"Thanks. You'd be about the only one. Not one other person has dropped by and offered to help."

Molly bit down on her guilt. Technically, she hadn't come to help, either.

"I need to get going. I'd be happy to pay you for the laptop if you're going to sell it anyway."

Gretta looked up, her eyes brightening. "Sure. Don't know what it's worth."

"Well, it's used and really, I just need the story off of it. But I could write you a check for a couple of hundred?" Something in her gut told her it would be money well spent.

Standing up, Gretta put her hand out. "Deal."

Molly wrote the woman a check, got the laptop, and headed for home. She still needed to call Jill. At this point, she was ready to hire the woman over the phone just to make sure the *Bulletin* had some backup. She should do that before she started digging. *Don't get your hopes up.* The police had checked the laptop, but their focus had been the emails...because Clay had sent them in that direction. Had he originally hoped Elizabeth would go down for the murder?

Too many questions. When she arrived home, she made two phone calls. One was to Jill, whom she left a message for. She hung up, hoping she didn't sound out of breath or frantic. Her pulse was determined to keep up with the racing thoughts in her mind. She hesitated on the next call, but couldn't get several things out of her head. One in particular: Clay had told his mother it was time one of them did something for the other.

Watching Tigger pounce around the backyard—knowing she owed the poor guy a walk—she dialed the number.

"Officer Beatty."

"Hi Chris. It's Molly. I wanted to let you know I was home, but I also have a big favor."

She hoped the pause she heard wasn't him rolling his eyes on the other end. "What can I do for you?"

"Did Clay say anything about the coffee mug that was used to kill his dad?"

"No. Why?"

Because maybe he didn't *know* what had been used to deliver the final blow. "You said you follow your gut and I get why you'd be wary of mine, but I'm asking you to do me this one favor and I promise, if he gives the right answer, I'll never stick my nose anywhere it doesn't belong ever again."

His sigh was easy to hear through the speaker. "Don't make promises you won't keep. What do you want? I'm not saying I'll do it, but what is it you want to know?"

Molly took a deep breath. "Ask Clay why, when he'd already punched his father, did he then hit him with the glass paperweight."

"What? What are you talking about?"

"Chris, I know I've been a pain in your behind. But I really, really need you to do this for me. I'll bring you cookies for a month."

"Stop trying to bribe me with cookies, Molly!"

She cringed at his tone. "Please? If he asks you what you're talking about or says he didn't hit him with a paperweight, end of story. But if he says something different, I'll do my best to explain when you get here."

"I can't decide if you're crazy, quirky, or brilliant."

She didn't get to offer an opinion as he hung up. Tigger came running in and she topped up his water, gave him some food, and a few good rubs.

"Sorry, bud. I know I'm not being the best company, but we'll hang out later. Go for a walk. Have some pizza. Well, you probably shouldn't have pizza."

She booted up the laptop while Tigger whined at her, clearly disagreeing with her thoughts on his dietary restrictions.

Molly's fingers shook as she waited. To help keep them steady, she grabbed her notebook. Starting on a fresh page, she jotted down the things that were bugging her most.

Vanessa Phillips acted almost scared to talk to me.
Clara said she'd enjoyed the interview, so why would she be
so abrupt when I went by?
Who did Vernon phone and why didn't he use his cell?
Why didn't Vernon bring the box of photographs into the
house if he was working on the story?
Why did Clay and Vernon really fight?

When Molly brought up the internet and Microsoft Word, both programs alerted her that they'd been shut down improperly and did she want to restore?

"Definitely," she said, pressing *enter* to both.

The police had been looking for the emails, thanks to Clay's tip. She double- clicked on that. First the interview, then the browser history. She found it no problem and read it twice to make sure she wasn't missing anything. He hadn't been lying. It was boring. Lifeless. Straightforward answers with no deviation from the question at hand. Biting her lip, Molly pressed the *back* button several times. Nothing happened. This was the interview that was last saved. She opened up her own email and mailed it to herself for later.

Breathing in through her nose, out through her mouth, she started to check the last pages Vernon had explored on the internet. The name Emilio Macintosh popped up in one of the searches. That name was familiar. Had it been on one of the letters in Vanessa's box? *Wait...Macintosh! The Post-it?* Molly's skin tingled. She'd thrown the note out, thinking it was nothing at the time. Maybe Vernon had been digging into a past flame? Several searches showed he'd been looking at the history of the Phillips family in the area: the brothers and their wives. He'd also done several searches on Vanessa's family and her life before marrying Charleston Phillips.

Molly was almost breathless when she clicked on the next bookmark. It was a Facebook page and Vernon had been messaging through it. Her eyes scanned the messages, trying to absorb the words and figure out if they meant what she thought they meant. The knock on the door jolted her out of her search with a frightened yelp. Tigger jumped up from his sleep and started to bark.

"It's okay. It's okay. Come on, let's get the door."

Officer Beatty was standing on the other side, an unreadable expression on his face.

"Hi. Come on in." Molly shut the door.

He did and crouched down to pet Tigger. "Hey, little guy. You're getting big."

Tigger rolled over and Chris laughed, but it was a weary sound. He stood and followed Molly into the living area. She walked to the counter and closed the laptop.

"Can I get you a drink?"

He shook his head. "No. Thanks. Let's start with your Jeep. I talked to both Hannah and Savannah about the paint. They were both over at Savannah's house, so it was one stop and their stories lined up. They borrowed the paint from the art teacher at school. When I stopped by said art teacher's house, sure enough, there was extra paint. Looks like you were right. It wasn't Clay on that score."

Molly's brows scrunched together. "Okay. I'm not following. Who's the art teacher?"

One side of his mouth quirked up. "Shannon Lester."

Molly groaned. Why would a woman she didn't know damage her Jeep? Was that where he was going with this?

"Okay, but Hannah and Savannah had access to the paint. Did they take it home? Could anyone at Savannah's house have had access to it?"

"Jeez, Molly. I don't think the mayor has time to deface your Jeep. I found paint that matches the color. Do you want me to move forward and see if there's grounds to press charges?"

Molly shook her head. Her Jeep seemed like the least of her worries. "No. What did Clay say about the paperweight?"

Chris came around the counter so there was less distance between them. "What's going on, Molly?"

Her heart sped. "What did he say?"

Irritation flickered in his brown eyes and he didn't look even a little bit happy when he spoke. "He said that he couldn't contain his anger so he picked up the first thing he saw on the desk and clocked his old man with it."

Molly sucked in a breath. "The paperweight?"

Chris ran a hand through his hair and sighed. "Damn it. Yes. The paperweight."

His eyes held hers and Molly's heart skipped a full beat. "He didn't do it. He doesn't even know what killed his dad. He lied when he confessed. He didn't kill Vernon."

"Then who the heck is he covering for?"

"I think I know."

Chapter 24

It was just after seven when Molly finished explaining everything to Sam. He paced the tiny square of her living room, running both hands through his hair, making it spike up at the front. Wearing jeans and a light gray sweater, he looked like the dark-haired boy next door. Looking at him reminded her that sometimes the best things came from what were perceived to be the worst. If she hadn't left L.A., she wouldn't be here.

"I don't like it, Molly. If all of this is true, meeting with a murderer doesn't seem smart. It puts you in danger and I'd really like you not to be in danger."

He stopped in front of her, where she sat—surprisingly calm—on one of the stools at the counter. "This person isn't a killer, Sam. They were pushed to their breaking point—maybe even one they didn't realize they had."

Sam took her hands. "And if you push again? Even harder?"

She turned her hands so their fingers linked. She liked the connection. "I need you to trust me. The wrong person has gone to jail."

Letting her go, he started to pace again. "Why would anyone do that? Why would Clay risk a sentence if he didn't do it?"

Molly slid off of the stool and walked into Sam's path to stop his pacing. "My theory is he thinks he's protecting someone."

"Gretta?"

Molly nodded. "I'm not sure if I'm right, but that would be my guess."

Shaking his head and giving a sigh, Sam just looked at her. She knew he could see there was no changing her mind on this. On top of finding the truth, she needed the closure on this as much as the rest of the town.

"I'll be up at the house. The second it's done, you call me." His voice was thick with concern, which Molly felt bad for.

Going up on tiptoes, she circled his neck with her arms. "Everything will be fine. I won't be alone. Will you take Tigger?"

Sam buried his face in the crook of her neck, sending a shiver down her spine. "Sure. He can keep me company. We can talk about finding you a better hobby."

Tigger pawed at their legs when he heard his name. Molly laughed. "I really need to take him for a walk later."

Sam touched her chin. "We'll do it together."

Her heart squeezed. "I'd like that. You need to go. The first of my two visitors is going to be here in ten minutes."

Sam's frown returned. "And the second?"

"Eight o'clock."

* * * *

Despite telling Sam she wasn't nervous or scared, her stomach felt like a salad spinner. If she was wrong about this, she'd look like a complete fool and probably make a lifelong enemy. Molly pulled the cork from the wine to let it breathe and set out two glasses. Just after eight, a knock came. Gripping the counter's edge, she counted to five, forcing herself to breathe. *You've got this.*

When she opened the door, she hoped her smile hid her anxiety. "Hi. Thanks for coming."

"No problem. I meant it when I said if there's anything I can do," Clara Phillips said, coming into Molly's small home.

She took off her long, dark coat and handed it to Molly. After hanging it, they went into the kitchen.

"Would you like a glass of wine? I was going to have one," Molly said.

Clara's smile was easy and bright. "No, thank you. But please, go ahead."

Molly poured herself a glass. Clara looked around the small space. Dressed impeccably in a pair of dark gray dress pants, a pale pink blouse, and kitten heels, she looked out of place in the cozy surroundings. Did she ever just wear yoga pants and sprawl on the couch?

"This is quaint. Katherine mentioned that Sam did a lot of the work," Clara said, turning to face Molly.

Molly didn't hide her surprise. "I didn't actually know that. I'm not surprised, though. He's good with his hands."

Clara's eyes flashed with amusement, making Molly realize what she'd said. Her cheeks warmed, but she didn't correct herself. "He fixed my Jeep up for me. It had to be repainted."

Walking to the counter, Clara set her purse on top. "I heard you had some trouble. That's terrible. I don't know what's happening with this town lately. I swear, it's always been a quiet, friendly little place. Officer Beatty came out to question Savannah and her friend about the paint."

Molly nodded, feeling as though the dance had begun. "Yes. He told me. Seems Shannon had the same paint at her house. They used it for signs for the pep rally. I guess she didn't know what to do with the extra."

Clara's lips tipped down and she gave a disapproving shake of her head. "Shannon has some troubles, I'd say. But don't judge Britton Bay based on a few incidents."

Molly sipped her wine, her fingers tight on the glass. "I won't. I'm happy here. I wasn't sure if I would be after Vernon died. I couldn't help feeling like I was sort of the catalyst of his death and that's a heavy weight."

Her guest pulled out a stool and sat. "Why would you feel that way?"

Taking a deep breath, Molly set her glass down. "I'm a big believer in signs, but not so much in coincidence. When he died after I pushed him to interview your mom, I just really felt like there was a connection."

Molly watched for any sign of reaction, but Clara kept her face passive. "That's ridiculous, Molly. I'm so sorry you put that burden on yourself. As I told you, my mother enjoyed chatting with Vernon. You obviously read too much into the timing and even if you don't believe in it, clearly it was just a coincidence. I can't imagine how Gretta is feeling. And Clay. Can you believe it? But at least he was man enough to confess and do the right thing in the end."

Nodding, heart beating fast, Molly worked to keep her tone even. "It's not always easy to own up to your mistakes. Especially if you made them during a moment where you weren't yourself."

Clara's eyes darted to the wineglass and she shifted in her seat. "Very true. Perhaps his willingness to plead guilty will make an impact on the sentence. I probably shouldn't stay too late. You said you had something for me?"

Molly smiled. "Yes. Let me grab it." She went to the entryway where she'd left the small box on the little side table. She had to work at keeping her hands steady.

"Oh. What is all that?" Clara's eyes widened.

Molly set it down between them. "It's a box of photographs and letters from your family. Your mother gave it to Vernon when he went to interview her."

"Really?" The pitch in her voice was the only indication of the woman's nerves.

"Yes."

Molly kept one hand on it, waiting.

Clara's smile was tight as her gaze met Molly's. "It's quite odd the police would give it to you, rather than the rightful owner. Was it in his home?"

"No. I stole it from his car," Molly said.

The woman's mouth dropped open. "Excuse me?"

Molly shrugged. "I told you, I couldn't help feeling responsible. I thought maybe there was something in this box that led to Vernon's death."

Clara's nostrils flared. Color darkened her cheeks. "So you just took something that wasn't yours? You realize that makes you a thief, right? Which, in my books, is no better than a vandal."

Molly let the insult slide, but Clara wasn't done, nor was she nearly as calm. Her fingers curled into elegant fists. "I really don't understand you, Molly. There's no connection between Vernon's death and my mother's interview. She didn't even say anything of consequence, which I'm sure you know seeing as you're his editor. And while I appreciate you returning this to me now, I don't see how I can avoid discussing proper protocol and procedure with Sheriff Saron. In fact, you'll be lucky if my mother doesn't want to press charges. I don't want to take that route, but it doesn't seem like you realize the line you've crossed."

Molly let her hand slide off the box. "I'd wait on that."

Clara stood, reaching out and sliding the box close to her. Molly was near enough to see that her visitor's hand trembled. "I don't think I will. I'm not sure if there'll be consequences for your actions, but I can't abide this. These items should have been returned to my mother. You seem like a nice enough girl, Molly, but I won't just pretend this is okay. You had absolutely no right."

When Clara rounded the counter, moving the box with her, Molly moved as well, blocking her path.

"You're very good at pretending things are okay, though, aren't you Clara?"

"What?"

The beating of her heart was almost painful in its intensity. "I couldn't let it go. I just felt like there was a connection. When Clay confessed, I thought, Well, so much for your intuition. But I still wanted the interview with your mom. Alan had the idea that we'd honor Vernon by sharing the last piece he'd written in addition to some of his older articles."

Clara's eyes cooled and her voice heated. "Would you let it go? My God. Our family has been in this town since the beginning. People know the story and while it's really nice you want to honor Vernon, I don't even see the point. No one liked him. Not even his own son, obviously."

Ignoring the woman's tone, Molly continued. "Your mother wouldn't return my calls. I went out to see her. She was quite abrupt."

Fire erupted in Clara's gaze, so fast Molly was lucky she didn't get singed. "She's a busy woman and seeing as she'd already given an interview, she probably had better things to do with her time. Which, clearly, you don't."

Molly nodded. "Maybe. That might be part of it. But when I stopped at the market and Archie—you know him, right? He told me Vernon made a call."

Clara's face paled. Her fingers tightened on the edge of the box. "Do you have a point?"

Molly leaned in a little. "In the age of cell phones, who pulls over to use a landline?"

Clara threw up her hands. "Are you asking me? I don't know and I'm done with your cloak-and-dagger. Maybe Vernon's cell died. I don't know and I don't care."

Molly walked to the couch, turned and leaned against the back with far more ease than she felt. "I think you do. Because I think it was you he called."

Turning slowly, Clara fixed Molly with an intimidating glare. "That's absurd. I don't even know the man other than the casual hello."

"Hmm. That might be true. But he found something in that box." Molly gestured to it. Before Clara could confirm or deny, she needed to lay out the rest of her theory and wrap this up. "He found something and he called you. He told you to meet him at his house the next day and you did. Whatever it was, it scared you. And sadly, even though I haven't been in town long, I got to know Vernon well enough to know that whatever he did find, he planned on using against you. He wasn't a nice man. Not at all. You're right there. Not a lot of people liked him. But he didn't deserve to die. And maybe you didn't mean for it to happen, but you hit him with the steel mug and it killed him. To keep your secret safe."

Jaw tightening, Clara straightened her shoulders. She practically hissed when she spoke. "You have no idea what you're talking about. I won't stand for this. You can't breeze into town and think you know everyone. I don't have any secrets. Do you have any idea who my family is, you insolent woman?"

Molly nodded. "I do. I know a lot about your family. Not from your mother, obviously. I'm not sure what you said to stop her from talking to me, but it worked. And not from Vernon. He really did a lousy job of the interview, but I suspect you may have altered her answers a bit when you had access to his laptop after killing him."

Clara advanced, rage pouring off of her like steam. "Stop it. Stop it right now! I won't let you just say these lies about me. Who do you think you are?"

Molly tried not to shrink back as Clara came forward. "Did you know, before Vernon stumbled across whatever it was he found, that Emilio Macintosh was your father? Have you always known or was it such a shock that you weren't really even yourself that night? I could see that. I could see the absolute horror of finding out your birthright from a man willing to blackmail you over it. I can't imagine how that felt. I'm sorry that he tried to use it against you, Clara. Truly. But it doesn't mean taking his life was okay."

Clara's arms came out as if to strike Molly, but instead, she buried her face in her hands for a moment. Molly's breath rushed out of her lungs as Clara's shoulders shook. When she looked up and met Molly's gaze, tears streaked down her face. Molly cringed at the anger still etched firmly into the lines of Clara's features, despite the tears.

"I didn't know. I didn't. And I didn't mean to kill him, Molly. It was an accident. I didn't even believe him at first. He's a horrible man and I thought he was lying to me. I'd never heard of Emilio Macintosh in my entire life. I told Vernon I refused to believe it and I certainly wasn't going to pay him to keep quiet about something that wasn't even true. But he had letters from this man—my biological father—to my mother. He'd found them behind a framed photograph of my mother. He called me from the store and told me he had something I'd want to see. I had no idea. I tried to reason with him, but he wouldn't listen. He just wouldn't listen. It was horrible."

Now Clara did reach out for Molly. She grasped her arms, her fingers pinching in, her desperation painted across her face like a mask. "Vernon wasn't a good man and neither is his son. He's already confessed to the murder, Molly. I promise you I didn't mean for this to happen. Please believe me."

Tears stung Molly's eyes more from Clara's nails pressing into her skin than sadness. "I do." She really did.

Clara wrapped her arms around her and held on tight, weeping against Molly's shoulder. "I promise you I'm a good person. It was an accident. It's only a matter of time before Clay follows in his father's vile footsteps." Clara leaned back. "Please. I'm begging you to just let it be. No one has to know."

Molly shook her head. "An innocent man is in jail."

Clara's eyes blazed. "Because he confessed! Obviously, he feels guilt over something and even if he didn't do this, he'll do something else. Look at where he comes from! I'm innocent too, Molly." She pointed at her chest and it was clear she believed what she was saying. "My whole life was a lie. When I confronted my mother, she said she was pregnant with me when she married my father, Charleston Phillips. Do you know, my own husband only married me for my connections? Because I was a true-blue Phillips and he believed the prestige of that would be better for his career than marrying for love. He said those actual words to me after we'd married. Can you imagine how he'd feel knowing I'm nothing. That there's absolutely nothing special about where I come from?"

Trying to keep up with the steady stream of words, Molly pushed off the couch. It didn't escape her that Clara clearly tied every bit of her self-worth up in her name and current position in the town. Perhaps if she'd seen herself as more— but Molly couldn't think about that now. "I'm sorry your husband said that, but I would imagine your mother knows something about your father."

Clara, not at all composed, nearly growled. "I don't *want* to know him. It's bad enough my mother lied and probably cheated well after she'd married Charleston. He was such a good man. He's the only man I'll consider my father."

Giving it one more chance, Molly tried to reason with her. "I understand that it's a lot. I know you want to keep the secret and there's no reason you can't. It's your story to tell, or not. But you can't let Clay stay in jail when he didn't do it. You have to tell the truth, Clara. Or it'll eat you alive."

The woman actually rolled her eyes. "God, you're dense. This isn't Shakespeare. I'm not going to see blood on my hands in the middle of the night. I didn't mean for it to happen, but I feel no regret. The only thing I have to do is keep living my life. I won't let you get in the way of that. I warned you to *leave*—why didn't you just do it?"

Molly froze. "You wrote on my Jeep?"

"Yay for you. You win the prize for being the nosiest newcomer ever. I didn't want any of this to happen. But you won't destroy my life."

Molly couldn't read the intentions in the hard set of Clara's jaw, but she could see the wrath in her eyes as she stepped closer.

The bedroom door opened softly, surprising Clara into whirling around.

"She doesn't have to. You've already done that yourself," Chris said.

Chapter 25

Clara was still sobbing when Chris put her in the back of the police cruiser he'd called after reading the frantic woman her rights. Sam hooked his arm around Molly's shoulder and tugged her into his side, kissing her temple, letting his lips linger. They stood on the pathway between the bed-and-breakfast and her place. Katherine and her guests had come to see the commotion.

"That half hour felt like two days," Sam muttered close to her ear.

Placing her hand on his stomach and leaning into him, she tightened her hold, grateful he'd been there within seconds of her text.

"You're shaking," he whispered.

"It got a little dicey for a second there," she admitted.

The crescent-shaped marks in her biceps still stung and the memory of how Clara's eyes had glazed over in her fury would stick in her mind for some time.

"I just can't believe all of this," Katherine said. She stood near them, watching on as Chris spoke to the sheriff, who was taking Clara to the station. The red and blue lights continued to pulse in the air. There were two couples and a single man staying at the bed-and-breakfast. They stood on the lawn, eyes wide. They probably hadn't expected much more than great views of the ocean when they'd booked their rooms.

"She felt like she had no other choice," Molly said.

"There's always another choice," Katherine replied.

Molly agreed and she still couldn't fathom how important a name and legacy were to Clara. *What if you'd found out your father wasn't your dad? That your mother had lied?* There'd be hurt and anger, for sure. But malicious anger? The need to kill rather than let it be known? No, Molly couldn't even begin to understand the woman's mind frame.

"I feel bad for her daughter," Molly said. If Thomas Black was as cold as Clara had suggested, what would happen to their daughter? Molly's neck was tight and a headache was inching its way up from the base. No more questions.

"Kids are resilient. Probably more so than adults sometimes," Katherine said.

In that case, maybe life would have been different if Clara had found out the truth when she was younger. When the sheriff left, Chris walked over to Molly, Sam, and Katherine. Fortunately, Tigger was still inside the main house or he'd be going nuts trying to get attention from all of the people.

"How you doing, Molly?" Chris asked.

She shrugged, once again appreciating the weight of Sam's arm around her. "I'll be okay. What will happen now?"

Chris glanced back at the empty driveway, then over to the guests. Two of them had gone inside and the others were turning to do the same.

Chris returned his gaze to Molly. "We'll release Clay. I gotta say, I'm not sure what shocks me more, that Clara Phillips would do this or that Clay Reynolds would do time for his mother."

"I guess you never know what people will do in a stressful situation until it slams into them," Sam said.

"That's the truth. You held your own tonight, Molly. You're a very brave woman," Chris said.

His tone was curt, letting her know that while he meant it, he also hoped she wouldn't be in the middle of anything else. As if she'd wanted to be. The adrenaline was catching up with her and the cool night air left goose bumps on her skin.

"Thank you. For saying that and for believing me tonight. For trusting me."

He nodded, reached out to shake Sam's hand and said good night to them.

"How about some hot chocolate?" Katherine asked after they'd watched him go.

Sam looked down at Molly. "Actually, I'd really like a shower. But thank you," Molly said.

"Okay dear. If you need anything, you let me know." Katherine nudged Sam aside and pulled Molly into a hug. Without warning, tears strained to set themselves free, but she bit her lip to staunch them as she returned the hug.

Following her into the carriage house, Sam shut and locked the door behind them. When they walked into the kitchen, her eyes landed on the wineglasses. She moved to clear them, but Sam put a hand on her arm.

"I'll clean that up. You go shower."

Molly nodded and turned to go to the bedroom and grab some pajamas first. As the water ran hot over her skin, Molly washed her hair and thought of all of the things she had to be grateful for. She hadn't really been in any danger this evening—at least, she didn't think so, but the effort it had taken to appear calm and strong had worn her out. By the time she'd dried off, tucked her hair up in a bun, and pulled on her soft cotton pajamas, Molly felt like her legs were weighted down with anchors.

Sam had lit the fireplace and dimmed the lights. He'd also made tea for both of them. Looking up from his phone, he smiled at her when she walked in.

"Feel better?"

She rounded the couch and took a seat beside him, her knee tucked up so it rested on his lap. "Mostly. I'm tired. Thank you for being here. For trusting me. And for staying."

He reached out and played with a strand of damp hair that had fallen loose. "You're welcome. I'd like to stay until morning."

While the thought wasn't unwelcome, her eyes widened at his suggestion. One side of his lips tipped up as if he'd read her mind. Wrapping a hand around the back of her neck, he pulled her in for a light and easy kiss.

"I'll sleep on the couch. I'd just feel better if you weren't alone tonight. If you're not comfortable with that, you could go sleep at my mom's."

Resting her head on his chest and snuggling in, she half sighed, half yawned. Yes, she had a lot to be grateful for. Now if she could just sleep for a week straight, maybe she could formulate coherent thoughts.

"I'd rather stay right here," she whispered.

Sam pulled the blanket from the back of the couch and tucked it around her and over himself. The fire crackled and she no longer felt cold. As her eyes drifted shut, she felt his lips in her hair.

"Then that's what we'll do," he said.

* * * *

A week later, Molly sat at her desk—once again, the last one at the office. She enjoyed the quiet hum of the computers, her dog snoring at her feet, and the feeling that she really was settling into a routine. She finished the edits on Jill Alderich's first story for the *Bulletin*, pleased Alan had hired her. She'd come on board at a time like no other the newspaper had seen.

Clara Phillips-Black, as she'd been named in the paper, was awaiting trial without bail. Molly had written that story herself, along with the truth about Vernon's murder. She'd spoken with Alan and Elizabeth, as well as Clara's family, about keeping the truth of her parentage quiet. It made explaining the murder a little trickier, but with Vernon's history of antagonizing people, no one questioned it.

Thomas and Savannah Black had left town a couple of days after Clara's arrest. No one was quite certain where they'd gone, but Sheriff Saron had stepped into the mayor's spot temporarily.

Clay had gone back to Portland, temporarily, with his mom to help her get settled. Turned out, he'd wanted to talk to Molly about his argument with Vernon. He was feeling guilty for fighting with his father before his death and thought maybe Molly, with her outsider's perspective, might be a good person to talk to.

Hannah was still having a hard time with Savannah being out of town and hoped she'd return, but Molly wasn't so sure. Clara would be a long-term story, even if it was just word of mouth. No teenage girl deserved to always wonder if people were whispering about her or her family.

Her phone buzzed and she smiled at the sight of Sam's name.

How about a walk on the beach and a pizza? We never did grab one.

Happiness—true, unrestricted happiness—blossomed in her chest. She'd found her home and in doing so, she'd regained some trust in her own judgement. She'd forgotten how much it mattered to follow her heart and her gut. Once she'd started, it had led her here and despite all of the things that had happened, there was nowhere else Molly wanted to be.

She replied to Sam and woke Tigger, closing down her computer. As she locked up the *Bulletin*, she couldn't help but think about Katherine's question. She'd been good at telling other people's stories, but she was finally starting to feel like she was living her own. And it was a good one.

About the Author

Jody Holford is both a contemporary romance and cozy mystery author. She lives in British Columbia with her family. She's a huge fan of Rainbow Rowell, Nora Roberts, Carly Phillips, Lori Foster, Sarah Fox, and Agatha Frost. She's unintentionally funny and rarely on time for anything. She has an equal amount of love for writing and reading the sigh-worthy moments in a book.

CPSIA information can be obtained
at www.ICGtesting.com
Printed in the USA
LVHW11s1523201018
594267LV00001B/109/P

9 781516 108695